# Local
# Knowledge

*A Unionville Mystery*

By: F. Edward Jersey

## ALSO BY
## F. EDWARD JERSEY


(non-fiction)

*Softwhere*

*The Viking 200 Challenge*


(fiction)

*Paines Creek Mystery*

*ObitUCrime*

*Cougar Attack*

*Unfinished Business*

*Monomoy Mystery*

*The Mid-Cape Open*

*Dangerous Waters*

# Local Knowledge

*A Unionville Mystery*

## By: F. Edward Jersey

Copyright © 2014 by F. Edward Jersey
First Edition

Edited by Wendy H. Jersey, Victoria Jersey, Stefan Kramer

ISBN: 1495401340
EAN-13: 978-1495401343

This book is dedicated to the good folks at the 'O' Bar. Thanks for the good times, good people, great food and entertainment.

# Local Knowledge

# Chapter 1

Every town in the country has one. A local joint where the food is pretty good, the beer is cold and the atmosphere makes you feel happy. On Friday night around five o'clock, the local establishment in Unionville, Connecticut, known as the 'O' Bar was just filling up with a colorful mix of patrons on their way home from work, just heading out for dinner, and generally looking for a good time.

Jake Wilson and Ron Alderman were serving the patrons at the bar. Bobby Rose was a bar back; he worked behind the bar for Jake and Ron cleaning up and doing whatever needed to be done. Jake had been working there for just over three years and Ron for the past two. They know the regulars by name, and by five o'clock, there were already ten people bellied up to the bar. By six o'clock, the place would be standing room only. They all knew this, because it was Friday, and that's what it's always like on Fridays. The wall behind the bar had a number of flat screen televisions all turned to various sports stations. On the far side of the room away from the bar, there were a number of tables for small groups of four to six people who wanted to sit as a group away from the bar. At the end of the room was a fireplace that in winter months would have a glowing fire.

The routine at the 'O' Bar was pretty much the same every Friday night. Regulars stop in for a cold one on the way home giving them some time to unwind. It seemed like every week there were a few new people who stopped in and then there were always the seasonal workers; landscaping and construction crews who stopped in at the end of their dusty days.

On this day, a crew of four from Harttt Landscaping had come in after a busy day outdoors, digging, mowing, planting, and raking. They took up seats closest to the door and talked about their weekend plans over beers. Frank Johnson, Lou Adams, Sam Marino and Pete Harttt had been doing this for as long as they've all worked together. Years.

"Pete, I made a tee time for four at Tunxis Plantation for ten tomorrow morning. Are you going to be able to make it?" Frank was always the one making plans for everyone else.

"I haven't checked with Heather yet. I'll have to let you know."

"Can't you make a decision Pete without checking in?" Without waiting for a response, Lou continued, "She has you so whipped."

As Pete sat contemplating the rudeness of Lou's comment, Sam piped in, "Pete, I know what you mean by having to ask the little woman. But some guys are more considerate of their significant others, and some aren't." As he brought his beer up, he nodded in Lou's direction.

"I can make a decision Lou, but tomorrow's our anniversary and I'm sure she has things planned. I just don't know what or when."

"We'll be done playing by three. We need to get in some practice if we're going to be competitive in the golf tournament. Plus, it won't take more than a few minutes to complete those planned things so maybe you can do them before ten," teased Sam.

Sam raised his mug, and Frank and Lou each raised their mugs as well.

"I'll drink to that."

"Jake", Frank shouted, "Give us another round."

Jake took out four fresh mugs from the freezer and poured. He brought the mugs over to the end of the bar, "Pete, don't listen to these guys. Take care of your personal business first. These guys are all hot air. If they were in your situation, they would be singing another tune."

Pete pushed his empty mug to the edge of the bar, and grabbed the cold one, "Thanks Jake. I know they're just kidding me."

Frank looked at him, "Call me tonight and let me know if you're gonna play or not. I'll need time to get someone to take your place."

"I heard young Tommy Benson trying to get Big Ed to play golf tomorrow. If you're looking for a fourth, I'm sure you could get Tommy to play." As the bartender, Jake didn't miss a thing.

"I played with him before Frank. He hits the ball a mile. I think he's a three handicap," Sam said.

"Well, if Pete can't make it, I'll take Tommy as a partner," said Lou.

"Nothing's going to help your game Lou," said Frank. "Even a three handicap partner will not have enough of an impact on your one twenty something."

"Why would you say that?"

"I'm just saying you'll need more than a three handicap to compensate for your crappy golf game. You'd be better off going bowling."

"Ha ha Frank. Where would you be if you didn't have me to beat up?"

"I'm sure I'd find someone else."

"Back to golf guys, I'll be there if I can. But if I can't make it, I'll see if Tommy can take my place."

Pete got up from his stool and went to the other end of the bar where Tommy was sitting.

"Tommy, Jake said you're looking for a golf game tomorrow?"

"Hey Pete. Yeah, I'm trying to get Ed to play. Why? You looking to play?"

"Nah. The guys have a ten o'clock tee time for four at Tunxis, and I'm not sure I can make it. They're looking for a possible replacement. Tomorrow's my anniversary and I haven't checked with Heather yet so I don't know if I can play or not."

"You'd be done by mid-afternoon. Not early enough?"

"I don't know. Sometimes she makes plans for the entire day, or lunch, and I don't want to disappoint her."

"I know what you mean."

"I'll get back to you as soon as I talk with her if you're available."

"Call me as soon as you can. I'm trying to get a game and I'll take the first one that offers."

"I'll call you on your cell as soon as I get home and ask."

"OK. I should still be here for a while."

"I'm leaving in a few minutes so I should be able to get back to you soon."

4

Pete turned and went back to his friends. Walking back, he could hear them laughing. "What's so funny?"

"We were just talking about your situation."

"Like Jake said, if any of you were in my situation, you'd be doing the same thing."

"Yeah Pete," Frank nudged Lou, "If I had a woman like yours, I'd be home right now."

"You wish you had any woman, Frank," Sam said laughing.

Frank frowned. He hadn't had a date in months and they all knew it.

"Hey, all of you wish you had a woman like Heather," Pete said.

"I wish I had just one night with a woman like Heather," Lou said.

Heather was a model, five foot ten inches and one thirty five. Her figure was Barbie perfect. She had long flowing brunette hair, and her eyes were a blue-green color that could see into your soul. Sprinkled across her nose and cheeks was just the right number of freckles that would keep her young looking forever. Walking into a room would typically mean a change of subject for most men.

"Don't talk about Pete's girlfriend like that guys. He might take it personal." Sam was pretending to be sensitive. The guys knew he was anything but most times.

"You bet I take it personal. You guys are just jealous."

"Just remember to give me a call and let me know if you're going or not," said Frank. "If I don't hear from you, I'll assume Tommy's taking your place."

"You'll hear from me. I'll get back to you as soon as I talk with Heather. Gimme a break. You're a nag."

"Fine. Then I'll talk to you later."

Pete paid the tab for himself and his crew with the company's card. "I'll see you later Jake."

"Have a good night Pete."

When he had left, Lou said, "I wasn't kidding. I would love to have a night with Heather. I see her in my dreams all the time."

"Dream on." Frank wasn't sympathetic at all.

"Some day," reflected Lou.

"In your dreams," Sam added.

"Yeah, in my dreams."

The three turned back to the bar and ordered three more beers.

Jake looked at Lou, "Why do you taunt Pete like that? You know how sensitive he is about Heather."

"Because I can."

"If you keep it up, you might just lose your friend, and your job."

"No, Pete isn't that thin skinned. I've known him since we were kids. We both worked for his dad in their landscaping business before he took it over. We go back a long way. He isn't offended."

"I hope he isn't. He's a nice guy."

As Pete was leaving, a cute blond named Trish Howland was coming into the bar, and Pete held the door for her.

"Hey Trish."

"Thanks Pete. Leaving so soon?"

"Yeah. I've got other plans."

"Too bad. I'm on my own tonight." She winked.

"Trish, cut it out. You know I'm seeing Heather."

"Yeah, I know. I just thought…" She stopped in mid-sentence.

"Maybe in another lifetime."

Trish walked in without looking back. "Just let me know."

Trish surveyed the bar and saw all of the stools but one were taken. She walked to the open stool and said to the men seated on both sides, "Hi guys, is anyone sitting here?"

Lou took one look at her, "It's your seat if you want it."

Trish turned to Frank and asked if he minded if she sat there. "It's open if you want it. But I have to warn you, Lou is kinda girl crazy."

"Lou, I'm game if you're."

Thirty years old, but looking twenty-five, Trish was polished. Her well fitting slacks didn't detract from the low-cut tank top, and her turquoise statement necklace was perfect against her tan. Her blond hair hung down to the middle of her back, and it looked like she had just rolled out of bed. Trish stood five-six and weighed about one-forty and had no problem getting Lou's attention.

"Honey, what're you having?" Lou asked as he put his hand on her shoulder.

"I'll have a martini, extra dry."

"Jake, one martini extra dry for the lady."

"Hi Trish, how're you doing?"

"I'm good Jake. This fine gentleman is buying me a drink, so it can only get better."

"I've known these guys for a while, and I don't think I've ever heard any of them called *fine*."

They all laughed as Trish claimed her seat. Jake went about making the martini and brought it over when he had finished. Trish took a sip, "Perfect."

"Glad you approve."

Trish turned to Frank, "You guys just stopping in after work?"

"Yeah. Pete worked us over pretty good today doing the landscaping at a new office plaza on route 4."

"That's Pete Hartt. All work and no play."

Lou touched Trish's shoulder again, "How well do you know Pete?"

"I've known him for years."

"I didn't know that," Frank said, trying to get Trish's attention.

Trish turned back to Lou, "Yea. I went to school with Pete's younger brother, and grew up a few houses down the street from them."

"So you know about his business."

"Yup, Harttt Landscaping. Most of the guys on the street worked there are one time or another while they were in high school and after. And I had something to do with the slogan."

"And what was that?" Frank asked again trying to get Trish to focus on him. She turned slightly and then turned her back to Frank. Something about him just turned her off. Although she wasn't sure what it was, but she wasn't even comfortable being rude.

"Well, one day when we were in high school, Pete's father who had founded the business, had us all around the table asking us to help him come up with a slogan for it. I said he should use something like *Put Some Harttt Into Your Yard* and he liked it so much he made it the company slogan."

"I never asked Pete where the slogan came from," Sam said.

"And did Pete or his brother put any Harttt in your yard?" Lou coyly asked.

Trish put her hand on Lou's leg, "I never got anywhere with Pete, although I've tried. But that brother of his, we were real close."

"Do you think we could get to know each other a little more? Maybe get real close?"

She moved her hand from his knee up a little, "You never know."

"You really shouldn't lead Lou on like that Trish. You never know what will come of it. I, on the other hand, am harmless."

"Well, after a few more martinis, I might find out who is and who isn't harmless." Trish threw back the last of her martini like a shot.

"That's all Lou has to hear and he'll be all over you."

"Then it might be a productive night after all," Trish said in a teasing kind of way.

"I'm meeting someone here in a little while. Until then, I'm just going to have a good time with Lou."

"Ok, just don't say I didn't warn you."

"I'll consider myself warned." She turned back to Lou and put her back to Frank, again.

Lou was completely taken in by Trish. From time to time she would lean over to fix her shoe or something and each time, Lou looked down her top.

After the second time, Lou finally said to her, "I couldn't help but look when you bent over and I must say you have an impressive body."

"So you like my breasts, is that it?"

"I think they're perfect."

"Well, maybe we'll have more show and tell later."

"Right here in the bar?"

"We could go somewhere just you and me for a little while."

"I'll come up with something."

When Trish got up to go to the ladies room, Lou leaned over to Frank, "Did you get a look at her body?"

"Not really."

"But we see you did."

"What do you mean?"

"If she bent over one more time, I swear you would have fallen off your stool right into her."

"She came on to me."

"Are you sure?" Frank asked.

"Yeah. She told me I might get to see even more later on tonight."

"She told me she's meeting someone here."

"You're just saying that Frank. You're jealous."

"No, she really said that to me when she first came in here."

"I hope you're wrong because I think I might get lucky with her tonight."

"Don't get yourself too worked up Lou. She did say she was meeting someone else here later."

"We'll see. Maybe tonight will be my night."

Just then, Trish came back from the ladies room. She took up her seat again and said to Lou, "So, anything happen while I was gone?"

"What do you mean?" Lou asked.

"I know how guys are. If they think they can put the moves on a woman, they boast about it."

"Well, we did comment about how fine looking a woman you are."

"Be patient Lou.  You won't be disappointed."

Trish was tapped on the shoulder.  When she turned around, she screeched, "You're here, you're here!"

"I couldn't get out of work early and it took me over an hour to get through the Friday night Hartford traffic."

"Well, you're here now.  Let's get you a drink."

Trish turned to Lou, "Lou, this is my friend Jenny.  Jenny this is Lou."

"Hello Lou."

"Nice to meet you Jenny."

Then Trish turned the other way and introduced Jenny to Frank and Sam.

"Jenny knows Pete also."

She turned to Jenny, "Weren't you and Pete in the same class in school?"

"Yes."

"So you know Pete's whole family?" Lou asked.

"Sure do."

"We'd better be careful what we say guys.  These ladies know the boss, and could be plants for information."

"How lame Lou.  Is that supposed to be a joke?" Sam asked.

"What?"

Then he thought about it, "Oh, I get it.  Plant, Harttt Landscaping."

They all laughed.

"It seems Pete knows all the beautiful women," Frank said looking Jenny over.

"He sure does," Lou added.

Jenny was dressed in tight black jeans, cuffed at the ankle with a pink striped blouse.  The sleeves were rolled up and most of the buttons were not buttoned.  Her brown hair was pulled back into a ponytail. She looked like the all American girl, five foot four, but petite in stature. There was something very gentle about her face; her long eyelashes accentuated her blue eyes, the tip of her nose was turned up, and the small gold hoop earrings drew attention to her perfect ears. In fact, her face had no flaws.

"Jenny had a crush on Pete for the longest time. Then, Heather came along. After high school, Jenny went on to college and moved away."

"Yeah, I recently took a new job in Hartford and moved back here from Boston."

"So, you here with anyone?" Sam asked.

"Just Trish. Girls night out."

Jenny turned back to Trish, "Yeah, til Heather came along."

"So you know Heather?" Lou asked.

"I know who she is but that's it. She seems to be the only woman Pete's interested in anymore."

"You got that right," Sam said.

Trish broke in, "We need to get Jenny a drink."

Sam waved to Jake to call him over. "What will you have?"

"I would like a Coors Light Draft."

"Frosted?" Jake asked.

"The colder the better."

"Coming right up."

Jake took out a frosted mug from the freezer and pulled her a beer.

Jenny picked up her beer and touched Sam's, "Thanks for the beer."

"My pleasure. Frank, why don't you give Jenny your seat?"

Frank quickly took the, got up from the stool and went to the other end of the bar.

"I'm Sam Marino."
"Jenny Connors."

Trish's shoe had fallen off and she bent over to put it back on. Jenny saw Lou looking down Trish's top, and when Trish sat back up, Jenny leaned over and whispered something into her ear. "That's alright. He has been looking at my breasts all night. In fact, I told him if things worked out, he'd get to see a lot more."

Sam just looked into his beer and when Jenny turned back to him, he pretended he hadn't heard them talking. "That Trish, she isn't shy about anything. That's why I like her."
"My friend Lou, he isn't exactly the most discrete person in the world either."
"I hope he's up to the challenge."
"He's been looking for an aggressive woman for some time now."
"Well, he found her. And she's about as aggressive as they come. She'll give him the workout of his life if he plays his cards right tonight."
"Don't let him hear that."
"Well then, this should be interesting."
"Let's have another beer and watch."
"Why not? It's a free show."

Sam asked Jake for another fresh beer for himself.

# Chapter 2

At the far end of the bar sat Ed Martin, also known as Big Ed. He comes into the bar every night around five. Not just Fridays, every day. He has a few beers, talks to Jake and Ron, flirts with a few of the waitresses and then leaves around six-thirty to go home for dinner. A creature of habit if there ever was one.

Tommy Benson, who drives a big rig, was sitting next to Ed. He had arrived a few minutes after Big Ed and the two immediately struck up a conversation about the weekend sports schedule. They didn't see each other every Friday, but many Fridays were spent catching up.

The two had been friends since Tommy was a standout basketball player having grown up in Unionville and attending the local high school. Big Ed was about twenty years older than Tommy and had been an ardent fan of the local sports teams since he was a kid himself. When Tommy led his team to the state finals in his senior year, he and Big Ed became friends. Now the two talked about sports every time they got a chance.

"Tommy, tell me again why didn't you go to college and play basketball?"

"When I was in my senior year, after the basketball season was over, I kind of had a run-in with the law."

"What was so bad it kept you from playing in college?"

"I got a girl pregnant."

"Yeah, well, that happens all the time."

"I know, but the girl was the principal's daughter. Word kind of got around and my scholarship offer got pulled. Then I couldn't get anyone to even consider me, and without a scholarship, no college."

"You mean the father got you blackballed?"

"Yep. Every school I contacted, ended up sending me a rejection letter right after they contacted my high school."

"I guess that was a stupid thing to do, especially with the principal's daughter."

"Yeah, it was. I didn't think beforehand, but I never thought anything like that would happen."

"Didn't you use a condom?"

"Nope I didn't. That was the second stupid thing I did that night."

"You had the nicest jump shot. You might have even been able to play pro ball."

"That's all history now. I don't think about it much. It won't get me anywhere."

"You're probably right. Why don't you do something with your golf game?"

"Like what? Tryout for the Nationwide Tour?"

"Why not? You're a natural athlete and you might be able to make it."

As the two were talking, a couple came in from the front door and stopped by Big Ed.

"Excuse me sir, are these seats taken?" the woman asked.

"I don't think so," said Ed.

The two pulled out two stools and sat down.

Jake promptly came over, "Hi Hal, Mary. How're you two doing this fine night?"

"Fine Jake," Hal Carson said.

"And you Jake?" Mary Carson asked.

"Pretty good. Things are just starting to get busy."

"We see. Last two seats at the bar and it's still early."

"Will it be the usual?"

"Please," Mary and Hal said in unison.

Jake made Mary a vodka gimlet and got Hal a beer.

Hal and Mary kept to themselves having a quiet conversation.

Frank Johnson come over and stood by Tommy and Ed.

"Tommy, Pete said we should ask you if you want to play golf tomorrow if he can't play."

"I told Pete I would take the first game I could get for tomorrow and he said he would call me as soon as he talked to his lady."

"Tomorrow's his anniversary and I'm going to bet he can't play."

"Well, if he calls in the next half hour and says he can't play, I'll let you know."

"We've got a tee time for ten in the morning at Tunxis."

"Yea, Pete told me that already. I'll get back to you as soon as I hear from Pete."

"Thanks."

Frank turned and went down the bar a few people and started to talk to another patron known to everyone as Pops who was sitting on a stool by the beer taps. As one of the "elders" he earned the nickname with nothing but respect.

"Hey Pops, what's shakin?"

"Hey there Frank, things are good. I see you're in here with the guys. On your way home from work huh?"

"Yeah, we stopped in for a cold one. Plus I'm looking for someone to replace Pete tomorrow in golf. It's Pete's anniversary and he has other priorities."

"I know all about it. The woman comes first."

"Yeah, but he should be able to get a round in during the day and take her out tomorrow night."

"That's not how it works Frank. You guys need to get your testosterone under control and think about things a little more from a woman's perspective."

"That'll be the day."

"Well, you would find things would be a lot better between you and your woman if you took my advice."

"Well, it's Pete's problem right now, not mine."

"It's everyone's problem Frank, not just Pete. You guys just don't get it."

"If Pete doesn't do the right thing, he won't get it."

"See, that's the kind of thinking I'm talking about. You only think about one thing."

"So what's wrong with that?"

"Frank, you need to think outside your pants. Sometimes being thoughtful isn't about sex."

"If you say so Pops. You've got a lot more experience than me."

"And if you don't lose the bad attitude, I'll always have more."

The two laughed, and then Frank whistled at Ron and asked Ron to get each of them another beer.

Once delivered, Frank picked up his mug, "To more sensitivity and less testosterone."

"Go ahead and make a joke about it Frank. But if you think about what I said and actually tried, you might find things a lot easier. You know what they say, fake it till you make it."

"Maybe I'll give it a try."

He put his drink down in front of the empty stool next to the Professor to continue his education.

Tommy was still considering the option of trying out for a professional golf career, and shared his thoughts with Ed.

"If I worked at it Ed, I could probably get myself into tournament shape in few weeks. But I'm not sure I want to go and live out of a suitcase for a few months trying to make it into the Pros."

"But Tommy, you're a three handicap right now. You could easily be a scratch golfer and with a little luck, you could be right there with the guys on the tour."

"Yeah, but I'm making some good money right now and my life is the way I want it."

"Just think about it kid. You have the talent."

"Thanks Ed. I'll think about it. Let's get another beer."

As Ron was bringing the beers over, Tommy's cell phone rang.

"Tommy here."

"Ok Pete, you have a good anniversary."

"Huh? Yea, he's still here."

Tommy motioned to Frank who was only a few people away from him talking to Pops. Holding up his cell phone, "Its Pete," then Tommy slid the phone along the bar to Frank's seat.

"Hey Pete."

"Ok. Tommy said he's ready to play. I'll see you on Monday. Thanks for letting me know."

Frank walked the phone back to Tommy.

"Pete said he can't make it tomorrow so if you can make it, we'd sure like you to join us."

"You said ten o'clock at Tunxis, right?"

"That's it. Lou wants you to be his teammate if that's ok with you."

"What kind of game does Lou have?"

"Not good."

"What kind of handicap does he get?"

"As much as he can negotiate."

"Well, without knowing how the rest of you play, I'll be his teammate if he gets a 25 handicap."

"I'll have to ask Sam before I can commit, but I don't think that'll be a problem."

"How much are we playing for?"

"Fifty per player."

"Ok, then with a 25 handicap, I'm in."

"Be there at ten. I'm sure we can work it out."

"Ok, see you at ten."

Tommy turned to Big Ed who was smiling.

"Does he have any idea how good a golfer you are?"

"I'm sure Pete told them. But I don't really care. If the guy they pair me up with a guy who can play at all, this'll be an easy fifty."

"See what I mean Tommy, you have that competitive streak in you. You should really think about giving it a try."

"Yeah, Yeah, there's a big difference in playing a few hackers for fifty bucks versus playing someone who can actually play the game for a million bucks."

"You're right, but you're that good."

"Tell you what Ed. I'll think about it."

"You do that."

"Now I gotta get going. I have a date tonight and I don't want to drink too much. It might mess up my game."

"By that do you mean your date or your golf game?"

"Both."

Tommy smiled as he put a twenty on the bar, chugged down the rest of his beer, slapped Ed on the back and left.

Ron came over to Big Ed and asked if he wanted another beer.

"No thanks Ron, I got to get going too. Have a great weekend. I'll see you on Monday."

"Going away for the weekend?"

"Nah, but I have plans that will keep me pretty busy."

"I get it. A new woman huh?"

"Something like that."

Ed added another twenty to Tommy's, handed both to Ron, and left.

# Chapter 3

Professor Tim Ryan had been drinking his scotch and soda and was finishing his appetizer. Frank had moved on, and he was ready for dinner.

"Jake, what's good on the menu tonight?"

"If you like sole, there is a stuffed sole on the special menu that's very tasty."

"What does it come with?"

"Your choice of pasta and vegetables, plus soup or salad."

"That sounds good. Let me have it with a salad. And I'll have vinaigrette dressing."

"Do you want rolls and butter also?"

"Sure."

Jake went to the register and entered the Professor's order. As he left, a couple asked the Professor if anyone was sitting on the two empty stools next to him.

"Nope."

They pulled out the stools and sat down just as Jake came back with the Professor's napkins and silverware for dinner.

"Welcome folks. Here for dinner or just drinks or both?"

"Both," John Walden said, looking back at his wife.

"We'll have a cold draft, Bud, and a glass of house chardonnay. Oh, and two menus."

The Waldens were an older couple probably in their mid forties. Both wore khaki slacks; he with a blue blazer and light green striped button down shirt; she with a dark green buttoned cashmere sweater over a white and navy polka dotted collarless shirt. They could have been cut from the cover of the latest J. Crew or Gap catalogs for older folks.

Pat Walden turned to Professor Ryan, "You're Professor Ryan from the college aren't you?"

"Guilty as charged."

"I'm Pat Walden. This is my husband John Walden. We met you last year during the commencement ceremonies at the college."

"Oh, did you have a child there who graduated?"

"No, John was a guest speaker at the commencement last year. He's the president of the Regional Chamber of Commerce."

"Oh, now I remember. How are you?"

"We're fine. We've never been here before, but have only heard good things. How's the food?"

"I'm typically just stopping in on my way home. But I haven't heard any complaints, and the service is good. Jake's the best."

"Do you come often?"

"The college is just down the road. So it's convenient for me to come here in between classes to get something to eat if I have time."

"Do you have classes on Friday nights?" John asked.

"No. No classes on Friday nights. The school knows better. What kid will sign up for a class on a Friday night?"

The group laughed.

"But once I'm done grading papers and such, sometimes I'll stop by on my way home so I don't have to cook. And since peanut butter and jelly is my specialty, this is better."

Jake brought the Professor's salad over and put it in front of him along with a basket of warm rolls. Pat and John were discussing the specials, and what each was hankering for when the Professor offered a suggestion.

Professor Ryan stopped eating his salad, "If you like eggplant, try the Rollatini. It's very good."

"Thanks, I just might," John said.

"Well, I'm going to order the clams casino appetizer to start while we try to decide what else we want," Pat said.

"Go ahead."

Jake come over and took Pat Walden's appetizer order.

"Anything for you to start?" Jake asked Mr. Walden.

"What's the soup of the day?"

"It's a beef barley."

"I'll have a cup."

"Would you like to order dinner?"

"We'll wait for the apps, then order."

"John, why not try one of the veal dishes. You like veal" Pat said.

"I'm thinking about it. The veal parm is speaking to me."

"I'm getting the chicken cacciatore. That, plus the clams and a salad will be more than I can eat."

"Ok. I'm going to get the veal."

Professor Ryan had finished his dinner by the time the Waldens had placed their order. He had asked Jake for another drink and had just taken the first sip when Jake brought the Waldens their second round.

Bobby Rose came behind the bar with a rack of clean glasses; Jake said, "Put those away Bobby and then take the dirty dishes to the kitchen if you would. The dishpan is pretty full."

Ron put Professor Ryan's dishes in the dishpan. It was almost flowing over. Bobby carefully put the wine glasses and other glasses away. As he picked up the overflowing dishpan, a glass perched on the edge fell out shattering on the floor.

"Sorry Jake."

"It's ok Bobby. I shouldn't have put any more in there."

"I'll be right back and clean it up."

Mr. Walden turned to the Professor, "So Professor Ryan, how are things at the college these days? Every time I go by the lot its full."

"It's getting to the end of the semester so things are pretty busy."

"I can imagine. Final exams, preparations for graduation and things like that," Pat said.

"Yea, plus trying to help the seniors decide on what they do next takes up a lot of time."

"Do you get involved helping the students try to decide what to do next?"

"Since I'm a department head, I spend quite a bit of time working with the outgoing students helping them make job connections or transfer into a four year school."

"That must take up a lot of your time."

"Just a part of the job. But I like it all."

As Mr. Walden was about to say something else, a young woman arrived and stood on the other side of Professor Ryan. She didn't say anything and waited for the Professor to turn to her. As Mr. Walden looked at her, the Professor turned and saw the young woman standing next to him, "Hello Carla."

Carla leaned over and gave him a kiss on the cheek. Professor Ryan turned back to the Waldens, "Carla Simmons had been one of my students. I was able to help her out with her career and she shows her appreciation by taking an old man to a movie from time to time. Carla, this is Mr. and Mrs. Walden. My new 'O' bar friends."

"Nice to meet you," Carla said.

"Nice to meet you too," the Waldens said in unison.

"If you'll excuse me," said Professor Ryan.

Carla Simmons was a tall woman. At six foot, she was a good three inches taller than the Professor. She dressed in skinny jeans along with a light striped cashmere sweater. There were sequins sewed onto the various stripes of the sweater making it sparkle as she walked towards the fireplace. She wore a pair of ballet flats trying to minimize her height. Her figure was slender and even looked downright skinny. She couldn't weigh more than one hundred forty pounds. Her hair was shoulder length jet black, as were her eyelashes. They were the perfect color and length to draw your attention to her hazel-green eyes. As a student, she must have been very successful.

When the two walked away from the bar, Mr. Walden said, "I guess the Professor has a special interest in some of his students."

"You don't know anything John. Don't assume."

"Well, she's much younger than he is."

"So what does that mean? He said she was a student. Of course she'd be younger."

"I've always wondered about the relationships that exist between students and professors. Some of these girls are very good looking and can be rather naïve. They're easily impressed, and not minors."

"So you think sex is involved?"

"Could be. The circumstances just lend themselves to things like that happening."

"Well, I wouldn't assume anything.

Jake brought their dinners over and Pat said, "What do you make of the Professor and his guest?"

"Oh, that's Carla Simmons. She used to be a student of the Professor. She graduated about ten years ago and the Professor helped her out getting her career started. Then she was in a bad car accident and he took it upon himself to help rehabilitate her from the injuries she received."

"Really?" Mr. Walden said.

"Yeah, she didn't have any family in this area. She was one of his favorite students. So when she needed help, he was right there to help her. And ever since her recovery, she stops by and takes him to the movies or something. They have become pretty good friends."

Mrs. Walden turned to her husband, "See John, you shouldn't jump to conclusions."

"You're right. But when I see an older man with a younger woman at a bar who acting kind of friendly, I can't help but think there's something going on between them."

"Well, you shouldn't," Pat said.

26

"You're right again."

The two started in on the food. John looked past Pat from time to time looking at Professor Ryan. For some reason, John couldn't get it out of his mind that something was going on more than camaraderie between the Professor and Carla.

At one point, he saw Professor Ryan say something to Carla and she had put her hand on his leg under the table.

"See there, there's something going on with them."

She turned and looked at Carla, "You're imagining things."

"I'm telling you, it's more than a platonic relationship."

"Sure John, sure. What else do you see in that crystal ball of yours? Eat your dinner."

# Chapter 4

A little after five thirty, Kelly Jones, Sue Walker and Karin Ascroft came into the bar. The three were having a good laugh. Ron walked over to them and waited for the laughing to stop.

"Looks like you three are having a good time," Ron said to them.

"Oh, Sue was just telling us about Lou Adams trying to hit on her last Friday," said Kelly.

"Yeah, she said he kept trying and trying, but when it came time to commit, he backed down," Karin said.

"Oh, really?" Ron said looking down the bar in Lou's direction.

Sue followed Ron's gaze, "Looks like he's working someone else tonight."

"Good. We shouldn't have to worry about him then," Kelly said.

"What can I get you ladies?" Ron asked.

"I'll have a martini, desert dry with olives," Karin said.

"Me too," Sue added.

"I'll have a cosmo," Kelly said.

Ron went to the back of the bar and made the drinks. He put them in front of the women who were laughing again."

"Now what's so funny?"

"Oh, nothing," Sue said.

"We were just commenting on Lou's technique," Kelly added.

"Technique at what?" Ron asked.

"For gathering information. Watch the next time I tell you to, Ron," Karin said.

A few minutes went by and then Karin said, "Quick Ron, look."

Ron looked at Lou. The woman next to him had bent over to pick something up off the floor and Lou was going out of his way to look down her blouse.

"Did you see that?" Sue said.

"Yeah. I guess," Ron said as he went over to another patron.

"What can I get you?" Ron asked.

"I'll have a beer."

Ron reached over the bar extending his hand. "Ron Alderman," he said.

"Mike Smith," the patron said shaking Ron's hand.

"Any particular kind?"

Mike looked over the various taps, "I'll have a Blue Moon."

"With or without fruit?" Ron asked.

"Without."

"So Mike, you new to the area?"

"I'm in town on business. I have to stay the weekend and someone told me this is a good place to relax."

"Yeah, it is. Most of the people who come in here are regulars who come in every week to decompress."

"We've got a place like this where I'm from."

"Where's that?" Ron asked.

"I'm from Paramus, New Jersey."

"Where about is that?" Ron asked.

"In north Jersey, not far from New York City."

"What kind of business are you in?"

"Computers."

"You sell them?"

"Nah. I'm into programming."

Ron looked around the bar. "I think Professor Ryan is into computers but I don't see him right now."

"What's good for dinner here, Ron?"

"Most everything. The portion sizes are pretty big and everyone says the food is great."

Mike looked through the menu Ron had given him.

"I'll have the Chicken a la George that's on the Specials menu."

"Good selection," Ron said. "Soup or salad?"

"Can I have a salad, Italian dressing?"

"Sure."

Ron went to the register and put the order in.

When Ron had walked away, Lou Adams introduced himself.

"Lou Adams."

"I'm Mike Smith. Nice to meet you."

"I heard you telling Ron you're into computers."

"Yeah. It's a living."

"I can never get the damn things to do what I want them to do."

"Oh, you'd be surprised what you can get one to do.

"I see the commercials and hear a lot of people in here talking about their smart phones and laptops. I guess I'm just not geek enough to keep up with the modern day technology."

"Do you have to be a geek to understand computers?"

"Probably not. But everyone seems to have a smart phone or laptop," Lou said drinking his beer.

"Mike, this is Trish Howland," Lou said as Trish sat back down after having gone to the ladies room.

Mike looked in her direction.

"Nice to meet you Trish."

"Same here, Mike."

"Mike's here on business."

"Isn't everyone?"

Mike wasn't exactly sure what that was supposed to mean, so he was glad Lou sat between the two. He just nodded and smiled.

Trish turned the other way to listen to something her friend Jenny was saying. When she did, Lou whispered to Mike, "She's a hot ticket."

"Really?"

"Yeah. I think I might get lucky with her tonight."

"Well good for you Lou."

Mike listened for the next hour to the conversations going on around him. He picked up quite a bit of local information.

At around seven o'clock, Trish had been working on Lou two hours, when she finally said, "Lou, finish your drink and let's take a walk."

"Give me a minute and I'll be ready."

Lou turned and looked at Mike, "Here we go."

Trish took Lou by the hand and led him out the door.

Ron came over to Sam Marino, "Where's Lou going?"

"Trish is taking him for a walk."

"Are they coming back?"

"Yeah. Give her twenty minutes. They'll be back," Jenny added.

"Ok. Lean their stools against the bar if you would Sam."

Mike turned the other way to see what was going on in that direction. The stools next to him were open.

"Sir, is anyone sitting here?"

"Nope. There was a couple sitting here a little while ago but I think they got a table."

Ron quickly came over, "Those are open."

The man sat down.

"I'm Don Pennington."

"Mike Smith."

"Nice to meet you Mike."

"What can I get you Don?"

"I'll have a Guinness."

Ron poured the beer.

"You from around here?" Don asked Mike.

"Just visiting. I'm here on business."

"That's what I figured. Friday nights are pretty much regulars this early."

"That's what I'm hearing."

"What kind of business you in Mike?"

"Computers."

"Oh, me too," Don said as he took his beer from Ron.

"I do some programming, not sales or hardware."

"Me too. I work for one of the big insurance companies in Hartford. Who are you in town visiting?"

"I'm an independent contractor. No allegiance to any one company, or any one place."

"What does that entail?"

"I write computer code for other people and they use it in their business."

"Oh, really? What kind of code is it? Like, what does it do?"

"Stuff that runs in the background on laptops, desktops and smart phones."

"Sounds interesting. I just write application code for big insurance administration systems. Typical insurance related transactions."

"Good money in that?"

"Yeah. These systems are so big, it takes years to learn all about them. So they pay good money to keep the systems maintained. Once you know a package, they pay big to keep the expertise. Is there good money in your programming?"

"Can be when the application is right."

"Here's your dinner Mike."

# Chapter 5

Bobby carried a couple six-packs of off-brand beers behind the bar.

"Put those in the cooler Bobby and then straighten up the tables if you would?" Ron instructed.

"Got it boss."

Bobby looked like he lifted weights.  He was about five-five and had broad shoulders and pretty big biceps.  He wore shorts, sneakers and a tight tee shirt with a picture of a fish on the front.  He put the beer on the floor and carefully took each bottle out of the six-pack placing them in the cooler with labels facing forward.

Jake came over to Don Pennington.

"Can I get you a menu?"

"Yes, please."

Jake handed him the menu.

"Say Jake, you must know pretty much everyone in here.  What's the deal with the women here?" Don asked quietly.

Jake looked at the women seated next to Don, "Those three down the bar seem to be fun types."

"These three?" Don nodded to his left

Jake nodded, and continued in more detail.

"Let's see, Kelly Jones, the one at the end, is single and pretty wealthy. She designed a clothing line for women between teenage and middle age, young adults I'd say, and then a cosmetics line to go with it. Both took off. Not bad for a woman who recently turned thirty-three."

"I'd say."

"And Sue Walker, in the middle, has been a friend of Kelly's since they were in college."

"And the other one?"

"Karin Ascroft. She's a friend of Kelly's who is into marketing. I think she's the brains behind a lot of Kelly's success."

"So they're in business together?"

"I know they're in here talking about business quite a bit, but I think Karin has her own company, and I think Sue is just a friend."

Karin, who was closest to Don, heard her name.

"Are you talking about me Jake?"

"Don was just asking me about you three and I was giving him some background."

Karin looked at Don.

"I'm Karin Ascroft."

"Don Pennington."

"Don, instead of talking with Jake about us, why don't you join us?"

"Kelly and Sue, this is Don Pennington," Karin said turning to the other two women.

"Hi Don," Sue said. "I've seen you in here before."

"Don," Kelly said.

"Yeah, I come in from time to time."

"Jake was giving Don a little background on us. I thought if he wanted information, better get it from the source."

"What are you looking for, Don?" Sue said.

"I was just asking Jake about some of the people in here tonight. He was just telling me about you three. Because he was starting with the prettiest."

"And what did he say?" Kelly asked.

"Not much. Just that you have your own company and have had some business with Karin and that Sue and you're old college friends."

"What else did he say?" Sue asked.

"That's as far as he got when Karin introduced herself."

"Too bad," Sue said. "He didn't tell you anything more about me?"

"No."

"Sue, you're flirting with Don," Kelly said.

"No I'm not. I'm just trying to find out what he knows and what he wants to know."

"Well, ask away Don. What can we tell you?" Karin said.

Don was a little embarrassed. He didn't know how to proceed.

Mike Smith leaned in towards Don, "I'd like to know a little about your business."

Kelly got up and walked down between Don and Mike.

"Kelly Jones."

"Mike Smith."

"Well, Mike Smith. What would you like to know?"

"I heard Jake say something about you owning your own clothing line and cosmetics company."

"That's right."

"Is your business local?"

"Yes. It's set up in Cheshire."

"Is that near here?"

"Not far, thirty minutes maybe."

"Do you have an app for your businesses?"

"Why would I want an app?"

"To reach all those women out there with smart phones. Tell them about sales, new items, let them purchase online, post reviews."

Kelly thought for a minute.

She turned to Karin, "Maybe Mike is on to something. Wouldn't it be nice if a woman could click on an app and find out what's new in fashion, where to get it and the price?"

Karin closed her eyes for a minute, "I'll put someone on it next week and see what develops."

"Why not have Mike talk to your people? He has a better verbal grasp of the idea and potential. Plus, maybe there's something in it for him as well," Don said.

"Good idea Don. Mike, do you have a business card?"

Mike produced a card and handed it to her. Karin took one of her own cards out of her purse and handed it to him.

"I look forward to hearing from you." Mike put the card in his shirt pocket, and turned back to his almost empty plate.

Kelly went back to her seat. The women started up a conversation between themselves.

Don turned to Mike, "See, you never know who you might meet."

"Yeah. And maybe something will come out of it."

"Maybe."

# Chapter 6

Trish and Lou walked outside. She took a cigarette out of her purse along with a lighter. Lou reached for her lighter and then flicked it. She leaned over and lit the cigarette.

"Isn't it a nice night?" Trish said looking up at the starlit sky.

"Sure is. It must still be over seventy."

"Want to take a walk down by the river Lou?"

"I thought we might go for a ride in my van."

"Let's walk a little. It's a nice night."

"Whatever you say boss." He took her free hand as they walked.

They walked across the parking lot and past the pharmacy. Then, they turned left.

"Let's cross the street Lou and go down by the river."

"The bank is pretty steep over by the river. We might want to walk the other way a little."

"Ok. How about down by the school field?"

"Yeah. We can walk right up to the river over there."

The two crossed the street and then walked back in the direction from which they had come. They passed the old factory buildings now refurbished and housing a number of new businesses. At the end of the street, they turned left and walked across the school field.

Trish walked down to the river. She took her shoes off and walked into the river. They could see a few lights from houses through the trees across the river and could hear the traffic crossing the steel bridge to their left.

"Want to skinny dip?" She asked Lou.
"Now?"
"Yeah. It'll be fun."
"I thought we'd get to know each better."
She interrupted, "Patience Lou."
"I guess."

Lou started to take his clothes off. As he set his shirt on the riverbank, he looked at Trish. She had all her clothes off and was wading into the river.
"Come on in Lou. It's nice."
Lou quickly took the rest of his clothing off and walked in. Trish was already standing waist deep in the water. The river even in summer was a little cold and he could see it affected her.
Lou looked at her, "Cold huh?"
"Come here you fool. You'll forget about the cold in a minute or two."
As Lou got to Trish, the water level rose to his waist. Trish put her arms around him and kissed him.

"See, I said you would get to see more of me."
"And I'm impressed."
"Ever make love in the water Lou?"
"No."

"Want to try?"

"I don't think it'll work. Water's pretty cold."

"I see what you mean," Trish said looking down.

"Why don't we go for that ride now, and warm up?"

"Maybe some other time Lou. Let's go back to the bar and have another drink."

"But Trish...."

"You need to compose yourself Lou. I doubt this night will work for you. I don't mean to be direct, but that's what I am."

"I guess you're right."

She came close to him and put her arms around him again. She looked up into his face and kissed him. Then, she turned and started to walk to the shore. His arms slowly left her, lightly touching her breasts as she turned.

"Patience Lou, Patience."

They walked back to the riverbank and dressed. Their clothes were a little wet in places, as they didn't have any towels. They walked across the school field and back down the street to the bar.

Lou walked back to his stool.

"What happened?" Sam said.

"We went swimming."

"Oh really?"

"Yeah."

"So, did she come through?"

"She did, I didn't. That damn river water was too cold."

"Wow. And you were so looking forward to her."

"I still am."

"Here she comes Lou."

"Well, Sam. Did Lou tell you what we did?"

"Something about going into the river?"

"Yeah. We both went skinny dipping."

"That's what Lou said."

"Probably would have led to even more but Lou got cold feet."

"It wasn't my feet at all."

"They all react the same in the water."

Sam and Jenny laughed.

"She sure taught you a lesson Lou."

"What lesson?"

"Don't be so sure of yourself."

"Oh, you think that's what she was doing, teaching me a lesson?"

"Just knocking you down a peg or two, teaching you a little patience," Sam replied.

Lou picked up the new beer Ron had put in front of him.

Jenny said, "Don't let them tease you Lou. It wasn't your fault."

"I wanted to go for a ride."

"I'm sure you did."

"Ok. You win."

"It's not about winning or losing Lou. It's about doing things the right way."

"So you think my approach was wrong?"

"Not wrong per se, but not her style. A little pampering perhaps?"

"Huh," Lou said taking another drink of his beer. "I think I can do that."

"If you do, you won't be disappointed."


Jenny turned back to Sam, "Patience pays off Sam. You'll see as will Lou."

"I guess. I've never been accused of impatience."

The four had a few more drinks, sharing stories and laughter.

The makeup of the people at the bar changed a little around eight o'clock. Big Ed had left. Pops had finished his daily visit and had gone home. The Walden's table reservation was for seven and a waitress had come for them. Professor Ryan and Carla Simmons were sitting by the fireplace finishing their drinks. They were going to an eight o'clock movie. Frank Johnson had given up his seat to Jenny some time earlier and was now seated along side Sue Walker.

A man appearing to be around thirty years old came in through the back door. Wearing jeans, Sperry sneakers, and a bowling shirt made popular by Charlie Sheen, he looked freshly showered and ready for the night. As he walked the length of the bar, the women would turn to look. He was tall, but fit, not lean at all. His hair was dark with just a hint of gray at the temples, and his face was cleanly shaved. He took up the seat vacated when Pops left.

"How are you tonight Paul?" Ron said.
"Ok Ron. Looks pretty busy tonight."
"Mostly the usual crowd. What can I get you? Red, white?"
"I'll have a Sam Summer I think. Still pretty warm and a beer will takes good."
"Menu?"
"Nah. I've already had dinner."
Ron took out a cold mug, poured the beer, and put it in front of Paul.
Paul Aaron was a local attorney. He had an office just off the green down the street from the bar. Hal Carson, was in the seat next to Paul, "How are you this fine day Paul?"
"I'm sorry Hal. I didn't see you there." Then, he looked past Hal, "Hi Mary."

"Hi Paul," Mary said and smiled.

"Just getting out of work?" Hal asked.

"Yeah. I've been in court all day. I had to finish up a few things at the office after court for Monday, and just wanted to unwind a little."

"Are you having dinner?"

"No. I had dinner brought into the office. I wasn't sure how long it would take for me to finish things up."

"I know the grind. I did what you're doing for forty years."

"The town just doesn't pay enough to keep a full time attorney so I have to take on additional clients."

"That's the problem with a small town."

"It'd be one thing if I could get all of Farmington's business, but I only get the Unionville stuff. And there isn't much going on in Unionville."

"Don't have to tell me."

"That's right Hal. Your firm handled Unionville before I got it."

"We did."

"Why did you give it up?"

"There wasn't enough money in it for the firm. We were growing and my partners wanted bigger things. Every job was a small job."

"I'm getting to that point too."

"Well, don't let the job put you in the ground."

"I know. That's why I come in here from time to time. This is a good place to unwind."

"Hal, let Paul relax a little. Stop talking shop," Mary insisted.

"We're just talking."

"You've been talking to him since he sat down. Maybe he just wants some peace and quiet?" Mary suggested.

"It's ok Mary. Hal understands what my life is like."

"Paul, you just need to find a nice lady."

"Oh, I'm not sure I could take that on right now."

"You'd be surprised how comforting it might be," Mary said smiling at Hal.

"She's right Paul. Mary has been a blessing for me. She keeps my head level."

"I'll have to keep that in mind, as soon as I find mine."

The four laughed and toasted to finding the good life.

Hal turned to Mary and they began a conversation between them as Paul glanced down the other end of the bar.

Frank Johnson was sitting next to him and Sue Walker was next to Frank.

"Hello Paul," Sue said leaning behind Frank.

"Hi Sue. How are you?"

"Just fine. Are you here with anyone?"

"No. I just left the office after a busy day."

"Want some company?"

"I don't know."

"Frank, change seats with me," Sue said as she got up.

"Hal and Mary were just telling me I should look for a good company," Paul said to Sue.

"You thinking about getting married Paul?"

"Not me. Hal was just saying how being married to Mary helped him throughout his career. You know he's an attorney as well."

"I know. He did work for my dad years ago."

"I just don't think I can give the proper attention to someone at this point in my life other than my clients."

"I can't say I disagree with your thinking. Plus, you'd have to find the right woman."

"And I just don't have the time to look right now."

"What about someone like my friend Kelly?"

"Kelly Jones? I don't know."

"Paul, she's successful, wealthy, good looking and available."

Paul looked past Sue and could see Kelly seated next to Karin.

"I can't disagree with you there. She's attractive."

"Plus, she's busy as well. She'd understand your career demands."

"Maybe you have something there."

"Want me to see what she thinks?"

"You playing matchmaker Sue?"

"You never know."

Sue got up and went over to Kelly. She talked to her quietly for a few minutes and then pointed at Paul. Then, Kelly got up and came over to Paul.

"Sue says you want to ask me something?"

"Like what?"

"She didn't say. She just said you might have a proposal."

"I think Sue's getting way ahead of herself."

"Mind if I have a seat?"

"Please do. Can I buy you a drink?"

"Sure. I'll have a cosmo."

"Ron, can you get Kelly a cosmo?"

"Sure."

"So Kelly, Sue says you're a successful business woman?"

"I do ok."

"Ok. She said you have over fifty people working for you in your clothing business."

"That sounds about right."

"Who does your legal work?"

"I use one of the firms in Hartford."

"Well, if you ever consider hiring your own counsel, I might be interested."

"I thought Sue said you work for the town?"

"On a retainer basis. I'm always looking for other opportunities. I'm not sure you noticed, but it's a small town."

"I'll keep that in mind. Glad to help another small business owner out."

She picked up the drink and took a sip. Her lips barely touched the edge of the glass. She closed her eyes savoring the taste. Kelly could be an actress, the way she carried herself. She had perfect skin, dark blonde hair that almost glowed, and she was dressed in a black wrap dress that tied flatteringly at her tiny waist. Her choice of shoes was clearly her pop of color: pink and teal brocade with 3" heels most women would avoid. She, however, had no problem working them. And the scent of her perfume as she arrived was just faint enough to be noticed, and subtle enough to be enticing.

Paul had taken notice of her appearance when she first walked over.

"So, Kelly, are you dating anyone?"

"Dating? That's such a limiting phrase."

"I was just wondering. Wouldn't want to step on any toes."

"Paul, if you're trying to ask me out, just ask."

"Ok. Would you like to go out sometime?"

"Sure. But, we can't talk business."

"That's not a problem for me. I do that all day."

"Me too and when I get out, I just want to put all of the business stuff aside."

"Do you get to go to the Bushnell?"

"Sometimes. I like opera."

"There's a good one coming up next month. I have season tickets. Want to join me?"

"That sounds good."

"And, I'll take you to a good restaurant in Hartford."

"Which one?"

"Salute. It's down by the park."

"I know the place. It has a good reputation."

"Then, it's a date. Let me have your cell number and I'll text you the exact date to set things up."

Kelly called his cell to exchange numbers, kissed him gently on the cheek, and got up and went back to her group.

Jake looked at Paul, "Good news?"

"It's one date Jake. Even I need to get out sometime, but it's a start, and she seems worth the effort."

"Make it count Paul."

# Chapter 7

Sue was still talking to Frank, when the back door opened again.

"Here comes Tim Stone."

"Who's he?"

"He's just some creepy guy who roams town a lot."

"Is he homeless?"

"No. He has an apartment across the street past Stop and Shop."

"Why does he bother you?"

"He's always looking at me. He sits on the park bench outside and just stares at me when I go out and have a smoke. One time, he even followed me to my car when I had to park over by the post office."

"Did he ever do anything to you?"

"Not yet. But I think he's stalking me."

Jake had overheard the conversation.

"I'll keep an eye on him Sue. You let me know if he bothers you."

"Thanks Jake."

"Want me to have a talk with him?"

"Thanks anyway Frank. But, I don't want to bring any attention to myself from that guy. And I certainly don't want to antagonize him."

"Ok. You just let me know if you want me to intervene."

Frank wasn't a big guy; only five foot six or seven, and about one fifty. He looked like he had pretty bad skin as a kid, and the scars remained. Although confident in personality, physically, he was not an intimidating presence.

"That's nice of you Frank." Sue touched his hand.

"I used to be a bouncer at one of the clubs in Hartford. I know how to handle troublemakers."

"You a bouncer?"

"We don't want any trouble in here," Jake responded.

"Oh, don't worry Jake. I won't start anything in here. But if he bothers Sue, I'll take it outside."

"Thanks in advance Frank." Jake rolled his eyes. Both Sue and Frank saw it.

"No problem."

Tim Stone took up the stool next to Don. Jake didn't pay any attention to Tim.

"What's a guy have to do to get a beer around here?" Tim hollered.

Ron came over, "Do you have any money Tim?"

Tim put a ten-dollar bill on the bar. "Is this green enough for you buddy? Get me a bud draft."

Ron poured a draft and put it in front of Tim. He took the ten and made change. Tim put the change in his pocket.

Don looked at Tim, "Tim, what brings you in here?"

"I'm just doing like everyone else. Having a drink.. Got a problem with that?"

"You know you have a drinking problem. You shouldn't be in here."

"I don't tell you what to do," Tim said, picking up the beer.

"We've known each other since we were kids Tim. I'm just trying to look after your best interest."

"I can take care of myself."

"Ok. Just trying to help."


Don turned back to the bar.

"What's his problem?" Mike asked.

"Oh, nothing serious. He's got issues."

"You know him?"

"Yeah. I've known Tim since we were kids. He's had bad luck all his life."

"What kind of bad luck?"

"Oh, he's been in and out of trouble with the law."

"What'd he do?"

"Drugs, alcohol, robbery to support both, you name it and Tim has probably done it."

"Well, keep him away from me if you would."

"Don't worry. Jake knows all about Tim and he'll be watching."


"Bobby!" Jake yelled from one end of the bar to the other, where Bobby was chatting it up with a couple younger girls. "Could you clean up around the stools at the end of the bar. We're starting to get pretty busy and people will be looking for clean seats."

"Sure Jake," Bobby hollered back.

"Anything you say boss," Bobby whispered under his breath.

Bobby went around straitening up stools, picking up glasses, coaster, napkins and plates from the bar, and dropping everything into either the dishpan or the trash. He got a broom and dustpan and swept the floor. Then, he sprayed the bar with a chemical mixture in a spray bottle and wiped the bar down.

"All set Jake," Bobby said as he headed to the kitchen with the dishpan. Jake nodded in his direction.

"Bobby, drop that off and then clear out the happy hour food area for the music."

Just after Bobby had finished, Rick Taft and his wife Sally seated themselves at the clean and recently vacated stools.

"How are you two doing tonight?" Ron asked the Tafts.

"Just fine Ron," said Sally.

"What can I get you?"

"I'll have a Jack and diet Coke," Rick said.

"I'll have a glass of Chardonnay."

Ron got their drinks.

He put them in front of the couple, "Menus?"

"We put in for a table so I think we'll just have drinks."

Rick turned to the couple next to them, "And how are the Carsons doing this beautiful evening?"

"Good Rick. Out for your usual?" Hal inquired.

"Yeah. We like coming here Friday nights."

"So do we," added Sally.

"Who's playing tonight?" Rick asked.

"I'm not sure. Jake, who's on the schedule to play tonight?" Hal asked Jake.

Jake picked up a piece of paper from next to the register, "Simon Rules."

"Oh, we've heard him before. He's pretty good," Sally said.

"Yeah. He plays a mean guitar," Hal added.

"And has a pretty good voice," Mary added.

"How are you doing Mary?" Sally asked her.

"I've had my days," Mary replied.

Sally and Mary knew each other from around town. Sally knew Mary had been ill with cancer for some time but didn't know every detail.

"Good to see you out."

"We try to get out from time to time."

"Mary seems to be getting past her problems. Her doctor has encouraged her to get out as much as possible."

"Good for you Mary," Rick said.

"Yeah. I'm not going to let some illness take me down."

Jake came over to the group, "I see Simon coming in and setting up by the door. Your entertainment should start in a little while."

Simon set up his PA system and amplifier. He had two different guitars with him and put them both in stands behind a stool he had placed behind a microphone. Bobby helped move things around by the door and in fifteen minutes, Simon was set to play. A small plate of appetizers and a beer had been brought to him while he was setting up, and he quickly ate the food and drank the beer.

"Good evening everyone. I'm Simon Rules. I'll be playing for your enjoyment for the next few hours. If anyone has any requests, let me or one of the bartenders know and I'll see if I can accommodate your request."

He picked up the twelve-string Ibanez guitar and started to play. He was good.

Sally leaned back, "Anything you want to hear Mary?"

"I wonder if he can play Don't Let The Sun Catch You Crying?"

"Let's see," Sally said.

"Rick, can you see if Simon knows Don't Let The Sun Catch You Crying?"

"Sure."

Rick got up and went up to Simon. He was still playing. He motioned to Rick to a pencil and paper on a table next to the PA system. Rick got the message. He wrote down the request and left it on the table. Rick returned to his seat.

"Do you think he'll play it?"

"There are a few other requests on the table already," Rick said. "But, we'll see."

They listened for the next half hour. Simon was really good. He played both guitars and had a powerful voice. After every song, everyone clapped.

"For the next song, I'm going to take you back quite a few years," Simon said. "If anyone wants to dance, come on up. There's plenty of room for you up here."

He started to play Mary's request.

"You should go up and dance, Mary. He's playing your song," Rick stated.

"Hal, what do you think?"

"Come with me. Fred Astaire is in the building," Hal declared.

Hal and Mary walked up to the soothing sounds of her request. They held each other close and danced.

"Isn't that nice?" Sally said to Rick.

"Yeah."

"She's had such a tough time. Hope the cancer is in remission."

"Cancer is going to get most of us sooner or later."

"You'd think with all our technology and medical advances we'd have solved that problem."

"Hey, our government doesn't want cancer solved. What would our country do if all of a sudden most of the population lived to be over a hundred? Think of the economic impact something like that would have."

"I guess. It's just so debilitating a disease."

"Yes it is."

Sally, pointed at Frank, "Look at Frank over there. He has skin problems, probably cancer, too."

"You don't know that."

"His face is such a mess. I think I read somewhere that skin cancer is one of the leading cancers."

"He looks more like he has a bad case of acne than cancer."

"I don't know, but he skin looks pretty bad," Sally said loudly just as Simon's song ended.

Frank overheard her comment, and blushed a little.

Simon quickly went into a new song, and the small group on the dance floor stayed there.

Sally stood up, "Let's dance Rick."

"I'm right behind you."

When the song ended, the couples all went back to their respective seats.

"Let me get us a round," Rick offered to both Sally, and the Carsons. Everyone agreed, and Rick waved Ron over.

"Ron, we'll all have another."

"To a good evening," Rick said making a toast to the group.

"Yes," Hal agreed.

While the toast was being made, Jake held up his hand motioning to Bobby to come over.

"Bobby, can you get another rack of mugs from the dishwasher? We're almost out."

"Sure. I'll be right back."

Bobby went to the kitchen. He came back a few minutes later with a full rack of mugs and began to put them into the freezer.

# Chapter 8

After keeping the dance floor full for at least an hour, Simon put down his guitar.

"I'll be taking a break for a few minutes folks. If anyone has any additional requests, please jot them down and put it on the table up here."

Trish, Lou, Jenny and Sam were all seated at the end of the bar closest to where Simon had been playing. Simon stood behind them and asked Jake for a beer. Trish turned to speak to Simon.

"Sounds pretty good tonight Simon."

"Thanks Trish. Glad you like it."

"Yeah, you're getting some following," Lou declared.

"And people are getting up and dancing," Jenny said.

"Simon, you're going to have to watch out. You become any better and all the women are going to be after you," Trish said.

"Are you one of them?"

"Maybe. Night's not over."

"Hey, what about me?" Lou said in a surprised tone.

"Don't worry Lou. I haven't forgotten about you."

"Oh. I just didn't want to get left out."

"You won't."


Sam said to Jenny, "Lou is trying to be on his best behavior since he went outside with Trish earlier. Now, he thinks he's threatened by Simon."

"He doesn't have to worry. Trish is only flirting."

"Maybe so. But, Lou is serious."

"Oh, all he has to do is hang in there. Trish has already told me she's leaving with him when Simon is done playing."

"Lou will appreciate knowing that."

"Don't say anything."

"Why not?"

"Well, things can change and I wouldn't want to upset either one of them."

"Ok. So in other words, don't listen to a word she says. I'll have to remember that."


"Trish, I'm going to the ladies room."

"I'll go with you."

Sam leaned over to Lou, "Keep it cool Lou. I have it on good authority that you're getting lucky tonight."

"Did Jenny tell you that?"

"Yeah. She said Trish is going home with you when Simon is done playing tonight."

Lou smiled.


The two women came back. Lou was the perfect gentleman for the rest of the night.

He couldn't wait for Simon to finish playing.

Jake had been at the other end of the bar talking with Frank Johnson and waiting on some of the other patrons. Ron had gone into the kitchen for something. Trish leaned over the bar to get Jake's attention.

"What can I get for you Trish?"

"Jake, can we have four lemon drops?"

"Sure."

"What are we celebrating?" Lou asked.

"Oh, nothing really. I just thought it would be a nice idea for the four of us to do a shot."

"Ok Trish. What's up?" Jenny asked her.

"Well, if you must know, you see those two guys in the center of the bar?" She was looking at Mike Smith and Don Pennington.

"Yeah."

"They keep looking at us."

"So?"

"Keep it down Jenny. I don't want Lou or Sam to hear us."

"Why not?"

"I think those guys are interested in us."

"Hey. I'm all set for tonight. I plan on going home with Sam."

"And I'm still planning on showing Lou a good time later. I just don't want to eliminate any options."

"Trish. I'd let it go if I were you."

"You're probably right."


The lemon drops came, with sugar and lemons, and the four quickly emptied their glasses. Trish could feel her insides warming up as the liquor went down.


Trish smiled at Mike the next time she looked over at him when she knew he was looking in her direction.

"I'm going to the ladies room," Trish declared.

"Weren't you just there?" Lou asked.

"Yeah, but I forgot to wash my hands."

Trish got up and walked away.

As she walked behind Mike's seat, she picked up a napkin that had fallen to the floor.

"I think you dropped this," Trish said handing the napkin to Mike.

"Thank you."

"I haven't seen you in here before," Trish said.

"I'm here on business."

"Are you here with anyone?"

"No. Just me by myself."

"How long are you in town?"

"Only for a few days."

"Well, if you're in town, maybe we could have a drink?"

"I'll probably be back here next week or the week after. Can I call you?"

"Sure. Ron, can I have a pen and a napkin?"

Ron took a pen out of his shirt pocket and handed it to her along with a cocktail napkin. She wrote a number on it and handed it to Mike.

"I'll call you next time I'm coming to town."

"Where do you stay when you come here?"

"At the Marriott."

"I know where it is. Maybe we can meet there?"

"Tell you what. Why don't we meet here for drinks and dinner next time I'm in town and then we can go to the Marriot bar if you'd like."

"Ok. That works just as well."

Mike tucked the napkin into his pocket.

Trish continued on to the ladies room. When she came back to her seat, Jenny said, "So what did you talk about?"

"What do you mean?"

"I saw you stop and talk to that man."

"Oh nothing. I'm just doing a little planning."

Lou overheard them, "What's the plan about?"

"Oh, nothing. I'm just thinking ahead and I was just telling Jenny."

"Does it involve me?"

"You're in my immediate plans, Lou. I'm not thinking much past later tonight and breakfast in the morning," Trish said to Lou in a sexy voice.

Lou smiled.

Jenny turned to Sam, "And what do you think Sam?"

"I saw Trish talking with that guy over there for a few minutes. I think I know what her future plans are and they don't include Lou."

"Don't say anything to Lou, Sam. I don't want to start anything in here tonight."

"I won't. Sam's being good anyway. He knows he's getting laid tonight."

"Yeah. Trish pretty much said so."

"See. There's no need to upset the apple cart."

"I'm glad you agree."

"Now, about us."

"Oh, you're getting it tonight also Sam."

"Can't wait."

Jenny looked in the direction of the two men seated in the center of the bar. Mike had pointed at Trish and was talking with Don. Don looked in Jenny's direction and smiled. Jenny returned the smile. She thought about what Trish did. Maybe she could pull off the same thing.

Simon started to play another song. This one was Unchained Melody. Sam excused himself to go to the men's room.

"Trish, want to dance this one with me?" Lou asked.

"Sure."

The two got up and started to dance. Jenny was seated by herself at the end of the bar right in front of Simon. She watched as Lou and Trish danced. Don tapped her on the shoulder.

"Care to dance?"

"I don't know."

"Come on. You'll like it."

"Ok."

Trish looked at Jenny and smiled giving her approval. They started to dance slowly and very close.

"I'm Don Pennington."

"I know who you're. I've seen you in here before. I'm Jenny Connors."

"See, this isn't so bad."

Jenny looked up at Don. His six-foot-four height left the top of her head under his chin. He leaned back a little to look down at her face.

"I'd like to get to know you better."

"I'm sure we could arrange something."

Sam came back from the bathroom to find Jenny dancing with Don. He sat at his seat and watched. When the song was done, Don said, "Thank you for the dance."

"You're welcome."

"Can I call you?"

"Sure." She gave him her number.

Don turned around and Sam was sitting right there looking at him and Jenny.

"I didn't know you wanted to dance Jenny?"

"I didn't but this man asked me when you were in the men's room."

"You could have said no."

"I did. But he insisted. Plus I love that song. It's over now Sam. Don't worry; I'm still leaving here with you."

Sam turned to the bar and asked for another round of drinks.

Trish leaned over to Jenny, "So, what did you think?"
"I gave him my number. Let's see if he calls."

When Jake brought the round over, Lou made a toast.
"To good friends and good times."

# Chapter 9

Paul Aaron and Frank Johnson had known each other for some time. They had met at the 'O' Bar about a year ago and had become friends occasionally golfing or fishing together.

"Frank, you here with Sue?"

"No. She's here with her friends Karin and Kelly."

"You trying to hook up with one of them?"

"I'd like to, but someone would have to entertain the other two while I'm finding out."

"Which one you interested in?"

"Karin Ascroft. She's into marketing. The other woman, Kelly Jones has her own company and it's very successful. Sue's a college friend."

"I talked to Karin and Kelly a little while ago about business. We exchanged business cards. I didn't really get a chance to talk personal stuff. Just business."

"Yeah. Karin does marketing for her. I think they're in here after a busy day at Kelly's company."

"I'd like to get to know Kelly better. She's obviously smart, and I think smart women are very sexy. But Sue is pretty easy on the eyes, too. Probably less work. Kelly and I might get together next month for a show at the Bushnell."

Simon started to play another tune. This time, he selected a more current number. A few of the younger women in the bar got up and started to dance. Kelly was talking to the guy next to her, so Paul walked to Sue, "Want to dance?"

"Sure."

The two got up and started dancing right next to their stools as they were within a few feet of Simon.

Frank turned to Karin, "Would you like to dance?"

"I don't think it would be a good idea. I'm here with my friend Kelly and don't want to leave her alone."

"She seems pretty pre-occupied to me," Frank said looking at Kelly and the young guy sitting next to her. It was Tommy Benson who had returned to the bar. They were whispering in each other's ears.

"Well, I guess its ok." She tapped Kelly's shoulder, and motioned that she was heading over to dance.

They danced along side Paul and Sue.

When the song was over, they went back to their stools.

Kelly said, "We'll be right back Karin."

"I wonder what they're up to."

"They'll be back," Frank said. "She left her stuff on the bar."

Karin looked over and Kelly's handbag was on her stool.

"Hand her bag to me Frank."

He did. Karin put it on a hook under the bar in front of her seat.

"Now, no one will take it."

"I don't think she'd have to worry in here."

"I'm just being safe.  She's my client and I asked her to come here with me tonight."

"So, you two work together?"

"Yeah.  We just rolled out a new campaign for one of Kelly's product lines and it was a big success."

"Good for you."

"We both stand to make quite a bit of money from this campaign."

Simon started to play a slow song.

"Want to dance?"

"Sure.  Kelly's still outside."

The two started to dance.

Bobby was behind the bar, and in front of it.  Cleaning up the floor, wiping up seats and the bar, and picking up the floor, and the dishes and glasses left behind.  It was a constant battle with the turnover the bar saw on a typical Friday night.

Jake yelled over the music, "Thanks Bobby."

"No problem."

"I don't know why people can't pick things up when they drop them on the floor."

Bobby picked up a rack of dirty glasses and took them to the kitchen to be washed.

When the song was over, Frank tried to give Karin a kiss.

"Better not," Karin said.  "I'm here with my friend."

"I think she has other plans," Frank said looking out the back window seeing the two kissing.

"How about that?"

Still, she didn't return the advance by Frank.

Karin turned to say something to Sue who had also returned to her seat but not sat down.  Sue was talking to Paul and preparing to leave.

"Sue, are you leaving?"

"We'll be right back."

Karin sat back down and turned to Frank.

"Why is everyone going outside?"

"I think they want a little privacy."

"To do what?"

"It's so noisy in here plus if they want to have a little time alone, it's hard to do in here. Sue smokes too, so she probably would be doing that."

"Frank, take me outside so I can make sure Kelly is ok."

"She's fine. I saw her when we were dancing. She's out back with a lot of other people. And she's not a little girl Karin."

"Come on," Karin said getting up and pulling on Franks arm.

The two walked outside. Karin saw Sue and Paul standing over by the Firehouse embracing each other.

"Where's Kelly?" She asked as she surveyed the parking lot.

"They were right here a little while ago."

Karin started to walk away from the building. She got to the lot by the Pharmacy building when she saw two people in the back seat of an SUV. Kelly was one of them. Then, the two people dropped out of sight.

Karin stopped and turned back to the building.

Frank hadn't followed her into the parking lot and was standing on the steps to the bar.

"Did you find her?"

"Yes. She's in a vehicle over there."

"See, all they wanted was a little privacy."

"I guess."

"Do you want to go back inside?"

"Can we just walk a little?"

"Sure."

Frank came off the steps and started to walk in the direction of the Pharmacy.

"Not that way. Let's walk the other way."

"Anything you say."

The two walked along the Firehouse out to the street where they turned left. They walked a little ways and stopped at the gazebo on the green. Karin stood with her back against one of the support pillars. Frank approached her.

He put his arms around her and gently kissed her. She did not resist his advance this time. After a few minutes, their tongues touched and the foreplay became more passionate.

"What do you say we get out of here and go to my place?"

"While I'd like to Frank, I'm here with Kelly. Let's see where the night goes."

They walked back to the bar. When they got inside, Kelly was back drinking shots and a beer.

"Where have you two been?" Kelly said to Karin.

"Just taking a walk," Karin said.

"Sure."

"I went out to see where you went Kelly and saw you in an SUV in the other lot," Karin said quietly to Kelly.

"Yeah. I was getting to know Tommy better."

"I just wanted to make sure you were ok."

"Oh, I'm ok. I think I'm going to take Tommy home with me when we leave here later. Is that ok with you?"

"Sure Kelly. Why not?"

"That's what I figure as well. Hey, we had a heck of a day and I'm going to reward myself."

Karin didn't respond. She turned to Frank, "Looks like I'm free for the rest of the night."

Frank picked up his beer, "Great."

# Chapter 10

Tim Stone took a long drink of his beer. He had been into the bar many times in the past and most of the regulars knew who he was. After getting over his temper tantrum of earlier, he turned back towards Don.

"Just stopping in for a beer and looking to see what's going on around town."

"Doesn't look like much. Just the regular routine."

"Oh, knowing who's doing what and when, is information, Don. And information is valuable."

"You should talk to Mike, Tim. He's in the information business. Mike, this is Tim Stone."

"Hi Tim."

Tim was a little reluctant at first, but he did shake Mike's hand.

"Don said you're in the computer business, Mike. What do you do?"

"I program computers."

"I guess that means you're in the information business then," Tim replied.

"Guess so."

"What kind of programs do you write?"

"I'm a representative for a big computer software firm. We write applications for big companies. Don said you're in the information business as well."

"Yeah, but it's different than what you do."

"How's that?"

"I'm nosy. I sit back and watch. It's good to know who's coming and who's going and who they're coming and going with, and interesting things like that."

"So what information have you gathered in here so far Tim?" Mike was looking around at what he saw as an interesting and eclectic group of people.

"Let's see. You see that group at the end of the bar?"

"Yeah."

"Those women have been working the two men they're with for a while now and have told the men they're taking them home tonight."

"So?"

"So, Lou Adams just wants to get laid and it looks like he will tonight. That means they either go to his place or hers. I'm going to guess hers since she's calling the shots. The other couple is a toss up. Could go to either place."

"Why is that information important?"

"I'm from around here, so I know where people live, how they live, what they do."

"Why would that matter?"

"No reason. I'm just saying."

"And the other couple?"

"They aren't a couple. The woman, Jenny, is a rich widow. Her husband was killed in an industrial accident and she sued for a big sum. I'm not sure she's really happy though."

"Why wouldn't the guy with her make her happy?"

"Not the right way."

"What, you'd try to marry her?"

"Don't be silly. There are other ways to get everyone happy."

"If you say so."

"I've got to visit the pisser," Tim said standing and stumbling towards the men's room.

Don Pennington leaned in to Mike, "You had enough of Tim's bullshit yet?"

"He is a different character."

"That's an understatement."

"He seems to be gathering information on everyone in here. He knows a little bit about everyone. Like he's been watching and listening for a long time."

"That's Tim's routine. He comes in here from time to time and talks up a confusing game. I don't think anyone has figured him out yet."

Tim came back from the men's room and ordered another beer, pulling his change out of pocket. It was obvious he's had a few bought for him, too.

Simon Rules continued to play. He alternated songs from his play list and requests from the audience, and covered every decade from the 60s on.

As the evening wore on, some of the people changed their seats at the bar. Paul Aaron and Sue Walker were seated together. Karin Ascroft was next to Sue and Frank Johnson next to her. Kelly Jones was next to Frank and Tommy Benson next to Kelly. The Tafts and Carsons were seated at the far end of the bar. Lou Adams and Trish Howland were at the end of the bar directly in front of Simon Rules. Sam Marino was next to Trish and Jenny Connors next to Sam.

Tim Stone said to Don and Mike, "See, everyone is pairing up in here."

"So? You know that's what they do here every Friday," Don said.

"I'm just saying. The people you thought came in here alone are probably leaving with someone."

"What's your point Tim?"

"That means someone's vehicle isn't going to be where it's supposed to be tonight."

"What the hell are you talking about Tim?"

"Nothing you'd be interested in Don."

"You're a nut case Tim,"

"Not crazy Don. I just observe things. And I deduce things."

"No, you're crazy."


"Give me another beer, Jake," Don requested.

"Me too," Mike added.


Tim just picked up his beer, in slow motion, and turned around looking at everyone in the bar area. He was gathering information.

Don looked at Mike and just shook his head.


Someone put a hand on Mike's leg from the other side and he jumped a little.

"Did I scare you?" Trish said.

"Yeah. I thought it was Tim touching me."

"I'd be freaked out as well. Listen Mike, I'll see you tomorrow afternoon. I'm leaving right now and I wanted to talk with you before I left."

"Ok. I'll be here by two."

She turned and went to the door. Lou was holding it open for her.

71

# Chapter 11

Tommy Benson and Kelly Jones had been drinking and dancing for a few hours. Her friends Sue Walker and Karin Ascroft had turned their attentions to Paul Aaron and Frank Johnson.

"Tommy, I don't have any other plans for the night. Why don't you take me home?"

Tommy got up quickly and picked Kelly up off her stool.

"Sounds good to me."

"Put me down Tommy. Everyone is looking at us," Kelly said trying to be as quiet as she could.

Karin turned to Kelly. "I see Tommy swept you off your feet, literally."

"Ha, ha."

"I'll call you tomorrow," Karin said as Tommy put Kelly down.

"Ok, but, not before noon. I'm planning on a busy morning," Kelly said as she picked up her purse.

"I can imagine," Karin said as Tommy and Kelly started to walk out.

Karin turned back to the bar.
"Jake, put Kelly's tab on mine if you would please."
"Sure Karin. So thoughtful of you."

"Looks like Tommy and Kelly are planning a busy night," Frank said to Karin as he picked up his beer.
"She's always liked muscular men."
"How about you Karin?"
"I like a forceful guy every now and then. But, most of the time, I like a man who is thoughtful."
"Thoughtful, huh?"
"Yeah, like you Frank."
He smiled at her. She leaned in and kissed him on the cheek.

"So what are your plans, Karin?" Jake said as he brought the updated tab to her and tucked it into the spot on the bar in front of her.
"Business is taken care of so I can enjoy whatever comes my way."
"Hope that includes me," Frank said.
"We'll see."
"You let me know when you're ready to go Karin."
"I'm ready now Frank. Let's settle up with Jake and go over to my place."
"Jake, can I have my tab?" Frank requested.
Jake went to the register and came back with the tab a few minutes later.
"I'll get them," Karin said.
"Don't be silly," Frank said picking up both.
"No. I had Kelly's tab added to mine when she left."
"It's ok Karin. I'll get all of them."
"See Frank. You're such a gentleman. So thoughtful."

"That's me."

"I won't forget this.  Let's go."

Frank paid the tabs, and the two got up to leave.

"Have a good night."

"See you Jake.  You too Ron," she added looking at the other end of the bar as Ron was waving.

"Bye Jake," Frank said as they left.

The two looked around for Bobby, but he must have been busy in the back or kitchen.

"Looks like it's getting quieter," Paul said as they waved to Karin and Frank leaving.

"Guess so."

"You want to get going?"

"Nah.  Let's listen to Simon a little longer.  He's almost done with his break and I'd like to dance some more."

"Sounds good to me."

With his break finished, Simon turned on his amplifier and picked up his guitar.  He started playing.

Paul and Sue danced to a few songs and then sat back down a little winded.

"Ron, can we have another two drinks?" Paul requested.

"Sure."

Ron got them each another drink.

"I'm sweating a little from all the dancing."

"Me too.  A little practice for later perhaps?"

"Oh really?"

"Oh maybe."

"I can't wait."

The two listened to Simon for another half hour.  They each finished their drinks, and at around ten, Sue said, "Let's pay and get going."

74

"Sounds good. Ron, can I have the bill?"

Ron came back in a few minutes with the tab.

Paul looked at it and handed a hundred dollar bill to Ron.

"Keep the change Ron."

"Thanks Paul."

"See you later."

"You too."

Sue and Paul left.

Ron walked around the bar. Some things needed to be cleaned up around the area where the group had been sitting.

"Jake, have you seen Bobby?"

"He had to run out for a few minutes. He said he'd be back in a half hour."

"Where'd he go?"

"Something about having to pick something up. Here he comes now."

Bobby walked briskly back to the bar.

"Bobby, you have some catching up to do. Errands on the clock? Get busy."

"Sure Ron."

Bobby grabbed his cleaning towel and spray and did what he always does. Diligently wiping down surfaces, scooping up crumbs, stacking glasses, and repositioning the stools were his specialties on Friday nights.

Jake had walked to the end of the bar where The Tafts and Carsons were seated. He leaned on the bar, listening to the conversation for a few minutes. Sally Taft was telling Mary Carson about their house being robbed.

"Mary, they took all my jewelry. They got Rick's computer, our TVs and some of Rick's tools that weren't too heavy to carry."

"Wow. How did they get in?"

"The police said the robbers came through the front door."

"Wasn't it locked?"

"They literally came through the front door. They broke the door frame by ramming it."

"The door didn't keep them out?"

"No. We even had the deadbolt locked."

"The jamb split right down the middle," Rick added.

"Wasn't your security alarm on?"

"These guys knew what they were doing. They cut the phone and cable lines before trying to break in. The police said they have seen this kind of robbery quite a bit lately. Somehow, the robbers know when to strike. The homeowners are always away," Susan said.

"Do the police have any leads?"

"Not yet. They said they have some ideas but nothing solid yet."

"Do they know when the robbery took place?"

"Sometime last Sunday. We left for a six day trip on Saturday after coming in here for dinner and our house was robbed Sunday night."

"None of your neighbors saw anything?"

"You know our house. It sits quite a ways back off the street. It's hard enough just seeing the house let along seeing the door being left open or hearing anything."

"How did you find out?"

"Our paperboy told his parents our door was open when he went to deliver our paper on Monday. It must have happened after he delivered Sunday, but before Monday. His parents called the police. The police contacted us as they were securing the place, but at that point the damage was done. We came home as planned on Thursday to take inventory."

As they were talking, another couple came up to the bar.

"Jake, is anyone sitting here?"

"Nope. They're your's."

Kevin Haines and Amy Nevins sat down.

"What can I get you?"

"I'll have a Baileys on the rocks," Kevin requested.

"And I'll have a Chambord on the rocks," said Amy.

Jake poured their drinks and as he put them down on the bar in front, Amy said, "Jake, I lost an earring in here last week. Did anyone turn one in?"

"What did it look like?"

"It's a silver box with a diamond in the center," she said.

"Let me take a look."

Jake went to the back of the bar and opened up a cabinet under the register. He pulled out a box and brought it to the bar.

"Here's all the stuff we've found recently at the bar that hasn't been claimed."

There were eyeglasses, a cell phone, two rings, Amy's lost earring and a personal organizer.

"There it is!" Amy said excitedly.

When she clapped, Sally Taft turned to look.

She looked at the things on the bar.

"Hey, that's my ring! Where did you get that?"

"This stuff was all in the lost and found box," Jake said to Sally.

"Well, that's one of my rings stolen from our house last week when we were on vacation."

"I don't know how it got into the box. We usually find these things when we're cleaning the bar up at the end of a night. I can't even tell you when it was put in the box or by whom."

"Rick, you need to call the police and tell them we've found one of the stolen rings here at the bar."

"I'll do it in the morning."

"Why not now? The robbers might be in here right now."

"We haven't put anything into this box today Rick, so I'm not sure we'd even have an idea of who might have dropped the ring."

"Thanks Jake. I'll talk with the police tomorrow and we'll see what they say."

"Rick, why aren't you going to do something right now?"

"Like Jake said, he doesn't even know when the ring might have been put in the box. Let's wait until I talk with the police and see what they say."

"Ok. I guess."

"Sally, at least you have a lead now," Mary said.

"I just hope whoever robbed our house gets caught."

"Let the police do their thing," Rick replied.

"Jake, can we have another round?" Hal requested.

"Sure thing Hal."

# Chapter 12

Sally was perplexed. She knew her ring was one of the items lying on the bar in front of Amy Nevins. Jake took a picture of the ring with his cell phone, and then gave Sally the ring. She put it in her purse.

"Rick, I want you to take this to the police station first thing tomorrow."

"Ok Sally. I'll go there first thing."

"I wonder how it got into the lost and found box." Mary said to Sally.

"Who ever robbed our house must have dropped it here at the bar," Sally said.

"Maybe you dropped it when we were in here before we went on vacation?" Rick suggested.

"I'm positive it was at home Rick. I went through my jewelry before we went on vacation and remember looking right at this ring when I was selecting what I'd bring on the trip. I know I put it back in my jewelry box."

"If you're sure Sally, this might be the lead the police need to find the robbers," Rick suggested.

"I hope so," Sally replied. "Some of the stuff they took were family heirlooms and can't be replaced."

"I wonder if the robber is here right now watching." Mary said.

Sally looked around. She recognized most of the people at the bar from other times she and Rick had been there but didn't recognize a few of the men seated a few stools away from them.

"Do you think it was someone you know?" Mary asked.

"Who would do such a thing?" Rick asked.

"Someone who needs money and knew you would be away," Hal suggested.

"Did you tell anyone we were going on vacation?" Rick asked Sally.

"I'd bet everyone in here knew we were away," Sally said. "Remember how excited you were when we were in here having dinner just before we left. Anyone who was within listening distance that night would have known we were not going to be home for the rest of the weekend."

Jake was standing in front of them listening, "Yeah, I knew you were going on vacation."

"So who knows where you live?" Hal asked.

Sally looked around again.

"I'd guess most of the regulars in here know where everyone else who comes in here regularly lives," Sally replied.

"You're probably right about that," Jake said.

"So it could be anyone," Hal said.

Now Sally started to look long and hard at everyone in the bar.

"What are you doing?" Rick asked.

"Looking to see if someone is paying extra attention to us," Sally replied.

"We've already been robbed Sally. There wouldn't be any reason to be watching us now," Rick said shaking his head.

"Hey, don't make fun of me."

"Think about it Sally. What would a robber have to gain coming back to rob us again. They already got everything of value."

"Not everything," Sally said. "They missed the cash box I keep in the top of my closet. It had thousands in it."

"What are you talking about?"

"You know. The money I keep in the house for emergencies."

"I don't know what you're talking about."

"Can you keep it quiet Rick? I'm baiting a trap."

"So, you're some super sleuth now?"

"I'm setting a trap," Sally said whispering to Rick. "I know there isn't any money in my closet, but the robber doesn't know."

Rick decided to go along with her ploy.

"Oh, yeah. Good thing you didn't leave the money box out in the open."

Rick turned around quickly and accidentally spilled his drink knocking the glass on the floor. It shattered into many pieces.

"Bobby?" Jake turned towards the bar looking for the bar back. He again was hanging out at the end of the bar, but this time no one was keeping him company.

"Sure."

Bobby got the broom and dustpan. He went around to where Rick had been seated and pulled the stool back. Then, he cleaned up the mess.

Sally and Rick had been standing for the time being behind Mary and Hal.

"That was careless of you Rick," Sally said.

"I guess I was just too excited about not losing the cash box in your closet," Rick said as he winked at Jake and Sally.

"Let's hope someone heard us talking about the cash box," Sally said.

"You have a plan?" Mary asked.

"I do. We've arranged for security cameras to be installed at our house since we were robbed. Maybe the robber will come back for the cash box and we'll catch the thief on camera."

"Let's hope," Rick said.

"You'll have to let us know if your trap works," Mary said.

"So, what else was stolen?" Hal asked Rick.

"I had just gotten a smart TV recently. It was one of those fifty-five inch 3D models."

"Had you programmed it yet?" Hal asked.

"Yeah. It was a pretty neat thing," Rick replied. "We could get movies and access the Internet right from our TV."

"So the robber has some of your identity information in the TV?"

"I guess. Not good?"

"Watch your credit card Rick. If you see unusual things showing up, it might be from someone using your smart TV information."

"I never thought of that."

"If you see unfamiliar charges taking place, tell the police. They can back track the IP address and find out who is using the TV."

"They can do that?" Sally asked.

"Sure. The TV will utilize a physical address when it's connected to the Internet. That's how those things work."

Jake added, "Don Pennington is into computers. You should talk to him about what happened and see if he has any ideas."

Sally looked down the bar. She knew who Don was but didn't recognize the man on one side of Don. She also knew who Tim Stone was and didn't want to have anything to do with him.

"I don't know those other guys," Sally said to Jake.

"Let me see if he'll come talk with you," Jake said as he went down to Don.

A minute later, Don was standing behind Rick.

"Rick, I understand your place was robbed. Jake told me about your smart TV being stolen and your computers."

"Yeah. Something I have to worry about I hear."

"Well, Jake's right about the police being able to track your smart TV or computers. If anyone tries to use them, they can follow the path to a physical address."

"How do we find out if someone is using our stuff?" Sally asked.

"Usually you need some kind of transaction to occur. Like a purchase from a credit card or a service using a credit card."

"We'll have to pay attention," Rick said to Sally.

"If you see something suspect, make sure you tell the police right away."

"Can they catch the robber right then and there?" Sally asked.

"Not right away, but the sooner the information gets into the right hands, the quicker the process can start."

"What process?"

"Well, if a transaction occurs, the police have to request a warrant to serve to the company the transaction occurs at and then start from there. Getting a warrant takes some time."

"Could the robbers get away while all the time is going by?"

"Maybe, but probably not. Once someone starts using the identity information, they historically have continued to use it. Getting free stuff becomes addicting. Plus, it's probably someone from around here, sad to say, so they probably aren't going anywhere."

"Couldn't the robbers use the information for a lot of things while this is going on?" Sally asked.

"Sure. But once you notify the police, they will work with the credit card company to limit your exposure while they're working on catching the robbers."

"You got all that?" Sally said to Rick.

"Thanks Don for your information," Rick said shaking Don's hand.

Don went back to his seat.

"Jake, get Don whatever he's drinking," Rick said.

Another couple came into the bar a little after nine.

Ben and Michelle Mackey sat down.

Ron came over to see what they would like.

"Hey Ben."

"Ron."

"What can I get you guys?"

"I'll have a white wine," Michelle said.

"And I'll have a Bud draft."

Ron got them their drinks.

"We're going to get a table by the fireplace as soon as it's empty," Ben said.

"I think those people sitting by the windows will be leaving soon," Ron said. "I'll let the hostess know you'd like to sit there."

"Thanks Ron," Ben said as he picked up his beer.

# Chapter 13

Sam and Jenny danced to a number of the songs Simon Rules played. They were having a pretty good time together.

At a little after 10:30 Sam said, "Jenny, I want to get a pack of cigarettes and the convenience store closes in thirty minutes. Wanna go with me?"

"Okee Dokee."

"Jake, we're going to the store for a few minutes. We'll be right back."

"Sure Sam. Just lean your stools against the bar and I'll keep them reserved for you."

"Thanks Jake."

Sam and Jenny got up and walked out hand in hand.

Sam and Jenny got into his SUV. As he backed out, Jenny said, "Make a right over there by the Post Office."

Sam did as instructed.

When they reached the end of the street where it turned to the right, she said, "Pull into the parking lot on the left."

Again, Sam obliged.

"Let's stop down there at the end of the lot by the river," Jenny suggested.

Sam drove to the end of the empty parking lot and parked under a big maple tree next to the river.

"What now?"

Sam turned the vehicle off.

"Leave the radio turned on."

Jenny opened the door and got out. Sam followed suit.

Then, she opened the back door to the SUV and got in. Sam followed.

Jenny put her arms around Sam and started to kiss him. That was just the invitation Sam had waited for all night. He reciprocated. She slid her hand down. Then, she reached and found what she was looking for.

Sam wasn't completely ready yet, but he showed promise. While Jenny was occupied with Sam's improving stamina, Sam reached under her blouse. He was having a little trouble and she reached to help him.

"Here, let me help you with that," Jenny said.

He allowed himself the pleasure of touching her body. After a few minutes of pleasure, he slid his hand down. As he did he stopped at the right place. Slowly, he massaged her and she sighed. His actions, and hers, did the trick. Sam and Jenny were both ready.

Jenny maneuvered Sam into a relaxed sit-back position. Then, she found what she was looking for. Sam tried to listen to the radio as a distraction but found himself unable to resist her advances.

"Do you want me now?" Jenny asked.

"I sure do."

She did things to Sam where he was unable to control what would happen next. Jenny was in full control. When Jenny thought Sam was about to climax, she abruptly stopped and sat back up.

"Why did you stop?"

"I want to be included as well."

Sam caught on and followed her lead.

A minute later, they were moving in unison.

Again, Jenny abruptly stopped when she thought Sam was about to lose it.

"What now?"

"Wait a minute. Do you have a condom?

"Yeah. There's a one in the glove box."

"Can you get one?"

"Sure."

He leaned over the center console, opened the glove box and took out a wrapped condom. He tore it open. She helped him put it on. They went back to what they were doing. This time, she wanted to be on top.

It took a little doing but eventually, Sam was on the bottom and Jenny on top. She sat up and lowered herself. Then, she restarted where they were, moving up and down.

Sam didn't pay much more attention to the radio. He reached up and caressed her as she moved up and down. Jenny came down all the way and stopped. She put her head back and let out a sigh of ecstasy. At that moment, Sam let lose. She let out another sigh.

Jenny fell forward onto Sam's chest. They were both pretty sweaty.

"That was great," Sam said.

"See, I told you things would work out."

"You sure did."

"Sam, let's go get the cigarettes and then go back to the bar."

"Sure, but the store is probably closed now."

"Go across the steel bridge. The gas station is still open and they sell cigarettes there."

"Good idea."

They both dressed and got into the front seats.

Sam started the SUV up and drove to the station where he brought a pack of cigarettes. Then, they drove back to the bar.

"That took a little longer than expected," Jake said.

"We got side tracked," Jenny said.

"Side tracked, huh?"

"You know how it is."

"Yeah, I guess I do."

"Can I get a shot of Jack?" Sam asked Jake.

"Sure. Did you remember to get your cigarettes?" Jake asked Sam.

Sam produced the unopened pack and showed them to Jake.

"Ha, ha Jake," Jenny said as Jake put the shot down.

"I thought you might be gone for the night."

"We just took a little ride," Sam replied.

Ron came over to say something to Jake. He saw Sam and Jenny back at the bar.

"So you two decided to come back."

"Yeah."

"Have a good smoke?"

"I'd say things were definitely smoky, or should I say steamy," Jenny replied.

Sam didn't know what to say.  He was surprised Jenny said anything about their rendezvous at all.

Ron looked at Sam, "Sam, you're speechless."

"We just went for a little ride."

"Sure you did.  Was it bumpy?"

"Talk to me later," Sam said.

"Sam, I never thought I would see the day where you would meet your match."

"Oh she is; she surely is."

He took another big gulp of his beer and smiled.

# Chapter 14

Mike Smith took out a small notebook and wrote a few things in it. Tim Stone was still sitting next to Mike.

"What's with the book Mike?"

"I try to keep track of people I meet. You never know when an opportunity will arise."

"What kind of business are you in?"

"Like I told you, I work with computers."

"That's a pretty big field. What kind of computer work?"

"I visit companies and talk about their marketing. Then, I give them ideas about how computers can enhance their marketing."

"How can a machine do that?"

"It's all in how information is captured, analyzed and brought forward. You'd be surprised at how much information companies have at their disposal and don't utilize."

"Sounds complicated."

"Not really. It's all a matter of programming or rather mining the data."

"Did you get any leads in here?"

"I've met some interesting people. I find visiting the local pubs in and around white collar business firms can be fertile."

"Oh, there are a lot of fertile people in here."

"Yeah, I see that quite a bit as well."

"You'd probably be interested in Kelly. She's got her own business and it's pretty successful."

"I wrote her name down."

"And Pete Harttt who was in here a little while ago with the group at the end of the bar owns a big landscaping operation in town."

"I didn't hear his name."

"He was here earlier but left. That guy at the end of the bar works for him," Tim was pointing at Sam.

"Tim, you came in after I did. How did you know he was here?"

"I was outside sitting on a bench when Pete left. I was out there when you came in as well."

"Really? I don't remember seeing you when I came in."

"That's because I blended in and you had no reason to see me."

"Huh. It's good to have local knowledge I guess."

"Sure is. Too bad you haven't figured a way of how to mine the information in a person's brain. Then you'd have something."

"Now that's an interesting idea."

Don came back and sat at his stool. He waved Jake over.

"Can I have another beer?"

"Sure. And thanks Don for talking with the Rick and Sally. She can be a little high strung and you probably saved Rick some headaches. This one's on them."

"Aw, thank them for me. It was no problem."

"What was that all about?" Mike asked.

"Something about a robbery and they had questions about how to track someone down."

"Were you able to help them?"

"I just explained how computers work. I think they got the idea."

"Isn't it amazing how little people know about computers?" Mike asked.

"Sure is. You'd think people would take a greater interest in the things. They're everywhere. Not knowing what you're doing with a computer or a device with computer capabilities can be very risky. You take those people for example. Their TV was a smart TV and it had personal data in it. When they were robbed, the robbers got the TV and access to the personal data it contained. Now, the robbers can take advantage of the data they found."

"What can the criminals do?" Tim asked.

"They can access accounts using the data found in the TV and run up some charges."

"Happens all the time," Mike added.

"That's what I was trying to explain to them," Don said.

"Well, if the authorities are skilled with computers, they should be able to backtrack the TV."

"That's what I told them. We'll have to wait and see if anything comes of it."

"I was just telling Tim something similar. People don't realize how easy it is to steal identity information from computers, smart TVs, smart phones and things like that."

"And the smart criminals know. And its funny, the guys who are doing these crimes have no formal education and could probably get good jobs if they really applied themselves. But they take the easy, no integrity route to getting what they want."

"I hope they informed their credit card company and the police."

"At least they did. Now, it should just be a matter of time before the police can find the stolen items and the criminals," Don said.

Mike made another entry in his notebook. Tim tried to see what it was, but with Don now sitting between them again, he couldn't see what Mike wrote.

"Did the robbery take place near here?" Mike asked.

"I think they live just north of here up by Collinsville."

"Yeah, they live just before the village in the left side off Route 177."

"Oh, you know were they live Tim?" Don asked.

"Well, not their exact address but one night after leaving here, they were in front of me going up 177 and they made a left going up the hill."

"On Route 4?"

"No, the next left just before the package store," Tim replied.

"Maybe they were just visiting someone."

Bobby Rose had been putting cleaned glasses away under the bar. "I think they live on the first street as you go up the hill on the left. I think it's the second house on the right."

Bobby picked up the empty rack and walked to the kitchen.

"I think I know the area," Don said. "It's kind of secluded up there."

"Yeah. The houses are pretty far apart and sit back off the road," Tim added.

"That's probably why the robbers selected the area to hit," Mike said.

"Well, it's in the hands of the police now. I'm sure we'll hear more next week."

Tim Stone stood.
"Time for me to be going."
Tim extended his hand to Mike.
"Nice meeting you Mike."
"You too Tim."
"See you around, Don."
"Bye Tim."
Tim turned and walked out.

"He's a strange character," Mike said to Don.

"He sure is. There's a guy who lives like a bum, has quite a bit of money and seems to know everything about everyone."

"Money, huh?! You'd never know it."

"Yeah. Tim was in trouble quite a bit. Some said drugs. Others said gambling. Anyhow, he was in a car accident some time back and got seriously hurt. He sued and won a big award. Now, he just wanders around town, sometimes walking, sometimes on his bike, sometimes in his old car. He comes in here from time to time. He's just kind of lost."

"Wow. You'd never know it from talking to him. He had quite a bit to say."

"Like what?"

"Oh, he talked with me about business and who in here I might want to take note of."

"That's Tim. He thinks he knows everything about everyone, and likes to share it. The women can't stand him."

"Why?"

"He brings up things about them that most of the women don't think someone knows."

"Kind of makes them uneasy?"

"Something like that."

"Well, he did seem to know something about everyone."

"The funny thing is that the guy is usually right."

"Huh. Maybe I'll run into him in here again."

"You plan on coming back?"

"I'm doing some business in this area and it'll require me to come back from time to time. Well, Don, it's been nice talking with you. I've got to call it a night. Early morning and busy day on the calendar."

"Nice talking with you Mike."

Mike paid his tab and left.

# Chapter 15

Kim Green and Janet Jensen, two of the waitresses in the dining room area came into the bar and took up the first two stools at the bar.

"My feet are killing me," Kim said to Janet as they sat down."

"You should have brought a pair of your old sneakers with you to work instead of wearing a brand new pair all night."

Jake came over to the two. "Done for the night?"

"Yeah. Things have slowed down in the dining room. The other girls can handle it." Janet said.

"What can I get you two?"

"I'll have a Coors Light draft," Kim said.

"Me too," added Janet.

Jake poured the two beers and set them in front of the women.

"Got anything for sore feet Jake?"

"I told her she should have brought a pair of her comfortable shoes in with her. But she didn't and wore those cute new shoes all night. Now her feet are sore," Janet said.

"Well, at least the new shoes are broken in now Kim." Jake commented.

"Oh, they hurt."

"Did you get the right size?" Jake asked.

"Yeah. But you know how new shoes can be. They're a little stiff at first until you break them in."

"You should have worn them yesterday, and with socks to stretch them out if you weren't wearing them with socks tonight," Janet said sarcastically.

"You don't have any socks on?" Jake asked in a surprised tone.

"No. I would have looked like a jerk if I had socks on with these sneakers," Kim said as she picked one of her legs up a little so Jake could see one.

"I see what you mean."

The sneakers were a dark pink color, a raspberry, with black soles and probably would have been hard to find a pair of socks that would blend in well with them.

"I've got a pretty good blister on my right foot."

"We've got some bandaids under the bar Kim if you want one."

"Ok. One might help."

"Bobby, can you find the box of bandaids under the bar and give Kim what she needs for her foot?"

"Sure Jake."

Bobby went to the other end of the bar and rummaged through the cabinet under the bar. He came out with a first aid kit and brought it to Kim.

"Thanks Bobby," Kim said as he handed her the kit.

Kim went through the first aid kit and took out a square bandage and an extra gauze pad. She put the pad under the band-aid and put both over the blister on her foot. Then, she put the shoe back on.

"How's that?" Jake asked.
"Feels better."

The two picked up their beers and took a drink.
"How's business been in here tonight Jake?"
"Pretty much as usual. Except that the Tafts were telling us about their house being robbed while they were on vacation."
"Really?" Kim said. "They live on the next street over from me. I didn't hear anything about a robbery in the neighborhood."
Kim looked around the bar to see if the Tafts were still there.
"If you're looking for them Kim, they left a little while ago."
"I think it's a little scary having someone robbed in the neighborhood I live in," Kim said to Janet.
"Yeah. And you live alone Janet. Do you have a security system?" Jake said.
"I don't have a formal security system but I do have my snub nose 38."
"You have a gun?"
"Yeah. And I know how to use it. If someone tries to break into my house and I'm home, all hell is going to break loose."
Kim handed the first aid kit back to Jake who handed it back to Bobby. Bobby went back to the other end of the bar and put it back where he had found it.

"Kim, would you shoot someone?" Janet asked.
"If they were trying to break into my house I would."

"I overheard one of the local police officers talking to some of the guys in here a few days ago and he told them if any of them had a gun and intended to use it, they had better make sure of the target and make sure the suspect was inside the house."

"That's a scary thought Jake. I'd have to wait until some burglar was actually inside my house before I shot?" Kim said in an annoyed voice.

"That's what the officer said. Otherwise, it might be construed as something other than a robbery or home invasion."

"What do you mean?"

"Well, what if someone was just coming to your door soliciting or something like that. If you shot the person, you'd be in the wrong."

"You know what I mean. I'd only shoot if someone were actually trying to break in," Kim insisted.

"Just be careful Kim," Jake said as he turned to go to wait on another customer.

"He's got a point Kim. You need to be careful with your gun."

"Don't worry Janet. If someone tries to break into my house, I'll make sure the police find the body inside my home."

"You're scaring me Kim."

"Janet, you know where I live. I can't imagine anyone coming down my winding driveway for any reason. You can't even see my house from the street."

"I don't know Kim."

"Plus, why would anyone want to break into my house. I don't have anything a robber would want other than maybe a TV and computer."

"Well, you have a gun. And don't you have a pretty big coin collection?"

"Yeah."

"If someone wanted a gun, they might break into your house to steal it."

"No one even knows I have it."

"Well, we do. And now anyone else in here who heard us talking knows."

Kim looked around. She knew everyone who was within listening distance.

"I'm not worried about anyone in here."

"That's what the Tafts said, Kim," Jake said as he came back to them.

"Just the same, I'm going to protect myself and my stuff."

"Oh Kim," Janet said.

The two finished their beers.

"Jake, can we another round?"

"Sure."

Professor Ryan and Carla Thompson had come back from their movie date, and took up the stools next to Kim and Janet.

Janet said, "Hello Professor Ryan."

"Hello Janet. How are you?"

"I'm doing fine. And how are you doing Carla?"

"Ok. Tim and I had dinner and took in a show tonight."

"That's good. How have you been?"

"Pretty good."

Janet turned to Kim as Jake put their drinks in front of them.

"You know her?" Kim asked.

"Yeah. Carla and I were in Professor Ryan's class together a few years ago."

"Oh."

"So, he's dating one of his former students?"

"Not dating. They're just friends. When she was severely injured in a car accident, the Professor came to her aid. He helped her recover and as a result they became good friends. She returns the gratitude by going to dinner and a movie with him from time to time. It's really a nice relationship."

"Do you think it'll develop into anything more?"

"Who knows? But if it does, that wouldn't be such a bad thing. They're both alone and single."

"I guess."

Simon Rules had just announced the last song for the night. A number of patrons got up to dance. Professor Ryan and Carla Thompson did as well.

When Simon finished, Carla looked up and gave Professor Ryan a kiss on the lips. They came back to the bar. Then, the Professor paid the tab and they left.

Janet looked at Kim, "Now what do you think?"

"I think it's great."

"But don't you think he's a bit old for her?"

"I didn't know love had boundaries."

"You're right Kim. He's just old enough to be her father."

"They're good for each other. Would you rather see a young woman like Carla with a guy who mistreats her?"

"I guess not."

"Janet, you need to revise your perspective. You've stereotyped too many things."

"Maybe."

101

# Chapter 16

On Saturday morning at 10 am, Lou Adams, Frank Johnson, Sam Marino arrived at Tunxis Plantation Golf Course. The three were taking their clubs out of their vehicles.

"So where's our fourth?" asked Lou.

"Here comes Tommy now," Frank said looking at a truck pulling into the parking lot.

"Tommy's my partner," Lou declared.

"Lou, if you think Tommy's play can save your score, you're kidding yourself."

"Ha, ha," Lou said as he turned to walk over to greet Tommy.

"Hey Tommy."

"Lou."

"You ready to kick ass on these guys this morning?"

"I'm a little shaky today Lou. It was a late night."

"Who did you go home with?"

"Kelly Jones."

"Oh, really?"

"Yeah. What a woman."

"You two looked kind of chummy when you were at the bar," Frank said.

"You guys are just jealous. She's got everything. She has money, she's in great shape, and she's really good looking and fantastic in bed."

"She is, is she?" Lou asked.

"Lou, you don't have a chance with her," Frank insisted.

"I don't know about that," Lou said. "What do you think Tommy? Think she'd go out with me?"

"Lou, she'd give you a heart attack. Sorry partner."

"You think Trish doesn't give me a workout?"

"Oh, she does. I've been with her as well and I can tell you she goes easy on a guy compared to Kelly."

"Tommy, when I went home with Trish, she insisted we do it three times during the night. Plus, she was all over me in the parking lot at the end of the street by the bar."

"So in total Lou, how much time would you say you were in the saddle with Trish last night?"

"Oh, an hour or so?"

"How about fifteen minutes?"

At Lou's expense, Frank had all the guys laughing.

"Who did you go home with last night Frank?" Tommy said sarcastically.

"I saw him leave with Karin," Sam said.

"Did you score Frank?" Tommy asked.

"We left together," Frank said quickly, hoping to get the subject changed.

"What's that mean?" Lou asked.

"I thought she was going to my place with me when we left but she asked to be dropped off at her place once we got into my car."

"So you didn't score, huh Frank? At least I did."

"Kelly had me at it 'till three in the morning. I finally had to tell her I had plans the next day and needed some sleep."

"It must be nice to be young and keep it up that long Tommy," Sam said.

"She made me use the magic pill."

"You Tommy?" Lou asked.

"Yeah me, Lou. What do you think? I could keep at it for four hours?"

"Yeah Lou," chimed in Sam, "You heard the commercial. If an erection last more than four hours, make sure you have a good woman with you."

They all laughed.

"Let's go check in," Frank said as he finished putting his golf shoes on.

The four walked into the pro shop and paid. "See the starter by the first tee and he'll get you going."

"Thanks," Frank said.

They put their clubs on the golf carts; Lou and Tommy in one cart, Frank and Sam in the other one.

"Tommy, you want a coffee or anything to get your game going?"

"No thanks Lou. I've got a few 5-hour energy drinks. That'll do."

"Ok. Let's beat the pants off these guys."

They drove up to the starter. "First tee is yours gentlemen when you're ready. Remember to keep the carts on the paths on par-3's and no closer than 25 yards from every green. You'll see signs, no need to measure."

This guy spends too much time alone, Frank thought.

"Got it," Frank replied.

They drove to the first tee.

"So, what are we playing for?" Lou asked.

"How about a dollar per hole for low team score and two dollars for the match?" Frank suggested.

"That works out to a max of twenty per man," Sam added.

"Works for me," Tommy said.

"Hey Frank, what happened to playing for fifty bucks a head?" Lou asked.

"That was when Pete was going to play. Tommy's quite a bit better. A buck a hole at least gives us a chance at winning something," Frank said.

"Ok."

"Lou, you and Tommy can have tee first," Frank said.

"Ok Tommy, you start things off. Make it a good one so these guys get the message right away."

"Lou, I'm going to play my game. Whatever it'll be, it will be."

"Ok. But, we need to stay ahead of these guys."

"We'll see."

Tommy took a few practice swings. Then, he addressed his ball. He only took his club back a short distance and then hit the ball. It sliced to the right ending up along the wood line.

"What was that?"

"I told you I didn't get much rest last night."

"Yeah, but you're shot was terrible."

"Lou, give it a rest," Tommy said as he took a 5-hour energy drink from his bag and drank it.

Frank leaned over to Sam, "Lou's going to drive Tommy crazy. This should be easy picking."

"Tommy hasn't gotten started yet Frank. You'll see, the guy gets in a zone and he's nearly unbeatable."

"You saw his shot. Tommy's either real tired or hung over."

"Well, he's doing something about it," Sam said as they looked at Tommy drinking his energy drink.

Lou hit his first shot about two hundred yards straight down the center of the fairway. He'd have a short shot to the green.
"Nice shot Lou," Frank said.
"Thanks."
"Looks like you'll be carrying your team," Sam said.
"We'll get better."
"Sure you will," Sam said.

Then, Frank hit his shot about twenty yards past Lou's ball. Sam hit his ball about the same distance but landed in the rough.
Tommy drove the cart to his ball. He took out a pitching wedge and hit his second shot to within ten feet of the flag.
Lou hit a seven-iron bump and run shot. The ball raced across the green ending up on the fringe on the backside of the green.
Frank and Sam both landed their second shots on the green about fifteen feet from the cup.
Lou tried putting from the fringe but left the putt short by six feet. Then, he missed the short shot and settled for a double bogey.
"You'll never beat us that way," Frank teased Lou.
"Hey, Tommy hasn't putted yet," Lou responded.

Frank took two shots to get his putt in. Sam left his first putt short by five feet and then missed as his second putt lipped out of the cup. He settled for a double bogey. Tommy, having the worst drive, finished with par.
Lou, with a big smile on his face, "Let's see. You guys got a nine, we got an eight."
They walked to their carts.

Driving to the second tee, Lou said, "Nice second shot Tommy."

"It was an easy shot."

"Even still. You won the hole for us."

"It's just the first one Lou. They all count."

"I know. But your play will make them get a little aggressive. And I know Sam. He becomes very erratic when he gets aggressive."

"Just play your game Lou. This isn't the PGA. You're gonna psych yourself out. Just play."

"Ok. And you too Tommy."


The rest of the round went pretty much as the first hole. Sam and Lou played about the same. By the time they reached the eighteenth tee, they had split the first seventeen holes with Lou and Tommy winning one more than Sam and Frank, 9-8.

Tommy had played both good and bad. He birdied a few holes but also had bogeys on a few. He managed to stay ahead of Frank by three strokes overall.

"Well, this hole will determine the match," Frank declared.

"We're up by one overall," Lou said.

"Yeah. We won eight of the seventeen holes played, so we could end up in a tie," Sam said.

Frank had struggled on the back nine. Thanks to Sam's consistent play, they were still in the match.

"Come on Frank, you're playing golf like you're with the women. You need to get aggressive."

Frank frowned.

"If we win this hole, we win the hole and tie for total score."

"What are you saying Frank?" Lou asked.

"I'm just saying its pretty close."

"Do you want to change the bet to winner take all on this hole?" Lou said smugly.

"What do you think Frank?" Sam asked.

"Sure why not."

"Ok Lou. Winner takes all. The low team pays the winning team the full twenty bucks. Per guy."

"You're on," Lou said.

"I hope you know what you're doing Lou," Tommy said.

"Just put it on the green in two Tommy."

"Frank, you're up first," Lou declared.

Frank took out his driver. He took a few practice swings and then hit his ball long and high. It landed about twenty yards short of the green.

"Nice shot Frank," Sam declared.

"Let's see you match that one Sam," Lou chided him.

Sam took his three-wood. After a few practice swings, he hit his shot to the left side of the fairway about a hundred yards short of the green.

"Playing a little conservative Sam?" Lou asked.

"Let's see you beat that one Lou," Sam retaliated.

Lou took out his driver. He took a few practice swings. Then, he addressed his ball and swung with all his might. He missed the ball.

"That's a one," Sam declared jokingly, but not laughing.

"I was just taking another practice."

Then, Lou addressed the ball again. He hit it into the rough about hundred and ten yards from the green.

Tommy took out his fairway wood again.

"What are you doing Tommy? You can reach this green from here?"

"Maybe I can Lou, but I thought you wanted to win?"

"You see where Frank's ball is?"

"That's why I'm playing my game."

Tommy took a few practice swings. Then he hit his ball. It went very high and pretty long for a fairway wood. His shot stopped about fifty yards short of the green.

"See, Frank's got you beat now."

"Not beat Lou. Just a longer shot. And I love a challenge in case you don't know that about me."

Lou hit his second shot on to the green about ten feet from the cup.

"Now, all you have to do is make the putt Lou," Tommy said.

"I can do it."

Sam hit his second shot and landed it just inside Lou's ball.

Then, it was Tommy's turn. He took out a sand wedge. After a few practice swings, he addressed his ball. He hit his shot sending the ball way up into the air. They all watched as it descended to the green. On the way down, the ball hit the flag on the flagstick and dropped straight down into the cup for a two.

"Nice shot Tommy!" Lou yelled. "Let's see you beat that one Frank. Woo hoo!"

Frank hit a short chip shot leaving his ball about three feet from the cup. They group walked up to the green. Tommy was in with a two. Frank and Sam were on the green with reasonable putts. Lou was furthest from the cup.

Lou addressed his putt.

"Give Sam a good line Lou. He's right in front of you."

Lou hit his putt. The ball had to break about two feet in order to find the cup. Lou had hit the ball too softly and it stopped about five feet below the cup.

Sam was next to hit. He lined up his putt and then sank it for a birdie.

The teams were now all tied since Lou had already hit his third shot, Tommy was in with a two, Frank was in with a three and Sam was about to hit his third shot.

"He gave you a good idea of what not to do," Frank said to Sam.

"He's still got to make it," Lou declared.

Sam hit his putt. It was right of the cup as he hit it. Then, the ball curved back to the left stopping right on the lip of the cup.

"Looks like it'll be a tie," Lou declared.

Then, Sam's ball dropped into the cup.

"What about the ten second rule?" Lou asked.

"How many seconds went by after my ball stopped?" Sam asked.

"I don't know but it must have been more than ten." Lou said.

"I think it's a good shot," Frank declared.

"Just make your putt Lou," Tommy said.

Lou lined up his putt. Then he hit the ball. It looked like it was going to drop right into the center of the cup until the ball turned slightly to the left a few inches from the hole. Lou had missed the shot.

Sam gave Frank a high-five.

"Looks like we take the whole thing," Sam said extending his hand to Lou, palm up.

Lou took out a twenty and put it in Sam's hand.

"I think I'll frame this one."

"Let's go get some lunch at the bar," Tommy said.

"I'm with you there," Lou replied.

"Come on Frank, let's go celebrate."

"You guys go ahead Sam. I'll be there in about a half hour. I've got to make a stop on the way."

"Ok. I'll have a beer waiting for you when you get there," Sam said.

"Ok."

Frank got into his vehicle and left.

The other three put their clubs into their vehicles and left.

# Chapter 17

On Sunday, Sam Marino stopped in at the bar. The place was pretty empty. Ron was bartending.

"Hey Sam. What can I get you?"

"I'll have a Bud draft, Ron."

"You're here early."

"Yeah. I had to go to the police station this morning. My place was robbed yesterday while I was golfing."

"You gotta be kidding. Really?"

"I don't know who would be so ballsy as to rob a place on a Saturday morning in broad daylight."

"Did a neighbor or anyone see anything?"

"I don't think so. I checked with my neighbors when I got home and no one saw anything."

"What'd they get?"

"The usual stuff. My TV, computer, some tools."

"Just like the Tafts. Except Sally Taft lost her jewelry as well."

"Well, they got my baseball card collection and it was worth quite a bit. Plus, my hunting rifles and a set of dueling pistols."

"Didn't you have a safe?"

"No. It's just me at my place so I didn't think I'd need one."

"Maybe with kids and stuff, but it might have deterred the burglars."

"Did the Tafts have one?"

"No, but they wish they did."


"It looks like they just drove up to my house, kicked in the front door and ransacked the place."

"Sounds familiar. The Taft's had a similar story."

"Well, I have one up on the punks, and I'm assuming there was more than one. Could one guy kick in a door? I don't think so. My computer had a GPS chip in it so I can track it as soon as I can get another computer and load the tracking software on it."

"Didn't you give that information to the police?"

"Not yet. I want to catch these guys myself first. Then, I plan on having a little chat with them before I turn them over to the police."

"Sam, are you sure that's a wise thing to do?"

"These guys have been hitting quite a few places lately. The law is pretty soft lately. Heck, they might not even serve any time even if they're caught red handed."

"That's probably true."

"Well, they robbed the wrong guy this time. I just want a piece of them first."

"You'd better be careful Sam. They have your guns and probably have guns from other robberies too."

"Oh, I'll be careful, up to a point."


Another patron came into the bar and sat at the other end of the bar. Ron went to wait on him.

The door to the bar opened and Bobby came in.  He took up a stool in the middle of the bar, where the taps were.  After Ron waited on the other person, he came over to Bobby.

"Hey Bobby.  How you doing today?"

"Just dandy Ron.  Looks pretty slow in here."

"Yeah.  But it'll get busy later.  Why're you in so early?"

"I'm due in for one o'clock but I wanted to get something to eat before I start work."

"What can I get you?"

"I'll have a burger, well done, and fries.  And a diet coke please."

"Got it."

"What'd you do on your day off?"

"I had a bunch of errands I needed to run, and clean up my place.  I hate cleaning."

"I know what you mean.  I have to take care of everything on my day off as well."

"I got rid of a lot of the junk I had laying around."

"I went to the dump yesterday too."

"I didn't go to the dump; I had some stuff I was able to pawn at the pawn shop."

"I've never been in one of those places.  They look so sketchy.  What do they take?"

"Almost anything and no questions asked.  At least the ones I go too."

"What does that mean?"

"Some of the places take your name and address from your license;   then they keep stuff set aside for 30 days for loan.  You get less money.  And if you sell it to them, they still set it aside in case the cops come looking for stolen stuff.  My place just wants the stuff, so the calendar and identification is not their thing.  They work with their customers."

"I wonder if the Tafts or Sam Marino checked with the pawn shops."

"Why would they want to check with the pawn shops?"

"They were both robbed recently."

"Wow."

"Yeah, I was just talking with Sam about it. He was hit yesterday."

"Any clues?"

"No. And he's a little pissed that someone would rob his place during daylight on a Saturday. He said it was like the robbers knew he wouldn't be home."

"Well, he does live in a pretty secluded place. I mean the street is lined with dense bushes and trees."

"So you've been there?"

"Nah. I heard him talking with someone in here a while ago and he was describing his place. The woman he was talking to was going to go over to his house and he told her where he lived and how to recognize the place. I heard him tell her you couldn't really see the house from the street because of the overgrowth."

"I'll have to mention to Sam about the pawn shops."

"They won't tell him anything. He'll only get lucky if he goes there and spots something belonging to him. Even then he might have to wait to get it back and pay to get it back."

"I'll tell him that as well."

Ron turned and walked to the end of the bar.

"Sam, I was just talking to Bobby about the recent robberies. He told me about a pawn shop he goes to that takes anything from anyone and doesn't care where it came from."

"I've heard of those places and there's one near here on Route 6."

"Did you check with them or any of the other pawn shops?"

"Not yet. I'm going to go around today and see if they got any interesting stuff in recently looking like what was taken from my place."

"Bobby said the people at the place he goes to wouldn't tell you anything. You'll have to see one of your things there in order to get them to tell you anything."

"Oh, if I see anything there that belongs to me, they'll talk."

"Be careful Sam. You never know who you're talking to. If they're willing to break the rules, they're willing to break the law."

"Yeah, I know. I've been around."

Bobby's lunch came out and Ron put it in front of him. He ate his burger and fries and was ready to go to work for his shift.

Sam asked for his check just as Bobby was coming behind the bar. Ron got it from the register and put it in front of him.

Sam said to Bobby as he got up to go, "Bobby, Ron told me what you said about the pawn shops. I think I'll go visit some of them. Any recommendations where I should start?"

"Nah. Hope you get lucky."

"Thanks buddy."

About a half hour after Sam had left, Rick Taft came into the bar. He took a seat.

"Hey Rick. How you doing?"

"Good Ron. Just finished a respectable round of golf. I could use a cold beer."

"Any particular one?"

"How about a Blue Moon, no fruit."

"Got it."

Ron poured the beer and put it in front of Rick.

"So, any leads on the robbery?"

"Not yet. And Sally has some crazy idea about putting in a security system to take pictures of anyone approaching our house."

"Does she think the schmucks'll come back?"

"Who knows? But she said if they do, she'll get their picture and turn it over to the police."

"Why would they come back again? Didn't they get everything already?"

"Yeah. But she's been blabbing to everyone about having a safe that the robbers didn't find."

"Do you have a safe?"

"No. She said she's just hoping to bait the guys into coming back."

"Don't you think she's taking a big risk?"

"You know Sally. She thinks she's a detective. She reads too many books and watches too much TV."

"Who knows, maybe she'll get lucky."

"Yeah."

Ron turned around to go to the other end of the bar. He had to lean over to get around Bobby who had just come out of the kitchen and was putting a few cases of beer into the cooler under the bar.

"Bobby, when you're done, can you clean up the tables over by the fireplace?"

"Sure Ron."

# Chapter 18

During the week, Mike Smith called the number Trish had given to him, and she answered on the third ring.

"Hello."

"Trish, its Mike Smith."

"Mike, how nice to hear from you."

"I wasn't sure if my schedule would free up time to give you a call this week but I finished up my work early and I'm not heading back to New Jersey until tomorrow morning."

"I'm glad you called."

"Do you have any plans for this afternoon?"

"No. What do you have in mind?"

"I thought we could meet at the 'O' Bar for a few drinks and possibly lunch."

"I'd like that. What time should I be there?"

"It's noon right now. Can you be there in an hour?"

"Sure."

"I'll see you then."

Trish hung up the phone, and immediately starting selecting clothes, jewelry and make-up. The weather was nice, and if they ate on the back deck, the sun would be warm, so she selected eggplant colored shorts, an ivory lace tank, and a multi-colored sweater, just in case. Jewelry was simple, diamond studs and her bold, gold chain necklace. Throwing open her shoe closet; she selected the dark brown raffia wedges. A brush through her hair, freshly brushed teeth, a spritz of her favorite sexy perfume, and she was date ready.

Mike came in first and sat at the bar near the back door. Jake Wilson was the only bartender on duty.

"How things going Mike?"

"Pretty good Jake."

"Good to see you again."

"I finished up my business this morning and I'm meeting someone here at one."

"What can I get you?"

"I'll have a Bud draft."

"Got it."

Jake took out a cold mug from the refrigerator under the bar and poured a beer.

He placed it in front of Mike.

"Trish Howland hasn't been in here yet today has she?" Mike asked.

"I haven't seen her yet but if she said she'd meet you, you can count on it."

Mike looking out the window into the parking lot, "Here she comes now."

Trish walked into the bar and sat at the stool next to Mike.

"Hey Trish. Can I get you something?" Jake asked Trish.

"Sure. I'll have a glass of white wine. And a glass of ice on the side."

"Pinot or Chardonnay?"

"Pinot."

"Having a good day?" Mike asked.

"Yeah. Just a little tired. I didn't sleep well last night."

Trish worked at the Health Center as a receptionist.

"We were pretty busy earlier today. I'm glad I only work the morning shift."

"Well, your workday is over now so you can relax."

Trish leaned over to Mike and kissed him on the cheek.

"That's just what I intend to do."

"Do you want to order lunch?"

"No. I have other plans."

"Oh, I thought we were doing something this afternoon?" Mike asked sheepishly.

"I should have said *we've* got other plans," Trish corrected herself.

Now Mike smiled.

"What do you have in mind?"

"Do you like Chinese?"

"Yeah."

"Then, let's get take out and go to my place."

"Sounds good to me."

"There's no mystery Mike. I plan on taking you to my place, feed you, give you a few drinks and then take full advantage of you."

Now Mike had a really wide smile on his face.

"Ooh, I like the sound of that."

"Oh, you'll like more than just the sound."

"When do you want to get this party going?"

"Let's finish these drinks and then I know of a good place for Chinese. We can stop on the way to my place."

Mike picked up his beer and chugged the contents. He placed the empty glass on the bar.

"You're really excited Mike, aren't you?"

Mike looked at her.

"I guess you are," as she glanced down at his crotch.

"Jake, can I have our tab?"

"Sure Mike."

Jake produced the paperwork from the register. Mike looked at it and then took out a twenty from his wallet, "Keep the change."

"Thanks. See you next time you're in town."

"Oh, I'll be back."

Mike and Trish got up and left.

Outside the bar, Mike said, "Want me to follow you to your place?"

"Leave your car here Mike, we can come back and get it later."

"Won't that be pretty late?"

"We can get it tomorrow."

"Ok. Then I can go to the hotel and get my luggage before I head back to New Jersey."

They both got into her car. Trish drove out the parking lot and east on Route 4. After a few miles, she pulled into the parking lot of a Chinese restaurant. They both went in. Trish picked up a menu and they looked at it.

"What do you like?" She asked.

"Chicken with cashews, fried rice and an egg roll works for me," Mike said.

"I'll order shrimp with snow peas, white rice and crab Rangoon.  With that much variety, we can share."
"Good idea."

Trish ordered.  They went to the small bar the restaurant had and ordered a drink.  It didn't take long and their takeout order was ready.  They finished their drinks and left.  It was just a little after two o'clock.

Trish drove west on Route 4 a little ways and turned into the road leading to the local cross country skiing facility and kids summer camp.  She lived in the last condo on the street.  They got out of her car and went in.  When she got to her front door, she was about to put her key in the lock and noticed the door was already open.

"What the hell?"
"What's the matter?"
"My door's open."
"Could you have left it open when you went to work?"
"No.  I always check it twice to make sure its locked."
"Does it look like someone broke in?"
"Not that I can see from here."

They both looked at the door especially by the lock, and it didn't look like there was any forced entry.

Trish slowly pushed door open.
"Let me go in first."
Trish allowed him to pass, and Mike went inside.
"Anyone here?" He said in a loud demanding voice.
There was no answer.
Trish came in behind him.
"Everything looks ok."
"Let me take a look around."
"I'll go with you."

The two looked around the living room, dining room and kitchen. The place was very neat.

"Everything looks in order," Trish declared. "Put the food over there on the counter," she said pointing at the island counter in the middle of the kitchen.

"Want me to make you a drink?" Mike asked.

"Sure. I'd like a martini."

"Where's the shaker?"

"Everything is right there in the liquor cabinet," Trish said pointing at a cabinet with wine glasses on top.

Mike opened the cabinet and found what he was looking for.

"Vodka is in the cabinet. I'm going upstairs to change."

Mike went about making the drinks. He had just added ice to the shaker and had begun to shake it when he heard Trish yell out.

"Mike, come here right away."

He put the shaker on the counter and ran up the stairs.

"In here," she called out from one of the rooms.

He went into the master bedroom and Trish was seated at a dressing table on the far side of the room.

"What's the matter?"

"Someone's been here."

"How do you know?"

"Look. You see that bottom drawer?"

"Yeah?"

"It's been opened."

"How do you know?"

She reached down and easily opened it.

"That drawer is always locked. I keep all my jewelry in there."

She held up a key.

"How could someone have opened it without a key?"

"I don't know but a few weeks ago, I lost a set of keys at the bar and never found them. I had another key to my condo at a friend's place so I was able to get in and then I had to have a full set of keys made from the backup keys I have, including that one."

"If someone found your keys you lost at the bar and knew where you live, that would explain why there were no markings on the front door when we looked at it."

"And how someone got into my jewelry."

"Did you have things in there of significant value?"

"Yeah. I'll bet there was over twenty thousand in jewelry alone in that drawer and now it's empty."

"Who would have known where you keep your jewelry?" Mike asked.

"I don't know. I've talked about my place with some of my friends from time to time but I can't imagine any of them doing anything like this."

"You think it might have been someone who frequents the bar?"

"I did lose my keys there and I'm sure someone there could have heard me talking to someone about where I keep my jewelry, although I don't make a habit of doing that daily or anything."

"And people there probably know where you live, where you work and what your schedule is like."

"So Mike, you think it's someone from the bar also?"

"I'm just saying someone at the bar might have all the information needed to do something like this."

"Well, I'm going to have to go to the police station tomorrow and talk with them."

"Don't you want to call them now?"

"Don't be silly Mike. I don't think anything else is going to happen that can't wait until tomorrow. We've got takeout down stairs and I want to eat and relax."

"I'll go finish making the drinks and get dinner set up," he said as he turned to walk away.

"Can you help me before you leave?"

Trish had started to pull her top over her head.

Mike reached up and pulled it completely off her leaving her standing there in her bra. She reached around the back and unhooked it. Then she placed it on her dresser. Mike just looked at her. She took off her shorts, folded them and placed them on the dresser as well. Mike came up behind her and started to slide her underwear down.

"We'll get to those a little later," Trish said as she turned around.

"I thought you wanted my help?"

"I do. Can you get me a sweatshirt out of the top of my closet? I'd have to go to the spare bedroom and get a footstool to reach it."

Mike went into her closet and retrieved the sweatshirt. When he came out of the walk-in closet, she had on a pair of yoga pants. She took the sweatshirt from him and put it on.

"OK, now I'm comfortable. Let's go downstairs and eat."

Mike finished making the drinks while Trish got out two plates, silverware and napkins, and set places at the center island. They took out their takeout, sat down and began to eat. The two shared the food and enjoyed the dinner. When they were done, Trish said, "Mike, why don't you see if you can find some music and I'll cleanup in here."

"Any preference?"

"Not really. Make it relaxing and sexy."

Mike went into the living room. He couldn't find the stereo. He went back into the kitchen.

"I didn't see your stereo in the living room."

"It's in the bedroom."

"Oh."

Mike went upstairs to the bedroom and found the stereo. He turned it on and went through the stations until he found one he liked. When he stood and turned around, Trish was standing in the doorway with nothing on. She pulled the window shade down. In a minute, he shed his clothing and the two were in bed.

# Chapter 19

The next day, Ron Alderman was tending bar. Sally Taft came into the bar with a friend a little after noon.

"Hi Sally."

"Ron. This is my friend Ted Summers."

"Nice to meet you Ted."

"What can I get you two?"

"I'll have a martini," Sally said.

"And I'll have a Blue Moon draft."

Ron got the drinks.

"Menus?"

"Please," Sally said.

"Where's Rick today?" Ron asked.

"He's working. Ted belongs to the same tennis club Rick and I belong to. We just finished playing so I invited him along for lunch."

"That's nice of you Sally."

"Well, a gal has to keep herself in shape."

The two looked through the menu. After a few minutes, Ron came back over.

"What can I get you?"

"I'll have a caesar salad with grilled chicken," Sally requested.

"And I'll have a steak and cheese grinder."

"Want onions or mushrooms?"

"No thanks."

"How about fries?"

"Just the grinder will be fine."

Ron went to the register and entered the order. When he turned back to the bar, Sally was whispering something into Ted's ear. The two looked a little too friendly to Ron; he had known Rick for a long time, and this felt awkward. He walked back over to them.

"So Sally, anything new on the robbery?"

"Yes. Remember I was saying things about our safe just after we were robbed?"

"Yeah."

"Well, someone tried to get back into our place to get at the safe. The cameras we installed showed someone trying to break into our house a few days later during the day. The robber was dressed in one of those hooded sweatshirts with the 'O' bar logo on it. Unfortunately, the camera didn't show the face of the person trying to break in but we think it's someone who knows us from here."

"Well that's weird. A worker? A customer?"

"Well, it was just two days after we were in here talking about the safe being missed and then someone tried to break in again."

"Did the robber get into the safe?"

"No. We don't actually have a safe. I had just said that hoping the robber would try again. In addition to the security cameras we installed, we had an alarm put in. I think the alarm scared the robber away because he didn't go into the house that we know of."

128

"Are you sure it was a robber?"

"Yes. Why else would someone be trying to break into my house?"

Ron went under the bar and came out with a hooded sweatshirt. He held it up for Sally to see.

"Did the hooded sweatshirt look like this one?"

"Just like it."

"This one was left here in the bar yesterday by someone."

"Then the robber could have been in here just yesterday."

"Or any one of the other one hundred people who have this sweatshirt."

Ted, who had just listened to the back and forth between Ron and Sally, said, "Maybe you shouldn't go home alone after lunch."

"That's a good idea Ted. Do you have anything planned for the afternoon?"

"Not really. I could go home with you and check things out just to make sure if you want."

"That would be reassuring."

"Then, I'll follow you home after lunch."

"Thanks."

Ron went to the end of the bar as a waitress approached with a tray of food. He picked up the plates and brought them to Sally and Ted.

"Can I get you anything else?"

"Not right now." Ted said taking the plates from Ron.

The two ate their lunches.

When they were done, Ted paid the tab and they left.

As Ted and Sally walked out, Bobby began to clean up the area where they were seated.

Ron said, "There goes trouble."

Bobby looked out the door at the two leaving. Ted had his arm draped over Sally's shoulder. He didn't say anything.

Ted followed Sally to her house, and they drove into the long winding driveway. Sally went to the front door and opened it. Everything seemed in place.

"Want me to come in?"

"Yeah. Just to make sure no one is here."

The two-walked from room to room allowing Sally the comfort of knowing no one was in the house.

"Let's check upstairs," Sally requested.

They went upstairs and checked the guest bedrooms first, then the bathroom.

"Looks ok to me," Ted said.

"Only the master bedroom left to check," Sally said leading the way to the far end of the hall.

She went in and looked around. Ted followed. Then, she went into the bathroom. She left the door open.

Ted could see her in the reflection in the mirror. She took her clothing off and placed the clothing she wore playing tennis into the hamper. When she stood back up, she turned around to put on a robe hanging on the back of the door. She had to close the door most of the way to retrieve the robe. Then she had put the robe on and opened the door, Ted was standing there on the other side of the door, naked and aroused.

"Ted, what are you doing?"

"I saw you taking your clothing off and thought you and I would..."

His conversation tapered off.

"You thought you and I would what?"

She stopped her words and looked down at him. Ted presented an interesting opportunity Sally hadn't considered.

But, looking at what he was showing her, she couldn't resist. She undid the robe allowing it to open. Then, she stepped forward and put her arms around his neck. He responded in kind allowing their naked bodies to touch.

Ted gently kissed her. She returned the kiss allowing her tongue to reach his. He pushed the robe back off her shoulders and in a minute, the two were on the king size bed making love. They were completely involved in each other, breathing heavily and moving in unison. They both reached climax at the same time.

"What the hell is going on in here?"

Sally looked over Ted's shoulder to see Rick standing in the doorway to their bedroom.

Ted quickly jumped up off the bed.

Rick looked at his wife, lying naked on their bed with another man.

"Rick, what are you doing home?"

"I forgot something I needed at work today so I came home to get it. How long has this been going on with you two?"

"This is the first time," Ted said as he was trying to get dressed.

"How could you do this to me?" Rick said to Sally as she got up and put on her robe.

"It just happened."

"Ted, you need to leave, right now," Rick insisted.

Ted grabbed the rest of his clothing and ran past Rick. He went downstairs and quickly dressed. Then, he went out, got into his car and left driving quickly down the driveway.

"Sally, what's this all about?"

"Ted came back with me after playing tennis. I didn't feel safe with the robbery and all and I asked him to check the house out with me."

"Well, you didn't have to get in bed with him."

"When we checked the bedroom, I went into the bathroom to get out of my sweaty tennis clothes. When I came out of the bathroom, Ted was standing there with nothing on."

"So you jumped into the bed with him?"

"He was aroused and when I saw that, I couldn't resist the temptation."

"And then when I came into the room, you seemed to be really into it."

"Well, I think with all the excitement of doing it with Ted got the best of me."

"And he got all of you."

"I'm sorry Rick. I never planned for this to happen."

"Sally, I don't know where we go from here. I don't think I can trust you anymore."

"Rick. This was the first time. I swear."

"Sure Sally. I'm going out for a while to think about things."

"Rick. Let's talk about this."

"Yeah. How Ted screwed my wife."

"No. Not about that. We need to talk about us."

"Sally, it's not us. It's you. You made that choice a little while ago with Ted."

"Rick."

"What do you want me to say Sally?"

"We just need to talk."

"About what? I come home from work to pick something up and here you're in bed with Ted getting it on."

"Rick. It's not like that."

"Oh no? What am I getting wrong?"

"Ted was just helping me out."

"Really? Well, did he help you out?"

"Yes. He checked the whole place out."

"So you rewarded him?"

"Rick, please."

"I know you and I haven't had sex for a long time now and I realize it's mostly my problem. But this? I really thought our relationship was stronger than this."

Rick turned and walked out of the house, leaving Sally naked and alone in the house.

# Chapter 20

Rick walked into the bar and took up one of the empty seats by the door. Jake came over.

"Hey Rick. By yourself?"

"Yeah."

"What can I get you?"

"I need a shot of bourbon and a beer."

"Coming right up."

Jake poured the shot and a draft. He put them in front of Rick as Ron came over from the other end of the bar and stood next to Jake.

"I saw your wife in here earlier today."

"Was she with a guy named Ted?"

"Now that you mention it, she was."

"Who's Ted?" Jake asked.

"She told me they had just finished playing tennis," Ron said.

"Yeah, tennis, and then they went home."

"Sally said she was a little nervous about going home alone with all the robberies taking place lately," Ron said.

"Oh, it wasn't the robberies Ron; she wanted to get into the sack with Ted."

"Sally?" Ron said as he looked at Jake.

"Yeah. I had to go home just after lunch to pick up something for work. When I got there, I found the two of them in bed."

"Wow," Jake said surprised.

"Imagine how I felt."

"What did you do?" Ron asked.

"I told Ted to leave and then I had to get out of the house to think for a little while."

"That's too bad," Jake said.

"I know I have my issues with Sally, you now, the age difference and all."

"How much older are you than her?" Ron asked.

"She's fifty-one and I'm sixty-four."

"Yeah, that's a bit of a difference."

"I know I have trouble satisfying her in some ways but I didn't think she would resort to another man."

"Have you ever tried one of those pills?" Jake asked.

"I've tried most of them. They work for a while."

"What will you do?" Ron asked.

"I don't know. When I saw her with Ted together in my bed, I just watched for a while."

"Why didn't you stop them right away?" Ron asked.

"She was really into it. I haven't seen her enjoying sex like that in some time. Then, when they were both done, she had this big smile on her face."

"Aren't you worried she might catch something and then give it to you?" Jake asked.

"I never gave it a thought but I guess I'll have to. I don't know about Ted, or anyone else she might be seeing."

"Did they use a condom?"

"I don't think so. When I surprised them, he got off her right away and I didn't see one."

"You've got a lot to deal with Rick. I don't envy you," Ron said as he turned to go to the other end of the bar.

Jake had been waiting on another patron and came over to Rick when Ron walked away.

"Yeah Rick. I don't think I'd be as calm as you if it were my wife."

"I'm pissed Jake. You can bet your ass. But I know I have my own shortcomings and Ted really satisfied her today."

"Do you think she'll do it again?"

"Who knows? I'll just have to pay attention for the foreseeable future and see what happens."

Jake looked at the door as it opened. Sally walked in. She walked over to where Rick was seated and took up the empty stool next to him.

"Rick, we've got to talk."

"Sally, I just want to be left alone for a while."

"Can I get you anything Sally?" Jake asked.

"I'll have a glass of Chardonnay, please."

Jake went to pour the wine.

"Sally, did you and Ted use a condom?"

"What kind of question is that?"

"I just need to know?"

"No. But it doesn't matter."

"What if you get something? It's not fair to me."

Sally hadn't thought about the consequences.

"Rick. I'm sorry I did what I did with Ted today. It'll never happen again. People make mistakes. They're not perfect. And neither am I. I do love you."

"Sally, I'm not blind. I saw the look on your face when you two finished. I haven't seen that look in many years. I know I haven't been able to bring you to that level in some time. You can't tell me you didn't like it."

"Ok, so I enjoyed it a little. It's been so long Rick. But, I can put it behind me and not go there again."

Rick wasn't so sure. He picked up his shot glass and finished it off. Then, he did the same with his beer.

"I'll have another Jake."

"Can we just go home?"

"Let me finish my beer," Rick said taking it from Jake.

The two sat for a few minutes not saying anything. Rick took his time drinking the beer.

"I'll see you at home Rick."

Sally got up and left.

Rick sat there quietly finishing another beer and shot. About twenty minutes later, he signaled Jake.

"I'll take the check, Jake."

"Sure Rick."

Jake put the check in front of Rick, and he took a twenty and ten out of his pocket and put it down with the check. "Guess I'll go home and see if we can work this out."

"Good luck Rick."

"Thanks Jake."

Rick left and drove home.

Sally was seated on their couch in the living room.

"I'm so sorry Rick. I shouldn't have brought Ted to our house."

"Bringing him here wasn't the problem Sally. Screwing him in our bed was."

"I know. How can I make it up to you?"

"Look Sally. I know you have needs I have trouble fulfilling. I've tried to think this over in my mind and remain calm. If I were in the same position, I'd probably do the same thing. Ted's a good guy and we've known him for some time. I don't think he'd ever plan to do something like you two did today so it had to be spontaneous. Don't get me wrong. I don't approve but I do understand."

Sally put her arms around Rick and hugged him. Then, she tilted her head up and kissed him. She lightly touched his tongue with hers. Rick returned the kiss. He felt something he hadn't felt in some time. They continued to kiss for a while.

Eventually, he reached around and undid her bra and began to touch her. Sally reached down and felt an aroused Rick. In a few minutes, the two were naked making love on their couch. Rick's stamina had returned from nowhere. Sally's breathing grew heavy. Sally held her breath and then let out a sigh as she reached climax. Then he did.

The two kissed again and again.

"Rick."
"Don't say anything Sally. Let's just enjoy what we can."
"I love you."
"I know Sally."

Rick got up and went into the bathroom to get a towel. He returned and cleaned himself up and then handed the towel to Sally. She did the same and then cleaned up the couch. Silently, the two picked up their clothes and went to the bedroom. They got into bed, pulled up the covers and cuddled together.

# Chapter 21

Ron was serving a few drinks to a couple who had taken up the table in the bar area closest to the door when a police officer walked in.

"Can I help you with something officer?"

"Yes. I'm Officer Cassidy. I'm working on a string of robberies that took place in the area recently and all of the victims indicated they come in here often."

"I have heard some of the patrons talking about the robberies. I think the other bartender, Jake Wilson, has as well. My name is Ron Alderman."

The two shook hands.

"Let me introduce you to Jake."

The two walked to the other end of the bar.

"Jake, this is Officer Cassidy. He's looking into the robberies some of the patrons have been talking about."

Jake extended his hand.

"Nice to meet you Officer Cassidy."

"How do you spell your name?"

Jake gave him the spelling. Officer Cassidy wrote it in a pad. Then Ron spelled his name for the officer.

"What can you two tell me about the robberies?"

"Not much," Jake said. "A few of our customers have been in here recently talking about them. I know the Tafts said their place was robbed."

"Yeah, Sally Taft was in here earlier today. She didn't want to go home alone for fear of finding the robbers there again," Ron added.

"Can you two provide me with a list of the customers you remember talking about being robbed?"

"Sure," Ron said. "Can we get it to you? We're getting pretty busy right now. Jake and I will work on it during our shift and I'll bring it over to the station in the morning."

"Thanks guys. I'll look for it in the morning."

Officer Cassidy shook their hands and then left.

"So Ron, why do you really think the police are coming in here to talk with us?"

"Officer Cassidy said the bar was the only common denominator he came up with when he interviewed all the victims."

"You think someone from here is doing the robberies?"

"Don't know but I think the police suspect someone from here."

"Well, let's start the list and I'll take it to the station in the morning."

"Ok, and I'll ask Bobby and the waitresses too if they heard anything."

"Good idea. That way we should get everyone on the list."

Ron went around the bar making sure every patron had what they needed for the time being. Jake took out a pad and started writing names down.

As Jake was writing, Bobby came behind the bar from the kitchen carrying a rack of glasses.

"Bobby, we're writing down the names of all the customers who told us about being robbed recently. When we're done, can you take a look at the list and see if we missed anyone you might have overheard talking about the recent robberies?"

"The recent robberies? You want me to look at a list?"

"Yeah. I think Ron and I can get most of them but it doesn't hurt to have another set of eyes look at the information and see if we missed anyone."

"I don't know. I'm not good at remembering things like that. And besides, I'm not really on the floor all that much."

"That's ok. Just see if you think we missed anyone."

"Ok."

Bobby put the rack on the cooler and started to put the glasses away. Jake returned to writing names on the list.

As the night went on, Ron and Jake took turns looking at the list. Every now and then, one or the other would remember a name and add it to the list.

Around eleven, Ron took one last look at the list.

"That's all I can remember."

"Yea, I think we got most of them."

"I've asked Bobby to take a look at the list and see if he can add anyone else," Ron said picking the list up and walking to the end of the bar where Bobby was storing glasses.

"Bobby, here's the list of names Jake and I came up with. See if you think we missed anyone who has talked about being robbed recently?"

"I'll take a look at it when I'm done putting these glasses away."

"Thanks."

Bobby dropped one of the glasses on the floor and it shattered.

"Shit."

"Need a hand Bobby?" Jake offered.

"No. I just took my eye off what I was doing."

"Try to be more careful buddy. Glasses aren't as cheap as they look."

"I will. Let me clean up the broken glass and then I'll look at your list."

"Just leave it by the register after you've looked at it."

"Ok."

Bobby cleaned up the broken glass and then went and picked up the list. He scanned it quickly. He didn't add anything and then put it by the register.

Ron went back to Jake, "What about the hooded sweatshirt?"

"You know, there used to be one in the lost and found box in the storage room," Jake said.

"Is it still there?"

"I'll go look."

Jake left the bar area and went into the storage room near the door. When he came back to the bar, he said, "I know I saw one in there recently. It's not there now. Maybe someone claimed it."

"Maybe. Weird timing though. It sits back there for weeks, and now it disappears?"

Ron saw Bobby drop the pad off at the register.

"Hold on a minute Bobby. Jake said he thought there was a sweatshirt in the lost and found box in the storage room recently. Did you see it?"

"No."

"Oh. I just thought you might have noticed it since you're in there more than anyone else in here."

"I don't recall seeing a hooded sweatshirt."

"Ok."

"Why are you looking in lost and found?"

"Supposedly someone wearing a sweatshirt with the bar name and logo on it was trying to pawn some of the stolen items recently. We just wanted to tie up a loose end of a missing sweatshirt."

"You know lots of people have those. I think we sold around a hundred."

"We'll have to ask the team members if they all still have theirs. That might eliminate some suspects. Although even the public can buy 'em."

"So you think anyone with one of those sweatshirts is a suspect?"

"I don't know for sure," Ron said. "It's just that one of the local pawn shops reported a person with a sweatshirt displaying our bar name and logo was attempting to pawn some of the items stolen in one of the robberies."

Jake turned and started to walk to the end of the bar. He pulled out a dishpan from under the bar and put it on top of the beer glass cooler.

"Bobby, can you take this to the kitchen?"

"Sure."

Bobby had been standing in the corner of the bar listening to Jake and Ron talk. He picked up the dishpan Jake had put on the cooler and slowly went back to the kitchen.

The back door to the bar opened.   In walked Don Pennington and Jenny Carson.

"Hi Jake," Don said.

"Hey Don.   What are you and Jenny out doing tonight?"

Jenny smiled at Jake, "Don gave me a call and asked me to join him for a few drinks tonight."

She reached for his hand as he pulled out a stool for her to sit at.

"What can I get you two?"

"I'll have a glass of Chardonnay," Jenny said.

"And I'll have a Blue Moon, no fruit," Don said.

Jake got them the drinks, and returned to the end of the bar where Ron was standing.

"They got together pretty quickly," Ron said.

"Yeah.   I saw her talking and dancing with Don when she was in here Friday night."

"Wasn't she with someone else on Friday?"

"That was Friday.   Today's a new day."

"Guess you're right Jake.   Must be nice to be single and free."

"Must be."

They want about their business for the rest of the night until closing finally came.

Jake picked up the list he and Ron had put together. Then he took out his cell phone and a card Officer Cassidy had given him.   He called Cassidy's number but got his voice mail.

"Officer Cassidy, this is Jake Wilson from the 'O' Bar. I only have four names on my list of patrons who have been robbed recently so I'll leave you this message instead of

144

coming by the station in the morning. The people I have on my list are the Tafts, Sam Marino, Trish Howland and Kelly Jones. If I come up with any other names, I'll call."

Jake put the phone away.

# Chapter 22

By Friday night, everyone at the bar was talking about the recent robberies. The usual regulars were at the bar by five. Sam was at the end of the bar with the rest of the Harttt landscaping crew talking about being robbed the last Monday while he was at work.

"So if the robbers got your TV, computer and other entertainment stuff Sam, what are you going to do for fun?" Pete Harttt asked.

"Hey, I still have a radio."

"Isn't that what it was like when you were a kid, Sam?"

"Ha, Ha."

Jake was taking orders for drinks. Lou had just come in, and stood behind Pete.

"What can I get you Lou?"

"I'll have a Bud draft."

"So Sam, did you find out anything about who robbed you?" Lou asked.

"Not yet. I'm still checking the pawn shops."

"You think you'll find something there?"

"I'm hoping."

"Have you checked craigslist?" Pete asked.

"Didn't think about checking there."

"You should. Maybe you'll recognize something stolen from your place being sold there."

"I'll check it out when I get home."

"I thought you lost your computer as well?"

"Oh yeah. Guess I'll have to wait until I get another computer."

"Can't you use your phone Sam?" Jake said.

"Yeah."

Sam took his phone out of his pocket, and was quickly on the Craigslist site.

"What category do you think I should look under?"

"Try General and then Electronics," Pete said.

Sam scanned the entries. There were quite a few.

"I don't see anything I recognize."

"Did you request to see the information by date?" Pete added.

"How do I do that?"

"Off to the right there are a few words at the top of the screen. Click Newest."

Sam did as told. The list now sorted the information in date order from the current date going backwards. As he scanned down the list, he saw something he recognized. There was a Samsung fifty-five inch TV listed for sale three days after he had been robbed.

"Hey, here's a TV matching my TV's description. And the listing was put up a few days after mine was stolen."

"What's the contact information say?" Jake asked.

Sam tapped the screen, "There's a phone number to call."

"Call it," Pete said.

"Absolutely I will."

"Hello."

"My name is Sam. I saw a post you had on Craigslist for a fifty-five inch TV. Is it still for sale?"

"No. It sold the next day. I guess I should have taken the post down but I forgot."

"Can you tell me how long you had that TV?"

"I had just picked it up at the Pawn shop the day before and had put it up for sale. Figured I could make a quick profit."

"Do you mind telling me what pawn shop you bought the TV at?"

"Was there some problem with the TV? Are you the person who bought it?"

"No I didn't. I just have a few questions about the TV."

"Are you a cop or something?"

"Nothing like that but my place was robbed last week and my TV was stolen. It was the same size and model as the one in your post."

"Do you know who you sold it to?"

"Some guy. He came by the next day and paid me three hundred cash."

"Do you have a phone number for the guy?"

"No. I didn't think I needed one."

"So you don't have any idea where the TV is now?"

"No. I don't know anything about a stolen TV. I only bought the thing at the Gold Digger pawn shop because of the price they were asking and I knew I could sell it for twice as much on Craigslist."

"Do you mind if I ask what you paid for it?"

"A hundred bucks."

Sam had everyone's attention at the bar as he talked on the phone.

"I'm working with the police to find out who robbed me. I'll give them your phone number and they may contact you. Can you tell me your name?"

"I'd rather not be involved."

"It really doesn't matter since I have your phone number and the police can contact you if they need to."

"My name is Henry Grey."

"Well, thanks for the information Henry."

Sam put his phone back in his pocket.

Jake was the first to speak.

"Sounds like you might have a lead."

"Yeah. This Henry guy brought a TV from the Gold Digger pawn shop during the week and planned on making a quick sale."

"Do you think he was involved in the robbery?" Pete asked.

"Doesn't sound like it. I'll turn the info over to the police and let them handle it."

"Does he still have the TV?" Jake asked.

"Nah. Said he sold it the next day."

"What are you going to do now, Sam?" Pete said.

"I think I'll stop in at that pawn shop tomorrow and see what I can find out."

As the group gathered around Sam pondered that idea, only Frank Johnson said something. "Sam, you might want to just turn what you found out over to the police and let them handle it." Ron, Jake and few others nodded in agreement.

"You know me, Frank. I like to deal with things head on."

"Yeah. I know. But there were other people who were robbed as well and if the robbers are using the Gold Digger to get rid of stuff, the police might want to widen the scope of questioning the personnel at the pawn shop." Jake said.

"I agree with Jake, Sam," Ron said.

"Listen to them, Sam," Pete said."

"Well, I'll bring it up to the authorities and see where things go."

"Good idea Sam," Pete said. "Give everyone a beer on me Jake."

"Thanks Pete," Frank said.

Ron and Jake poured the beers placing them on the bar in front of the group of men. As they stood back, Ron said, "Let's see. Sam, the Tafts, and Trish were all robbed."

"Yeah. That's very strange. Sure looks like someone who frequents this place might be playing a role in all the robberies, or it's an incredible coincidence."

"I can't imagine who would be involved in such a thing. I like to think of these folks as friends."

"Me either. But you can't overlook the commonality of these robberies. All the victims are here, right now."

Ron looked around. "Wow. Who ever is doing these robberies might be right in front of us right now."

"You have any suspects?" Ron asked Jake.

"Let's see."

Jake scanned the crowd.

"You know. Tim Stone is a strange character. You think he might be involved?"

"He's strange but I don't think he's a thief."

"If the opportunity presents itself, Ron, see if you can get any information out of Tim."

"Oh, now you going detective on me, Jake?"

"Nothing like that. But if the police come back in and start asking questions, it might be helpful if we can add something."

"I'll see what I can find out."

Jake went back over to Sam.

"Sam, didn't you say your laptop had a GPS tracking device in it?"

"It did."

"Were you able to locate the laptop using the GPS tracker yet?"

"No. I need to get a new computer first."

"Can't you use someone else's?"

"Probably. But, they would have to have the tracking software installed."

"Is that hard to do?"

"No, if you have an account with the tracking company."

"Can't you use your account on someone else's computer?"

"Probably. I'll have to see if someone will let me use their computer if I don't get a new one soon."

"Can't you use your smart phone?"

"I don't know."

Jake looked around the bar. He saw Don Pennington sitting at the other end of the bar.

"I wonder if Don might know how to access your GPS tracker?"

"I don't know."

"Let me see if he'll come down and talk with us about it?"

Jake walked down to Don.

"Say Don. Sam and I were just talking about his laptop that was stolen. He said he had a GPS tracking device installed on it. He thinks he might be able to find the laptop if he can figure out a way to use the tracking software without the laptop."

"He can probably use anyone's computer to track it."

"Yeah. That's what Sam said but he hasn't done that yet. He thought he needed to get a replacement computer first."

"Nah. He can use any computer. All he needs is his account ID and password and then he can go to the software company's site and download a copy of the tracking software."

"Could he use his smart phone?"

"I don't see why not. The company probably has a smart phone app he could download for free."

"Can you come over to where Sam is sitting and help him out?"

"Sure."

Don got up, picked up his drink and walked over to Sam.

"Hey Sam."

"Don."

"Jake says you're trying to find your stolen laptop by accessing a GPS tracker you had on the machine."

"That's right. I bought one of those trackers that looks like a small battery and had it put inside the laptop case."

"Then, you should be able to locate it."

"I know but I thought I'd have to buy another laptop in order to do that."

"You can just use your phone."

Sam took out his phone, and handed it over to Don.

"You think I could find the laptop using this? Have at it."

"Sure. What's the name of the company you got the GPS tracking software from?"

Same gave him the name and Don entered it into Sam's phone using an Internet connection. When the site came up, Don said, "What's your account ID and password?"

Sam thought for a minute.

"My e-mail address, sammarino@hartt.com and my password is onirams30."

"What's that, your age and name spelled backwards?"

"Yeah, something like that. It's easy for me to remember."

Don typed the information in and was granted access to the site. He looked at the tabs at the top of the screen: Home, Account Profile, Updates and Find My GPS. He selected the Find My GPS.

It took a minute or two and then the screen showed a map of the area with a red dot brighter than the rest of the screen.

"What's that?"

"That's the location of the GPS tracker."

"Where is it saying the laptop is right now?"

Don widened the screen. It showed Route 177, Route 4 and the Farmington River. Highlighted was the word Unionville.

"See the red dot is just off the side of Route 177 and below Route 4?" Don said pointing to the screen.

"Yeah."

"It's telling you your GPS tracking device is right there."

"Isn't that the parking lot outside the bar?"

"Looks like it."

"You're telling me my laptop is outside here right now in the parking lot?"

"I don't know about the laptop, but the tracking device is near by."

"I had it taped inside the hard case of the laptop," Sam said.

"Then, it might still be there."

"How can we find out exactly where it is?"

"The software probably isn't that specific. I think just getting you into the general vicinity is about the best you can expect."

"So you think my laptop is outside here right now in someone's vehicle?"

"I'm not saying that. The GPS is. So I'd say definitely probably."

Sam looked around the bar. Most of the regulars were there. He didn't know what to do next. Jake came over to them. "Find anything?"

"Yeah. Sam got the tracking software to tell us where my laptop is right now."

"And?"

"And it's outside right here. Probably in someone's car."

"No kidding?"

"Look."

Sam turned the phone to Jake so he could see.

"Look at the red dot. That is where the tracking software says my laptop is right now."

"I see it. Can you get the exact position?"

"The technology isn't that precise yet. It'll only get you within a few hundred feet," Don said.

Sam looking out at the parking lot said, "There have to be over fifty vehicles out there."

"And there's no way of telling which one the laptop is actually inside," Don said.

"Well, at least we know someone in here has my laptop."

"Or at least has your GPS tracking device."

"Who could it be?" Sam said. "I may have to wait for it to move, to find it."

# Chapter 23

During the week, someone broke into Kelly Jones's home while she was out of town on business. She had called the police when she got home and realized what had happened. Officer Cassidy came and met with her. She completed a statement for everything she could think of that was taken. The list included her jewelry, a laptop, two TVs and a box of sample products her company had been working on. When Officer Cassidy had finished making his notes, he said, "That's about all I need tonight, Ms. Jones."

"Thank you for coming over Officer. I appreciate it."

"Do you have any idea who might have done this?"

"No. But, some of my friends have been robbed recently too. We all know each other from the 'O' Bar so its weird."

"I've been looking into some of those situations. I think there's a connection here. I know there's no sign of forced entry, but can you try to keep everything exactly as it is until I can get some detectives out here for pictures and fingerprinting?"

"Sure. I'm ready to call it a night anyway. Listen Officer, this isn't going to be in the paper or anything is it?"

"Probably not. Is there a problem?"

"No, I guess not."

"Listen, I understand. Seeing it in public is like being a victim again. I'll do what I can to keep your information out of the limelight."

"Thanks Officer."

"I'll write up my report when I get back to the station. Would you like a copy of it?"

"Yes. Can you send it to my e-mail address?"

"Sure."

She handed him a business card. He looked at it and saw her e-mail address.

"I'll send it to this address as soon as its ready. It'll just be the first report, of course, but we'll keep you in the loop all the way."

"Thanks."

She'd take a look at the report when it came in.

A few days later, Kelly took a longer than normal lunch hour and went to the 'O' Bar. When she walked in, she saw Sue and Karen seated at the bar talking. She sat at the empty stool next to Sue and heard them discussion the robberies.

"My place was robbed the other night when I was out of town on business."

"No kidding?" Karen stated.

"Yeah."

"What was taken from your place Kelly?" Sue asked.

"I lost all of my jewelry, my laptop and two TVs."

"Now, I'm kind of afraid to be in my place alone. You know there aren't too many other people who live on my street and I'm the last house at the end of the cul-de-sac."

"Maybe you need to get a guard dog or something?" Sue said.

"Or maybe you need to find a permanent man," Karen added with a wink.

"I think I'll settle for being robbed before I go the man route Karen. I can recover from a robbery. I'm not sure about having just one man around the place all the time."

"I know what you mean," Sue said. "It's one thing to have a man around for some fun but they have a tendency to get possessive."

"So what's so bad about that?" Karen said.

"I like my freedom. I can come and go as I please and be with whomever I choose," Kelly said smiling.

"Guess it's a tradeoff you'll have to live with," Sue said.

"Maybe I'll look into a home security system or something."

"Yeah. You can always turn it off and you can't do that with a man."

The three laughed. Lou saw them laughing and walked over.

"Having a good laugh ladies?"

"We were just debating the merits of a good security system over having a man around," Sue remarked.

"And which one won out?" Lou asked.

"Let's just say getting a dog came in a close second to buying the security system," Sue added laughing.

"You know ladies, having a man around can have other benefits as well."

"Like what?" Sue asked.

"Odd jobs, heavy lifting, maintenance, things like that."

"Yeah, and laundry, messes, meals, cleaning and having to listen to complaining," Sue said.

"What about protection? With all these robberies going on, someone might get hurt," Lou said trying to improve his gender's position in this hypothetical contest.

"I've got my own protection," Karen said. "Break into my place will get to meet my gun and I'll use it if I have to."
"You have a gun Karen?"
"I do. It's a Smith and Wesson nine mil."
"And you know how to use it?"
"Lou, you don't want to be the person trying to break into my home if I'm there all alone. Trust me. I know how to use it."
"And like she said, she would if she had to," Sue stated.

Frank Johnson called over to Lou.
"Lou, come down here for a minute, could you?"
"Sorry ladies. Gotta go."
Lou walked back to the end of the bar to see what Frank wanted. When he walked away, Sue motioned to Jake.

"Can we have another round?"
"Sure. Same for everyone?"

They all nodded yes. Jake got them another drink. Putting the drinks on the bar, he said, "So Kelly, did you lose anything of value in the robbery?"
"Yeah. I had a necklace with a diamond in it. It was my grandmother's."
"I remember that necklace," Sue said. "It was beautiful."
"It was. I feel so bad losing it."
"A necklace with a diamond huh? You know Kelly, I thought I saw a necklace in the lost and found box. I think it has a stone in it. I thought it was glass. Let me get it."

Jake pulled a box out of the closet behind the bar and brought it over. He set the box on the bar and opened it. There was a cell phone in it, two sets of keys, a couple pair of glasses and some other stuff in the bottom. He turned the whole box over spilling the contents on the bar. On the top of the pile was a necklace.

"That's it!" Kelly said joyfully.

She picked up the necklace and held it up for everyone to see. Then, she poked through the rest of the stuff in the box to see if anything else of hers was there. But there wasn't.

"I can't believe the necklace I thought was stolen was here in that box."

"Jake, do you know how long it's been in there?" Sue asked.

"Could have been a day, a week or month. Any of the staff could have picked it up off the floor and would have put it in there."

"Can you ask the other people working here and see if any of them put it there? I'd like to know how long it's been here."

"Sure. I'll ask around and see if I can find out."

"Thanks Jake. I'm sure glad you checked."

"When was the last time you wore it here?"

"I never wear the necklace. It's an heirloom I don't want to lose."

"Then I wonder how it found its way into the bar?"

"Me too."

"Let's toast to Kelly finding her family treasure," Sue said holding up her drink.

The ladies toasted and had the drink.

"You know Kelly, the funny thing is Sally Taft had a ring stolen from their place and she found it in the lost and found box as well."

"You're kidding?"

"It's like someone is dropping some of the stolen stuff around the bar. Could it be a clue or just carelessness?" Sue said.

"Let's see if Jake can find anything out."

Jake took the necklace and left the bar area for a few minutes. He went into the restaurant portion of the building, and talked to a number of the other workers. Ten minutes later, he came back.

"Find out anything?" Sue asked.

"Yeah. One of the younger waitresses found this necklace a few nights ago near the men's room door."

"So it's one of the guys in here doing the robberies," Karen said.

"I didn't say in the men's room. She found it in the hall outside the men's room. That area is used by women, the kitchen, even kids for the party room."

"So someone dropped it there. I wonder if it was on purpose or by accident." Sue said.

"She said it was after closing a few nights ago so she just put it in the lost and found box. She also said she forgot to say anything to anyone else about it and had forgotten about it until I just showed it to her."

"Well, I'm just glad to get it back."

"I think you might want to mention it to the police Kelly. They'll be interested in the connection and in the fact you found it."

"I will."

Sally Taft had overheard the women cheering and saw Kelly holding up a necklace. She walked over to where the women were celebrating.

"What's the cheering for?"

"Kelly found a cherished necklace that was stolen from her place," Karen said.

"Good for you Kelly. So it wasn't stolen after all."

"Oh, it was stolen. Jake found it in the lost and found box here at the bar. I never take that necklace out so whoever robbed me must have dropped it or gave it to someone else who lost it here at the bar."

"That's funny. I found a ring that was stolen from my place in the lost and found also."

"That's what Jake told us," Sue said.

"Someone from here has to be involved in all these robberies ladies. We need to find out who is doing it," Sally said to the three.

They all looked around. They didn't have a clue other than the fact that two items from two different robberies showed up in the lost and found box at the 'O' Bar.

"You know, I had a security camera put in my house after it was robbed the first time. The day before yesterday, I was checking the camera and there was a picture of a person on my front porch I think was trying to break in again."

"Did you get robbed again?" Karen asked.

"No. I also had an alarm installed and it went off. Whoever it was ran off but I got a picture on the camera."

"Do you have it with you?" Sue asked.

"I sent a copy of it to my cell phone. I'll show you."

Sally took her phone out of her handbag and turned it on. She brought up a picture of a person at her front door. The person had a dark hood over his or her head so it was hard to figure out if it was a man or woman, and the size was no indicator. It could be a small man or a large woman. The angle of the camera had been at too steep an angle to see the face of the person. About the only thing that could be made out was that the person seemed to be over five feet but less than six, had on jeans and a hooded sweatshirt and black sneakers.

"Isn't that sweatshirt one of those sold at the bar here last year?" Kelly asked.

They all looked closely at the picture. It had the name of the bar and logo on the back clearly visible in the picture.

"Jake, come look at this picture. Isn't that one of the sweatshirts sold here last year?" Kelly asked.

Jake looked at Sally's phone.

"Yeah. That's one of ours. We had one in lost and found for a while, but it disappeared a few days ago. I should check to see if its back. This just gets weirder and weirder."

"Did you give the picture to the police?" Kelly asked.

"Not yet. I'm meeting with them again tomorrow and I'll give it to them at that time," Sally said.

"I wonder who it could be." Karen said.

They all looked around the bar.

# Chapter 24

Kelly saw Tim Stone standing by the door. He had gone outside to smoke a cigarette and was on his way back inside.

"I'm going to talk with Tim and see what he knows. He seems to know everything that goes on in town."

"Be careful Kelly," Karen said. "He might even be involved."

"You think so?"

"I don't know. He's just so creepy."

Kelly picked up her beer and walked over to Tim. He was waiting for someone to get up from the bar so he could get a seat.

"Hey Tim. How are you?"

"Kelly. I'm doing ok."

"Tim, do you mind if I talk to you for a few minutes about the robberies that have been going on?"

"I don't mind. But I really don't know anything about the robberies."

"Maybe not, but you seem to know a little about alot that goes on in town."

"I make it a point to pay attention to the comings and goings in town."

"Well, maybe you know something that can help figure this thing out."

"I don't know but what the heck."

The Tafts had just gotten up from their seats at the bar. Tim saw Rick pay the tab. He pointed to them leaving and he and Kelly went over to the empty seats. They sat down.

"Ron, get me another beer and give Kelly a refill."

"Sure Tim."

"Now, what would you like to know Kelly?"

"It seems everyone who's been robbed comes in here. I was robbed. The Tafts, Sam, Trish and who knows who else. Some of the stolen stuff ended up being found right here. Who do you think might be the culprit?"

"I really have no idea. If I was trying to solve the crimes, I would consider how the robber got the information he needed to commit them."

"What do you mean?"

"Well, let's say there's a conversation taking place between a few folks at the bar. Schedules come up and details of who will be where and when get discussed. If I wanted to rob someone and had information about that person's possession, place and schedule, it would be fairly easy to plan a robbery and be pretty confident about not getting caught."

"So you think those of us who have been robbed have openly given the robber information about our schedule so he or she could commit the crimes?"

"Would it work?"

"But could it be that easy?"

"I don't know for sure. But, think about it. Most of you who have been robbed are regulars here. So, your home location is readily known. Plus, I'll bet many of you have talked about your possessions from time to time, and talked about them openly. You'd be surprised at the things one can overhear in a bar like this. Just what you wear and what you drive says a lot about you."

"Karen had a security system installed at her place after she was robbed. She let it be known that the robber didn't get into her safe during the robbery. The camera took a picture a few days after the first robbery and showed a hooded person trying to break into her place again. Unfortunately, there isn't enough detail in the picture to identify the person."

"How can you be sure it was a robber and even the same robber?"

"Well, she had an alarm system installed also and the alarm went off when the person tried to break in the second time. It scared the robber away."

"What kind of information did she get from the picture?"

"An average sized man or woman dressed in jeans, sneakers and a hooded sweatshirt, the same kind the bar was selling last year. There's quite a few people in here who would fit a description like that."

"Well, think about the things that were taken."

"Mostly jewelry, TVs, computers and stuff like that."

"Stuff that can easily be pawned huh?"

"Yeah. Some of us that were robbed have been looking into the local pawn shops but nothing solid had come forward yet."

"I'd say you're on the right track. You might want to try to set a trap with some of the other regulars in here you think you can trust and see if it works."

"That's what Sally Taft tried to do but she didn't get enough detail in the picture she got."

"If it were me, I'd come up with something that would really interest the robber. Like having a large sum of cash on hand at home. Make up a credible story about how you came into the money and plan on getting it into the bank in a few days, like after a weekend. If you make it attractive enough, you might just fool the robber into taking risky action. Even the walls have ears I've heard." Tim laughed at what he thought was his own joke.

"What kind of story would work?"

"Why not say you hit it big at the casino? They payoff in cash."

"That sounds like a great idea. Thanks Tim for talking with me."

"You're welcome Kelly. I hope you succeed in catching the culprit. I'm not a big mystery fan, but I'd like to know how the story ends."

"So do I."

Kelly got up and went back over to where Sue and Karen were sitting.

"Did you get anything worthwhile out of Tim?" Sue asked.

"He didn't know specifically about the robberies but had some good ideas about how we might solve them."

"Like what?"

"He thinks there's a lot of information expressed freely in here that could be used to let a robber know when someone will be home, what possessions one has and what to look for while committing a robbery."

"What's he talking about?" Karen asked.

"Well, think about it. Like Tim said, most everyone knows everyone else in here. We know who lives where, things about each others homes, who will be home and when and even what we might have inside our places."

"So?" Sue said.

"So, someone who wanted to do the robberies just needed to have the information. He said it's like we invited the robber in."

"I see what he means," Karen said. "Nothing like telling a criminal when it would be a good time to be robbed, what possessions we have and where to find them."

"Yeah. It makes sense."

"But, what about the stuff that has turned up here in the bar?" Karen asked.

"I didn't get into it with Tim but he did say we should try to set a trap to catch the perpetrator."

"A trap?" Sue said.

"Yeah. He had a pretty good idea. Pick someone that hasn't been robbed yet and can be trusted. Then, make up a story about that person having a sizeable amount of cash on hand and needing to get it into the bank after a weekend. Pass the information around on Friday night with the person going out on Saturday night. Then, have someone hiding at the home where the cash is on Saturday night and see what happens."

"Who do you think would be a good candidate?" Sue asked.

"I'd say it should be one of the single females," Karen said.

"Why a female?" Sue asked.

"Because females are more predictable than males and we want to make sure the storyline laid out is as believable as can be," Kelly stated.

"Well, who hasn't been robbed yet and has a place that the robber would be inclined to take action against on short notice?" Sue asked.

"Why not you, Sue?" Karen said.

"Everyone knows I don't have much."

168

"Yeah, but what if you said you hit the lottery for ten grand or you hit it big at the casino. Everyone knows they pay off in cash. Then, if you bought everyone a round at the bar on Friday night?" Karen said as she let her voice taper off.

"Yeah Sue. And your place is pretty isolated at the end of the street up in Collinsville," Kelly added.

"I don't know."

"It's a perfect setup Sue," Karen added.

Jake had been standing behind the bar waiting on one of the patrons. He could hear the women talking about their plans.

"You gals taking to detective work now?"

Sue looked at Jake. "We've got to do something."

"Why not leave it to the police?"

"Jake, I think we have a good idea of how to find out who is doing all this stuff if the person is from here. And the police are so slow," Karen stated.

"Even so, who's going to capture this robber anyway?"

The three women looked at each other. Then, they looked around the bar.

"Why don't we ask Lou or Sam?" Kelly said.

"Why them?" Sue asked.

"Because Sam was robbed. He'll want the satisfaction of catching the robber," Kelly stated.

"Good idea," Sue said. "I'll talk to them."

Sue got up. She reached for her beer and knocked the glass to the floor behind the bar. It almost hit Bobby in the head as he was putting clean glasses in the rack under the bar.

"Sorry about that Bobby."

"No problem. Not the first time I've been beaned by a bottle or glass."

169

"Bobby, can you clean that up?"

"Sure Jake."

Sue got up and walked to the other end of the bar where Lou, Sam and the others from Hartt landscaping were sitting.

# Chapter 25

"Hey guys. The girls and I were talking about all these robberies and we think we might have an idea to find out if someone from here is involved."

"Oh you do now, do you?" Lou said.

"Yeah. I talked to Tim Stone for a little and he had some interesting ideas."

"Tim. He might be involved in these robberies."

"We don't think so. Anyway, he had a good idea of how to set a trap to catch the criminal."

"He did, did he?"

"Yeah. Someone who hasn't been robbed yet makes it known that there is a large stash of cash at home from winning at the casino or lottery and that the cash needs to be put into the bank after the weekend. Then, the person makes up a story about no one being home on Saturday night."

"And how does all this happen?"

"Well, Tim says it looks like all the information might have been obtained about the victim's right here at the bar. So, if a credible story gets out about the money and possible easy way to get it gets out, the robber might go after it."

"It all sounds good but you have no guarantee that whoever is committing these robberies will get the information."

"That's true but it's worth a shot."

"So why are you telling us all this, Sue?"

"We think you might be willing to help us catch the crook."

"Me or Sam? I'm no policeman and last time I checked, neither was Sam."

"But you're a pretty strong guy and if you play your cards right, Lou, there might be a reward."

He thought about it for a minute and then smiled.

"That's a good point. Ok. I'm in. Who are we going to set up as the next victim?"

"Me."

"Go ahead Lou. You can be the hero this weekend."

"Sam, you don't want to get involved in this anyway. Let me do the dirty work."

"So here's how we're going to do it."

"You've got my undivided attention Sue."

"Lou, come on. Pay attention."

"I am."

"Ok. So on Friday, I'll come into the bar and say I hit it big at the casino that day. I'll be with the girls and then you come over and ask me about my winnings. I plan on buying everyone a drink just to show I'm in the money. You ask me out for Saturday night and I'll accept."

"Sounds pretty easy."

"It will be. Then, on Saturday night, you pick me up. You and I will leave like we're going out on a date and then park a block away to sneak back to my place and wait and see if anyone shows up."

"What will we do while we're waiting?"

"Lou, I'm sure we'll find something to do."

"I think I've got it."

"Remember, it all has to look legit. Tim says not to overlook the obvious. Someone in here is gathering the information and then committing the robberies. Just be ready."

"Got it Sue. Oh, good luck at the casino Friday."

She gave him a hug, got up and went back to her friends.


Frank Johnson overheard some of the conversation and turned to Lou, "What are you getting yourself into Lou?"

"The girls think they have an idea of how to catch the robber committing all of the recent crimes if he's from here."

"And what's your role in all of this?"

"Who knows? I'm just trying to get laid and if things work out, Saturday night will be a nice long night."

"I just hope you haven't gotten in over your head."

"I'm not worried. I'm just a hired actor as far as I'm concerned. What's the worst that can happen? I catch the robber?"

"Well, what if the robber shows up while you're putting the moves on Sue?"

"Yeah, that wouldn't be good."

"Any idea of when these robberies are taking place?"

"Some during the daytime on weekends but mostly at night just after dark."

"So, you only need to get past the first couple of hours after sunset and then you should be able to work your charm."

"That's it. I'll work my charm."

"Good luck with that."

"Hey, this is Sue we're talking about. Luck's not required."

"Like I said, good luck."

After a little while, Kelly Jones came over to Lou.

"Lou, Sue told us you're in on our plan."

"That's right."

"Listen. I'm a little worried about Sue. She lives alone in a pretty secluded area. She's going to make herself a target to be robbed and I'm a little worried for her safety. Especially if he doesn't happen Saturday night while you're there."

Tommy Benson had taken the stool next to Kelly. "What's this all about Kelly? I overheard you talking with Lou about Sue. Is something wrong?"

"No Tommy. This doesn't involve you."

"Hey, if there's anything I can do, let me know."

"I was just talking to Lou. I'm concerned for Sue's safety."

"If you need someone to go home with Sue, I'm available."

"Tommy, you've been to Sue's place with her before haven't you?"

"Sure. A couple of times."

"Then, you know how out of the way her place is."

"Yeah. Even I get the creeps walking to her place at night from the corner. Someone could be hiding in any one of those buildings just before her house. I wonder why someone put that house there anyway."

"Sue told me it used to be owned by the family who operated one of the machine shops on her street."

"Well, those places are all shut down now. All that's left is the bar by the road and the antiques place inside the old factory."

"Yeah, and Sue's place at the end of the lot."

"Well, anyhow, if Sue needs someone to go home with her, I'm available."

"We'll keep that in mind Tommy. Thanks."

Kelly left the two and went back to the other women.

Sam and Pete Harttt had been involved in a conversation about the landscaping business, when Kelly walked away, Sam said, "Lou, I'm going to meet up with Pete and a few other guys Saturday and go to the Boat Show at the Convention Center. I can't believe you're not interested in going. Can't you do the detective thing a different night?"

"Nah. I've got a date next Saturday. Sam, you just heard her."

"You're not serious about what Sue was talking about are you?"

"Sure. I'm in. We're going to play detective over at her house."

"Ok. But, you're missing out on a good night out."

"Oh I'm going to have a good night. Sue's asked me to stay over and I'm sure we'll have a good time."

Sam went back to talking with Pete. Lou turned around and ordered another drink from Ron. Pops, who had been seated two seats away from Lou asked for his check, paid it and got up. As he left, Ed Martin came into the bar and took up a seat. He said the hello to the regulars he knew and ordered a Jack and coke. Ron put the drink in front of him.

"So what's going on Ed?"

"Not much. I got stopped last night by the police just down the street after leaving here. They wanted to know where I was going and what I was up to."

"Why would they stop you Ed?"

"It must have been a little after eleven. I pulled out of the parking lot by the firehouse and turned left. They were parked in the firehouse lot and immediately followed me. Just past the school, the lights on the cruiser started flashing and I pulled over. That's when I found out I was the person they wanted to talk to."

"And what happened?"

"The officer said I matched the description of the person who had been committing all these recent robberies."

"Really?"

"Yeah. They asked a whole lot of questions and then wanted to know where I got the hooded sweatshirt I was wearing."

"What hooded sweatshirt?"

"You know, the ones we bought here last year."

Ron reached under the bar and pulled his out. "Like this one?"

"Yeah. That's the one. I've got one in the back seat of my car and I guess they knew it was there."

"Someone left this one here this week. I just haven't put it into lost and found yet."

"The officer said they have a description of a suspect in the robberies. He said the suspect is about five-five, jeans, sneakers and a hooded sweatshirt like that one."

"Hell, that could be anyone, even me although I'm not five-five."

Ed looked around, "Almost any of these guys in here could fit the description give or take a few inches."

"Where did they leave it?"

"When I got out of my car and stood up, the officer knew he had the wrong guy."

"Why was that?"

"Look at me. I'm over six feet tall."

"He must have felt foolish."

"I guess. They just asked a lot of questions and then decided to let me go. I have to tell you it was a little unnerving."

"So they just pulled you over for questioning?"

"Yep. Said I fit the description. Once I told them of my alibi for last weekend and looking at how tall I'm they decided to let me go."

"What was your excuse?"

"Apparently, one of the robberies took place last weekend and I was away all weekend up in Boston. Once I told them my alibi could easily be verified, they let me go."

"So the police are at least actively pursuing the case."

"Looks that way."

# Chapter 26

As the night started to come to a close, Sam, Tommy and Ed were the only people left at the end of the bar. All the other guys had gone home. Kim Mason had cleaned up all of the tables in her area and was finished for the night. She took up the empty stool next to Sam.

"Busy night Kim?"
"Same as usual."
"Can I buy you a drink?"
"Sure, why not."
"Jake, bring Kim whatever she wants."
"What will it be, Kim?"
"I'll have a glass of chardonnay."
Jake poured her a glass of wine and put in front of her.

"So what are your plans now, Kim?"
"I just want to relax for a little while."
"What you need is a massage."
"Sounds great. Here?"

"Why don't we go out to my vehicle for a few minutes? I'll have you feeling like a million bucks in a few minutes."

"We'll be right back Jake."

They got into Sam's vehicle. He started it up and drove to the lot behind the school. He parked down by the water, kind of hidden from view from the street. Sam turned the vehicle off and suggested they get into the back seat. They did.

"Turn your back to me Kim and I'll help you relax."

She did and Sam massaged her shoulders, neck and back. She leaned forward a little and he massaged her lower back the best he could. Then, he reached under her blouse and unhooked her bra. At first, she resisted.

"This is in the way Kim. You'll feel better in a few minutes."

She had to admit, Sam's hands seemed to work magic on her muscles. She let him remove her bra and work on her back. Then, he reached around and softly caressed her breasts. She didn't resist.

"Why don't you stretch out on the seat and let me work on your legs?"

She did as instructed. Sam worked all the way down to her ankles and then up. When he got back to her neck, he coaxed her to turn over. When she did, he undid her pants.

"What are you doing?"
"You'll see. You're a little tight."

He massaged her in the area. She giggled a little as he tickled her. He tried to slide his hands down a little further.

"No Sam. Not here."
"Why not?"
"Someone might see us."
"There's no one around."
"I just don't want to take the chance."
"Kim."
"Sam. I have to work here. I can't afford for anyone to catch me doing something like this."

She sat up, pulled her pants up. Then, she put her bra on and her blouse.

Sam got the message.
"Can we go somewhere else and finish?"
"Not tonight Sam. Why don't we plan a date for another night and I promise you will not be disappointed?"
"I'm already disappointed. But, I understand. How about tomorrow night?"
"Sounds good. Why don't you come over to my place around seven and we can take it from there."
"Seven it is."

They both got into the front seats, and Sam drove them back to the bar parking lot. They went inside and sat back down.
After finishing another beer, Sam paid his tab.
"I'll see you tomorrow night Kim."
"See you tomorrow Sam."

Sam got into his vehicle and left. He went to the gas station and filled up. Then, he planned on going home or maybe stopping at the Wood n' Tap bar on his way home. He pulled into the Wood N' Tap parking lot but then thought about what had happened and decided to go back to the 'O' Bar.

Jake came over to Kim, "Where you been kid?"

"I went outside with Sam for awhile and we took a short drive down the street."

"Oh, to that parking lot behind the school?"

"Yeah. You know about it?"

"Sam, Lou and almost all of the other guys use that lot whenever they want to get a quickie. They think they're fooling everyone but I've seen all of them down there at one time or another."

"Don't tell anyone else about it. Will you Jake?"

"Your secret is safe with me."

"Thanks. I couldn't go through with it with Sam. Sex in the backseat of a car on top of a sweatshirt with your job's name on it seems so high school."

"Sam had one of our sweatshirts? I don't remember him buying one. The sweatshirt might be a lead into the robberies. But he was robbed also. So I don't know."

"Maybe he was, maybe he wasn't. Does anyone actually know if he was robbed or not?"

"That's a good point Kim. I'm not sure we actually know or not but I'll find out."

Jake went to the register and pulled out a list. He came back over to Kim.

"This is a list of all the people who ordered one of those hooded sweatshirts that wasn't an employee. The cops asked for it. And Sam's name isn't on the list. So, I wonder where he got the one you saw in his vehicle?"

"He didn't say and I didn't ask."

"I'll find that out as well."

"I'm beat Jake. I think I'll call it a night."

# Chapter 27

Right after Kim left, Sam came back into the bar to where Ron was standing.

"Is Kim still here?"

"She just left. Did you need her for something?"

"No. That's all right. I'll catch up to her tomorrow."

"I thought you had left for the night, Sam?"

"I did but I forgot to return something to lost and found."

"What's that?"

"When it was raining the other night, I didn't have an umbrella or coat and one of the waitresses let me use this hooded sweatshirt she got out of lost and found."

Sam put the hooded sweatshirt on the bar just as the bar phone rang and Ron turned to answer it.

Ed and Tommy were still in the bar and they looked at Sam.

"Hey Ed, didn't Sally Taft say she got a picture of the robber coming back to her place wearing a hooded sweatshirt like that one Sam has over there?"

"Yeah, that's what she said."

"You think Sam could be the one doing the robberies?"

"Now why would Sam rob anyone? He doesn't need the money. Plus, He's six-two and I thought Sally said the robber looked to be around five-five."

"Well, he has a hooded sweatshirt."

Jake heard them talking and added, "When Kim told me about seeing the sweatshirt in Sam's vehicle, she didn't know about the connection. She told me about it when she came back in here and I checked my list of people who bought one. Sam wasn't on the list."

"Let me see if Sam has a good explanation," Ed said.

Ed walked over to Sam.

"Sam, where did you get the sweatshirt?"

"What's it to you Ed?"

"Tommy and I were just talking about the robberies when Jake said you didn't buy one. So where did you get that one?"

"Not that it's any of your business, but I got it from one of the waitresses here a few days ago when it was raining out. And now I'm returning it."

Ed looked at Sam, then at the hooded sweatshirt. Then, he turned and walked back to Tommy.

"So?" Tommy asked.

"He says he got it from one of the waitresses a few days ago to put on because it was raining outside."

"Do you buy it?"

"Well, it did rain pretty hard a few days ago so I guess it could have happened that way."

"I'll check with the staff and see if someone confirms Sam's story," Jake said.

"That should put our suspicions of Sam to rest."

"Plus, he was robbed too, wasn't he?" Tommy asked.

"He said he was robbed, but I never saw any police report or anything," Jake replied.

183

"Ok, so Sam probably didn't do it," Ed added. But he was thinking to himself, "And if he was the robber, why would he work with Sue to catch the robber? Well, besides the sex of course." Ed chooses not to say what he was thinking, remembering what Tim had said about people at the bar. Tim might be smarter than he looks.

"Maybe whoever has been doing the robberies left that hooded sweatshirt here and it ended up in lost and found," Tommy speculated.

"I guess that's possible," Jake said.

"Let's give Sam the benefit of the doubt for now. We'll see what Jake finds out," Tommy said.

"I've got to get going Jake. Can I have my tab? I'll take Tommy's too."

"Sure Ed."

Jake printed Ed's tab and handed it to him. Ed paid it and left. Tommy wasn't far behind him.

Sam took up a stool at the bar, grabbed the sweatshirt that had been left behind, and handed it to Jake.

"Can you put this in lost and found? I borrowed it the other day. Can I have a beer?"

"Sure."

Jake picked up the hooded sweatshirt and placed it on the counter behind the bar. He poured Sam a beer and brought it over to him.

"It's on the house, Sam."

"Thanks. Wow. That's never happened before. Maybe my luck is starting to change."

Jake kind of felt bad. He had allowed himself to become suspicious of Sam based on the conversation he had with Kim and the guys. After hearing Sam's explanation, he thought he owed Sam something. Sam sat quietly for a few minutes finishing his beer. Then, he got up and left.

Jake and Ron went around the bar and talked to the few people still there. They announced Last Call and said the bar would be closing in a half hour.

John and Pat Walden had come in about a half hour earlier and were having a nightcap.

"Let's finish these up and head home Pat."

"Give me a minute. Say Ron, what's the status of the recent robberies?"

"Not much. Everyone has been talking about them. Why?"

John put his drink down on the bar, "Pat thinks we might be in line to be robbed."

"Why do you think you might be robbed Pat?"

"Well, we're retired now and we might look like easy targets."

"But I don't think we have anything a robber might want," John said.

"What about your collections John, and my jewelry?"

"Pat, who would want my collection of musical instruments or my collection of rocks? I don't think a robber would take the time to take that stuff. It's way too heavy."

"Is the stuff worth anything?"

"He has instruments over a hundred years old. One violin he has is worth thousands. And some of the rocks he has are worth a fortune."

"Even so, who would know what any of my stuff is worth and be able to pick the good stuff out and ignore the other stuff that isn't worth a thing?"

"I'm just saying John, we could become a target."

"I wouldn't worry too much. You two live just up the street from here by the church and all of the robberies have taken place in remote secluded areas."

"Thanks Ron for putting us at ease. I agree with you. We don't have much to fear."

"I still worry John."

"You always worry Pat."

Pat and John finished their drinks. John paid the tab. They got up to leave.

"Have a good night."

"You too Ron."

They were the last two patrons to leave. Jake and Ron went about their tasks of closing the bar down for the night. Bobby swept the floor around the stools and then arranged them in a neat order.

By two a.m. everything was done.

"See you tomorrow Ron," Jake said as he went for the door.

"See you tomorrow."

"I'll probably be a little late tomorrow. I want to stop in at the Gold Digger Pawn shop and have a talk with them. I don't think they open until noon."

"You getting involved in the detective stuff now also?"

"I think it might be worthwhile. Even if for nothing else, it clears our name."

"Ok. I'll make sure I'm on time."

"Thanks Ron."

"Bobby, you just about finished?" Jake asked.

"Yeah. I just have to put the broom away. I'll put the trash out on my way out the door."

"Thanks. See you tomorrow."

"I'm off tomorrow but I'll be in the day after."

"Ok. See you then."

Bobby put the things in the closet, picked up the black plastic garbage bags and left. He threw the trash in the dumpster and then headed home.

# Chapter 28

The next day, Jake got up early and went to the gym. He worked out for an hour and then stopped at the local Dunkin Donuts for coffee and a muffin. He returned home, took a shower and dressed for work. His shift normally started at noon but he wanted to stop at the Gold Digger before going to work. At eleven, he headed out.

It took him about twenty minutes to arrive at the Gold Digger pawn shop. Pulling into the parking lot, he didn't see another vehicle. He walked up to the door and read the store hours. The sign indicated the store hours were noon to nine pm. He got back into his car and drove down the street to a local convenience store. There, he purchased a newspaper and bottle of water. Then, he went back to the pawnshop, parked and started to read the paper.

When he was halfway through reading, a pickup truck pulled into the parking lot. A woman, about forty years old got out and went to the door. She opened it and went in. Jake looked at his watch. It was still another ten minutes until the store would open.  The woman who went in, turned on the lights.  She returned to the door, opened it and walked over to Jake's vehicle.  Jake rolled his window down.

"I know I'm early but I have to get to work pretty soon," Jake said.

"No problem.  You can come in if you'd like."

"Thanks."

Jake put his paper away and rolled up the window.  He went inside.

"My name is Jake Wilson.  I work at the 'O' Bar in Unionville."

"I'm Tracy Jones."

"Nice to meet you."

"What can I do for you Jake?"

"Some of our customers have had their homes robbed recently and I'm trying to help them find out who did it."

"Gee, I'm not sure I can help you."

"I'm not asking for you to tell me anything you don't feel comfortable telling me but I'd just like to ask you a few questions."

"What do you want to know?"

"Well, it seems the robber was caught by a security camera at one of the places robbed.  The image of the person looks like an average sized person wearing a hooded sweatshirt.  Here's a printout of the picture."

Jake pulled out a printout of a picture showing a person at the Taft's door.  The picture taken from above showed a person dressed in what looked like sneakers, jeans and a hooded sweatshirt trying to pry the door open.

"Why not take the picture to the police?"

"Oh, the homeowner did and they're working on it.  But, someone told me unless firearms are involved or unless someone was actually hurt, the police tend to put these cases on the back burner."

"I've heard that as well."

"If you look closely at the hooded sweatshirt, you can see the name of the 'O' Bar and our logo on the back in the picture."

She looked closely.

"I see it."

"Have you seen anyone in here wearing one of these?"

"Let me see."

"I'm not here all the time but we have a security system taking pictures of everyone all the time. Let's take a look at it."

She led him to an office off to one side of the shop. It wasn't a big office but had a desk, a computer, a shelf of other electric equipment, filing cabinets and a side chair. Jake sat at the side chair and Tracy sat at the computer.

"What day do you want to look at?"

"Let's see. Most of the robberies have been taking place on weekends so I'd guess Monday or Tuesday would be best."

"Any particular week?"

"Let's look at two weeks ago."

Tracy typed in a few commands and a video started to play. Jake could see a date and time stamp in the upper corner. The tape started right at noon.

"This could take a long time, couldn't it?"

"I can fast forward until someone shows up on the video."

Tracy pressed a key and the video moved in fast forward motion. Jake watched the counter as the clock moved to one o'clock. A man with a young boy appeared on the video. Tracy hit a key and the video went to normal speed. They watched for a minute and Jake said, "Not what I'm looking for."

Tracy pressed the fast forward key again. Another half hour went by before another person showed on the video. It was a woman. She didn't match the description either. They continued to watch the fast forward video when another person came into view. As Tracy slowed the video down again, Jake said, "There, that's one of our hooded sweatshirts."

The person was carrying a laptop computer into the store. The camera angle wasn't low enough to show the face of the person who had the hood up over his or her head but clearly showed the name and logo on the back of the hooded sweatshirt.

"That person might be the one doing the robberies," Jake exclaimed.

"I see Bob talking to the person," Tracy said as the two watched the person put the laptop on the counter and speak to the clerk.

Bob looked at the laptop and then went to the register. He handed the person a hundred dollar bill and the person left.

"Can I talk to Bob?"

"He's not working today. I'll try to get a hold of him and see what he remembers. Don't get your hopes up too much Jake. Sometimes, we don't take names or any other information and get quite a few people in here. Bob might not remember the person."

"I understand. But, anything Bob remembers might help."

Tracy picked up the phone on the desk and made a call. "Bob, this is Tracy. I have a man here who is asking a few questions about a laptop that was brought in here two weeks ago when you were working. I can see in the security video where you looked at the laptop and gave the guy a hundred bucks for it. Can you give me a call when you get this message?"

She hung the phone up.

"I got his answering machine."

"I heard."

"Give me a number and I'll call you if I get a hold of Bob."

"Thanks Tracy. I appreciate it."

He wrote a number down on a piece of paper and handed it to Tracy.

Jake looked at his watch. It was one o'clock. He was now an hour late and had to get to work.

"Do you want to look at the video some more?"

"I've got to get to work. I'm already a little late."

"Ok. You can come back and look at more of the security videos if you want."

"Thanks, but I've got what I came for. Now, I hope Bob can shed some light on the person in the video."

Jake left and went to work.

# Chapter 29

Jake started to drive back to Unionville. He called work. The phone rang once and Ron answered.

"Ron, its Jake. I stopped at the Gold Digger pawn shop and talked to a lady there who showed me their security tapes from two weeks ago. And guess what?"

"What?"

"Someone was in there that afternoon pawning a laptop."

"So what's so unusual about that? Isn't that what they do?"

"Yeah, but the person pawning the laptop had on an 'O' Bar hooded sweatshirt."

"You're kidding?"

"No."

"Could you tell who it was?"

"No, the person had the hood up and the angle of the camera wasn't low enough to see the face."

"Did the lady give you a description?"

"She wasn't the one working the day the pawn took place but she called the person who was working."

"What did that person say?"

"She called a co-worker named Bob but got his answering machine."

"So you didn't find out anything?"

"Not much. But, we know someone wearing an 'O' Bar hooded sweatshirt was in there pawning a laptop two weeks ago."

"Hey, didn't Lou say his laptop was stolen?"

"Yep. And he was robbed two weeks ago."

"Too much coincidence."

"I agree."


"Ron, I'm going to make one more stop on my way in. Can you handle things until I get there?"

"Sure Jake. We're pretty slow right now anyway."

"Thanks. I should be there in about a half hour."

"See you then Jake."


Jake went to another pawnshop known as Central Connecticut Pawn. The owner, Dave King, was a friend of Jake's from college.

"Hey old friend. How you been?"

"Dave."

"What brings you to my corner of the world?"

"I just came from Gold Digger Pawn and wanted to ask you a few questions about the pawn business."

"Sure, what do you want to know?"

"Well, a number of our customers have been robbed recently. Things like cash, jewelry, TVs, computers and stuff like that have all been taken."

"That's the kind of stuff we see all the time."

"Well, it seems a number of our regular customers have been the target for these robberies and I think someone else at the bar is involved."

"Why do you think that?"

"You know how it is at a bar. People talk. Some brag and when the booze flows, a lot of information flows."

"Yeah. I know what you mean."

"Well, think about it. Some let it be known when they will be out, what possessions they have and some even let it be known how to get into their home."

"I can see how an observant person might be able to use information like that."

"That's what I'm thinking."

"So how can I help you?"

"First, look at this printout of a person taken by a security camera at one of the houses that was robbed."

Dave looked at the picture.

"See the name and logo on the back?"

"Yeah."

"That's from a hooded sweatshirt the bar sold last year. We only ordered a hundred of them so the person in the picture had to get it there."

"Or someone gave it to the person in the picture."

"I guess. I went down to the Gold Digger and showed them the picture. The lady working didn't recognize it but did show me some footage from their security system from a few weeks ago. And someone was in the shop pawning a laptop while wearing a hooded sweatshirt like the one in the picture."

"Ok. So do you know who the person was pawning the laptop?"

"No. They didn't have any information."

"Did they at least describe the person?"

"The lady I talked to wasn't the one working when the pawn took place. She put in a call to the person who was working but he wasn't home."

"I know the drill Jake. Gold Digger has a reputation of loose record keeping and take no prisoners."

"What do you mean by that?"

"We're supposed to get information about everything being pawned. This industry is known for association with crimes. Gold Digger looks the other way on many deals if they think they can turn an item around quickly. That way, they don't have to report the transaction at all. They even scrub their security tapes just so there's no record of transactions."

"Doesn't the government do something about it?"

"They check on us from time to time but like everything else, they look the other way if the money is right."

"Oh, a crime covering a crime?"

"Something like that."

"I did get to see their security tapes from two weeks ago so I know someone was in there wearing one of the bar's hooded sweatshirts."

"Jake, don't be surprised if you go back there and find out the tape you looked at has been scrubbed clean."

"Why would they do that?"

"You asked questions. They don't like questions. And, if the owner of Gold Digger thinks your questions might bring him problems, that tape is history."

"Should I go to the police?"

"My guess is the tape will get lost real soon."

"So where do I go from here?"

"Maybe the lady will talk to the salesperson and get back to you before the Gold Digger gets wind of your questioning."

"I hope so."

"Don't. Look Jake, when someone walks through that door with more than one thing to pawn or even looks suspicious, alarms go off in my head. It doesn't happen too often, but does. People just don't do that. I usually figure a person trying to disguise him or her self is either a drug addict or is doing something illegal. Our policy is to make them show ID. Sometimes the person pawning something shows us an ID sometimes they turn and run. When they don't show an

ID, we know something's up.  Plus, legally, we're supposed to hold items for thirty days in case they're involved in a crime. If Gold Digger is buying and selling in less than thirty, that's illegal too."

"I wonder if Gold Digger does it like you do."

"Maybe sometimes.  But, it's easy to look the other way in this business."

"I see what you mean.  I've got to get to work Dave. Thanks for the information."

"Don't know if it's any help or not."

"I think I have a better picture.  Thanks.  And stop in at the bar sometime."

"See you Jake.  I might just do that."

# Chapter 30

Jake was an hour and a half late getting into work. Entering the bar, there were six people seated at the bar and one of the tables had three people at it.

"Sorry it took me so long."

"No problem. It's been pretty slow."

"After going to the Gold Digger, I stopped at Central Connecticut Pawn to talk with Dave King. Know him?"

"The name doesn't ring a bell."

"I figured he'd give me the real scoop about how those places operate."

"Is he one of the guys you went to college with?"

"Yeah. We go back a long ways."

"What did you find out?"

"Dave gave me the whole lowdown on pawn shops. He says they're supposed to get identification information on the stuff they take in but sometimes some pawn shops cut corners and are a little loose with information."

"What does he know about the Gold Digger?"

"He says the place is known for shaky deals. According to Dave, Gold Digger has been cited numerous times for failing to have proper documentation on hand for expensive things, especially electronics. He said those are the kinds of things easiest to move and if a shop owner thinks an item might sell quickly it can be tempting to make a quick transaction and not record anything."

"Did he know anything about any of the robberies?"

"Only what he had read in the paper. Dave said his store requires ID for everything they take in and he has records for everything. He said the questionable characters all know which shops have loose policies and which ones don't."

"So someone trying to make a quick sale of things taken in a robbery probably wouldn't go to his place." Ron stated.

"That's the impression I got."

"Did you show him the picture?"

"I did. He said he didn't recognize the hooded sweatshirt or the person even though you couldn't see the person's face. Dave said his camera is at the register and would have picked up the face even though the person had a hood up trying to cover-up."

"Too bad Gold Digger didn't do the same thing."

The phone rang as they were talking, and Kim picked it up at the waitress station.

"Jake, it's for you."

"Hello, this is Jake."

"Jake, its Tracy from the Gold Digger."

"Thanks for calling Tracy. Did you get a hold of Bob?"

"Yes, he called in a little while ago."

"Did he know anything about the surveillance picture you showed me?"

"He said he remembered a guy coming in like I showed you. He said the guy had been in a few times before because he always wore the same hooded sweatshirt."

"The same one I saw in the video?"

"The same one."

"About how often did he say this person came in?"

"He said at least four times while he was working. He said the guy usually had electronic stuff like a TV or a computer. He knows the guy was stealing the stuff because how many people come in over the course of three weeks with more than one TV or more than one computer."

"Did he get any identification from the guy?"

"No. He said the guy balked when he asked for ID and said he would take his business elsewhere."

"Did he?"

"No. Bob was told by the shop owner to offer half of what we'd normally offer for the stuff the guy was trying to pawn and the guy took the offer."

"What happened to the stuff the guy pawned?"

"I don't know but I'll bet it wasn't in the store more than one day."

"A friend of mine who owns another pawn shop said I should expect to hear something like that also."

"Listen Jake, Bob wanted to know why I was asking all those questions and when I told him I showed you the security video, he got rather quiet and suggested I do the same if I want to keep my job. He told me if our boss finds out I showed someone the security tapes without asking him first, he'll fire me on the spot."

"Well, thanks Tracy. I appreciate you calling me back."

"No problem. If you could Jake, keep my name out of anything you're looking into. And I'd appreciate it if you not mention our phone call to anyone. I don't need any trouble and need to keep my job."

"I understand Tracy. I'll do what I can."

"Thanks."

"So what's the scoop?"

"That was the lady I met with at Gold Digger. She said another person who works there remembers a guy coming in a few times over the past couple of weeks pawning stuff. The guy coming in didn't identify himself and only agreed to pawn the stuff he had after the clerk made him a low-ball offer in cash for the stuff he had and told him he didn't have to show ID."

"Did the clerk have any idea who the person was?"

"No. But, I have to think that someone coming in a few times over a couple of weeks would be easily identified by someone seeing the person again and again."

"You'd think."

"I'd love to get Bob, that's the guy Tracy said was working when the stuff was pawned, to come in here and see if he recognizes anyone."

"Do you think he'd do it?"

"Tracy said Bob told her she needs to keep quiet regarding the operations at the Gold Digger if she wants to keep her job. He told her the owner doesn't like word getting out about how his place operates."

"What do you plan on doing?"

"I don't know. I think I'll go back there one night this week and see if Bob is working."

"And then what?"

"I'd like to try to talk to him and see if I can get him to come in on Friday night for a little while."

"You'd ask him to come in here and try to ID the robber?"

"I'd ask him to come in and look around and try to identify the person pawning the stuff over the past couple of weeks. Then, we'd have to try to tie the pawn activity to the robberies."

"I get it."

"Why don't you take a break Ron and let me handle things for a while. And thanks for covering for me."

Ron went outside and sat at one of the tables on the patio. He had Bobby bring him a burger and diet coke. Jake took care of the patrons at the bar, and about a half-hour later, Dave King came into the bar.

"Hey Dave. What are you doing here?"

"My afternoon help arrived after you left so I made a few phone calls following up on our conversation. I wanted to get out for lunch so I drove over."

"What can I get you?"

"I'll have a burger and Bud draft."

"Ok. And it's on me."

"You don't have to do that Jake."

"You came over to talk to me didn't you?"

"Well, yeah."

"Then, the least I can do is spring for lunch. Plus, if what you tell me has anything to do with resolving all these robberies, my boss will have no problem with the bar buying you lunch."

"Thanks. I called a few of the other pawnshop owners I know and told them about our conversation. Seems your hooded sweatshirt robber has been a busy person."

"Oh?"

"Two other shops, one in New Britain and another in Hartford both remembered a man dressed in a hooded sweatshirt like the one you described coming in over the past few weeks pawning things, mostly electronics. The owner of the Hartford shop said the guy had electronics and jewelry when he came in."

"Some of the robberies did include jewelry."

"Those people might want to take a ride down to Park Pawn on Park Avenue in Hartford and see if their stuff is still there."

"You think their stuff might still be there?"

"I don't know. The shop owner is usually pretty careful and if he took stuff in, he might have ID information."

"I'll mention it to the people who had jewelry stolen."

"Both owners said the person bringing stuff in had on a sweatshirt with 'O' Bar logo on the back, so I'll bet it's your suspect."

"I wonder if they could ID the person if they saw him again?"

"Roger Skylar, the owner of Park Pawn, might be willing to come in and try to make an identification. You want me to ask him?"

"Would you?"

"Sure. When do you want him to come in?"

"How about Friday night. Around six?"

"Friday, huh?"

"I'll find out. Weekends are usually the busiest. That's the time when those in most need of money seem to show up. I'll ask and see what he says."

"Thanks Dave."

"No problem."


Ron came back into the bar with Dave's lunch.

"Who's this for Jake?"

Jake pointed to Dave. "It's Dave's. He stopped in to talk with me about the robberies."

"Didn't you stop in and see him earlier today?"

"Yeah. He made a few phone calls after I left and stopped in to talk with me about them."

"Dave, this is Ron Alderman. He's the other bartender here."

They shook hands.

"Jake stopped into my place earlier today and talked with me about the robberies that have taken place. I had some info to share with him and wanted to get out for lunch so I came over."

"Well, thanks for coming in Dave. We can use all the help we can get in solving these crimes."

"I'll let you know if I find out anything else."

"We appreciate it," Ron said and then turned and went down the bar seeing if anyone needed anything.

Dave took a bite out of his burger.

"I'll call you Jake and let you know if I can get Roger to come over with me on Friday night."

"Thanks Dave."

Dave finished his burger and beer. He got up, thanked Jake for the lunch and left.

# Chapter 31

On the next Friday night, most of the regulars were at the bar by five. Lou, Sue, Kelly and Karen were huddled at the end of the bar.

"Karen, you and Kelly make a fuss of me winning at the casino yesterday. Lou and me are going to fake going out on a date tomorrow night. Then, we'll go back to my place and be there when the robber tries to steal the money."

"Sue, are you sure you want to do this?" Kelly asked.

"Yeah. Lou will be there with me. It'll be ok."

Bobby was just finishing setting up the happy hour appetizer table near the door. He went to the kitchen to get the appetizers. He came out of the kitchen holding a platter containing a big pile of wings. Then, he put them into one of the chaffing dishes on the table. He returned to the kitchen and came back with a big bowl of mussels. As he was pouring them into the second chaffing dish, a few spilled on to the floor and bounced against the bottom of Lou's slacks, leaving buttery stains wherever they hit.

"Sorry Lou. Let me get something to clean this up."

Bobby went back to the kitchen and came back with a towel, spray bottle and sponge. He sprayed a little on the hem of Lou's slacks, sponged the spot and then used the towel to attempt to dry them off.

"It's ok Bobby. It'll dry in a little while."
"You can have them dry cleaned and send the bill to us, Lou. It was my fault."
"No problem. It doesn't look too bad."

Lou turned around and the back of his stool bumped Bobby in the back. He fell forward into the table holding the chaffing dishes. As he fell, he reached out to catch himself and caught his hand under one of the chaffing dishes in the sterno holder. He burned his hand. As he pulled it out, the smell of burning flesh was in the air. Bobby let out a yell. Lou turned and helped him.

"What the hell happened Bobby?"
"I fell into the table and burned my hand on the sterno."
"Let me see?"
"It looks pretty bad. You better have it looked after," Sue added.

Ron came around from the bar and looked at Bobby's hand. Better go to the clinic and let them take a look at it Bobby."
"Can you drive yourself?" Sue asked.
"I think so."

Ron asked Jake for the first aid kit under the bar. Jake handed it to Ron who took out the tube of first aid cream. He spread it on the burn, and then put a gauze pad on it. Then Bobby quickly left to have the wound looked at.

"I don't know what happened?" Lou said to Ron.

"Don't worry Lou. He'll have it looked at and I'm sure he'll be all right."

"I hope so."

Lou turned back to the ladies.

"Ok everyone. Ready to set the trap?"

Everyone was ready.

"Sue, I can't believe you won five grand at the casino today?" Karen said loudly.

"Yeah. I was playing a dollar slot machine and hit the three doublers."

"So what do you plan on doing with the money?" Kelly asked.

"I don't know."

She pulled out a roll of dollars and held it up.

"You shouldn't be carrying all that cash," Lou said.

"Oh, I only have a few hundred here Lou. I left the rest in my nightstand at home."

"You think it's a good idea to leave the money in your house?" Karen asked.

"The bank was closed by the time I got home and I wasn't able to deposit it today."

"Well, you better get there first thing in the morning and put the money in a safe place," Kelly said.

"I have plans tomorrow but I'll get it to the bank first thing on Monday."

"Want me to hold it for you, Sue?" Lou said.

"Fat chance Lou. The money would be safer right where it is."

"Ha, ha, ha. I am trustworthy ya know."

"So what do you plan to do with your winnings?" Kelly asked.

"Jake, I'd like to buy the bar a round of drinks on me. That's the first thing I plan on doing with my winnings. Then, I might treat myself to a vacation."

Jake went around the bar. He put a shot glass upside down in front of each patron and explained to them that Sue was buying everyone at the bar a round.

Sally Taft was sitting with her husband Rick at the other end of the bar. She got up and came over to Sue when Jake told her about Sue buying drinks.

"Sue, what's the celebration for?"

"I hit it big at the casino today."

"Oh, really?"

Sue said in a hushed tone she thought only Sally could hear, "Not really. We're setting a trap to try to find out who is doing all these recent robberies."

"Does anyone else know your plan?"

Sue motioned her head to Kelly, Karen and Lou. "We're all in on it. Lou is going to ask me out on a date for tomorrow night. I'll accept and then we're going to stake out my place and see who shows up to steal the money."

"How can you be sure someone will show up to rob you?"

"I can't but we're going to let it be known that I have a pile of cash in my nightstand that will be there tomorrow night while we're out on a date. If the robber is here, he'll come."

"Have you talked to the police about your plans?"

"Heck no. If it's someone from here doing these robberies, we'll know how to handle it."

"I'm not so sure of your plan.  But, good luck."
"Thanks Sally."

Sally returned to Rick.  She told him about the plan.
"What are they crazy?"
"I don't know.  Thinking about it, their plan might just work."
"What if the robber is armed?  What if there is more than one?  What if someone gets hurt?"
"Rick, stop asking questions. I don't have the answers. This is a plan Sue, Kelly, Karen and Lou have put together."
"I still think they're nuts."
"Let's hope they catch someone and no one gets hurt."

Everyone seated at the bar knew about Sue's winning at the casino within a half hour.  A few of the patrons made a toast to Sue thanking her for the drink.  Tommy Benson seemed to be real interested in talking with Sue about her success.  When Sue had gone to the ladies room, Tommy intercepted her on her way past him.

"Sue, thanks for the drink."
"You're welcome."
"So you hit it big at the casino today?"
"Yeah.  I hit the slots for five grand."
"Five thousand?  Holy shit."
"That's the most I ever won."
"What do you plan on doing with your winnings?"
"I'm going to put it in my bank account on Monday and then decide what to do with it from there."
"You probably shouldn't be carrying that much cash around with you.  You never know who might come after you."
"I left most of it at home in the nightstand.  It'll be safe there until I can get it into the bank."

"What if someone breaks into your house and takes it?"

"Oh, don't be silly Tommy. It's only five thousand minus a few hundred I brought with me tonight."

"Well, your place would be easy to get into."

"I wouldn't say easy."

"Don't you still keep a spare key outside under that plant on your porch?"

"Quiet Tommy. No one is supposed to know about that."

"But if someone does know, all they have to do is retrieve the key and open the door. It would be easy pickings."

"Tommy, I don't think anyone other than you knows where my spare key is."

"I hope for your sake that's true."

"I'm going out with Lou tomorrow night anyway so I don't think anything will happen."

"Are you planning on staying at Lou's for the night?"

"I might."

"Well, what about Sunday? You'll be home then, won't you?"

"Maybe."

"Sue, you need to be careful."

"Thanks for the concern Tommy. I'll be careful."

She turned and continued to walk back to Karen, Kelly and Lou.

"What was that all about with Tommy?" Lou asked.

"He wanted to know more about my hitting it at the casino."

"Nice of him to be concerned."

"Yeah. He seemed concerned about me having that much cash at my place. He thinks I'm being too vocal about having the cash and leaving it home."

"Let's see. About how tall is Tommy?"

"I'd say he's about five-seven," Kelly stated.

"Yeah. I'd agree," Karen added.

"Do you think Tommy might be the one doing the robberies?"

"Not Tommy. He's a lot of things but I don't think he's a robber," Sue said.

"Just who might fit the profile of a robber, Sue?" Lou asked.

"I don't know. But, I don't think it would be Tommy."

"I hope you're right."

"Do you think the word is out sufficient to get the robber interested in robbing Sue's place?" Karen asked the group.

"Well, everyone knows Sue hit the casino and she has the money at her place. Now we've got to sit back and see if someone tries to get it over the weekend," Lou said.

"You think someone would try to get it tonight?" Kelly asked.

"Probably not. We just put out the story just now. No one even knew about the money a half hour ago," Lou said.

"Plus, Lou and me are going on a date tomorrow night. That would set the stage for a robbery."

"That's right," Lou said. Then he said loudly, "Sue, why don't I take you out to dinner and to see a good band tomorrow night?"

"Where do you want to take me?"

"There's a good band playing at the Maple Leaf up in Simsbury tomorrow night at eight-thirty. We could catch a bite to eat and then go dancing."

"Oh, that sounds good to me. What time should I be ready?"

"I'll pick you up at seven."

"I'll be ready."

The girls stayed at the end of the bar having a few more drinks. Lou picked up his glass and walked to the other end of the bar and sat down at an open stool next to Rick Taft.

"Sounds like Sue's having a good time, Lou?"

"Yeah. She won some money at the casino. Who wouldn't be celebrating?"

"That's what she told Sally. She also told Sally about your plans for tomorrow so I know the date is a cover."

"Keep it down Rick. We don't want anyone to know."

Jake was close enough to hear them. He turned his head to look at Lou, and then at Rick, and then just shook his head.

So the information was out.

# Chapter 32

A little after six thirty, Dave King came into the bar with a person Jake didn't recognize. They walked to the end of the bar where Jake was standing.

"Hey Jake."

"Dave."

"Jake, this is Roger Skylar. He's the guy I was telling you about who owns Park Pawn."

Jake shook hands with Roger.

"Nice to meet you Roger."

"Likewise. Dave tells me you're trying to identify someone whose been robbing a number of your clients."

"That's right. Based on the information we've collected, it seems someone in here may be involved in the robberies."

"Dave told me about some of the things you two talked about a few days ago and I can't disagree."

"We feel strongly about the 'O' Bar connection, but we don't know who."

"He also told me you suspect it's the same person who has showed up at a number of pawn shops wearing a sweatshirt with the bar name and logo on it."

"That's right. Hold on a minute."

Jake went to the back of the bar, opened a closet and took out a hooded sweatshirt. He brought it back to Dave and Roger.

"Like this one."

He held it up so they could see the name and logo on the back and then held it up by the hood.

"I've seen a sweatshirt like that one on someone in my place before."

"That's what Dave told me when I asked him if you might stop in with him."

"So, what can I do?"

"Take a look around and see if you recognize any of the people in here."

"Ok."

"You might want to give Roger a beer so he doesn't look so suspicious while he's walking and looking around Jake," Dave suggested.

"Good idea."

"Make it a Coors Light, if you could."

"I'll have one also," Dave said.

Jake gave them each a beer, and put the check on the bar. "I'll get that, obviously, but for appearances…"

Roger started by the door. He walked around slowly appearing to look at all of the pictures and posters on the walls. As he went around, he took his time to look at each and every person as well.

When he finished in the bar, he walked up by the fireplace and looked at everyone seated at the tables. Then, he walked down the hall and into the restaurant.

"Can I help you?" a waitress asked him.
"No. I'm looking for the men's room."
"It's over there down the hall."

Roger walked down the aisle of tables and up the other side and then went in the direction of the restroom. Instead of going in the restroom, he went into the banquet room. There were only a few people seated in there so it didn't take him long to come back out. He returned to the bar.

"Anything?" Dave asked him.
"Yeah. I saw one person in here I recognize."
"Which one?"
"The third guy from the end of the bar near the door."
"He's young and looks like he might be the same height of the guy Jake showed me in a picture. He does look familiar to me too."
"I think his name is Tommy something. Park Pawn does ask for ID, so I've seen it."
"You remember his name?"
"Yeah. He's been in my shop a couple of times."
"Recently?"
"Not this week. I think he was in a month or so ago."

Jake had finished tending to the patrons at the bar when he saw Dave and Roger talking over by the door. They had just sat down at one of the high-top tables. Jake went over.

"Did you see anyone you recognized?"
"Maybe," Dave said.

"Don't rush or anything. The crowd can change a little as it gets later. Feel free to hang out as long as you like."

Roger nodded towards the end of the bar, by the door.

"How about you Roger? Anything so far?"

"Not definite. But that guy Dave pointed out, I might have seen him before. Third one from the end.

"That's Tommy Benson."

"Tommy Benson. That's the name. He's been into Central Pawn. But not recently."

"You sure Tommy has been pawning stuff? At both places?"

"A Tommy Benson was in my place in the last month. I forget what he was pawning but he was definitely there."

"Has he been in there more recently?"

"Not that I recall. But I'm not always at the register so it's possible he came in since then."

"Tommy Benson," Jake said.

"I'm just not positive that guy over there is the same person who was in Park Pawn. He doesn't look like the same person I saw."

"What do you mean?" Jake asked.

"His face is different. But, he showed ID and said his name was Tommy Benson when he was at my place."

"Did he have on a hooded sweatshirt with the bar logo and name on it when you saw him in your place?"

"Not that I remember. But to be honest, fashion's not my thing."

"Hmm," Jake said looking in Tommy's direction.

"What do you plan on doing about it?" Dave asked.

"I'm not sure. I'll talk with Tommy later and see what he has to say. Well, thanks Roger. I appreciate you coming over."

"You're welcome."

"And thanks Dave for helping me out."

"No problem Jake. Glad to be of help. And we'll keep an eye and ear out going forward."

"Listen guys, I've got to get back to my business. Friday nights can be busy," Roger said.

"Me too," Dave added.

"Well, thanks again."

They shook hands with Jake and left.

Ron had seen Jake sitting for a few minutes with Dave and another man. When they left and Jake returned to the bar, Ron said, "Who was that with Dave?"

"One of the other pawn shop owners. He said he recognized one of our patrons as being in his pawn shop recently pawning stuff, but more by name than by face."

"Really? Who was it?"

"Tommy Benson."

"Tommy can't be the person doing the robberies."

"Why not?"

"He's got excuses."

"Tommy's got excuses for everything. Maybe we're overlooking something about Tommy."

"I don't know Jake. I just don't see Tommy being involved in these things. What do you plan on doing?"

"I'm going to ask Tommy to go outside with me for a few minutes and ask him about the pawn shops."

"Ok. I'll tend to the bar while you talk to him."

Jake went over behind Tommy.

"Tommy, can I talk to you for a few minutes outside?"

"Sure Jake. What's this all about?"

"Let's talk outside."

The two walked out the door by the parking lot. Jake continued to walk around the corner by the firehouse. Tommy followed.

"What's up Jake?"

"Tommy, someone I know came in here tonight and said you've been using area pawn shops."

"So, I don't deny I have been in a pawn shop."

"Did you pawn any electronic stuff?"

"Probably. I've been in a few pawnshops from time to time pawning stuff. Whenever I go to a tag sale or flea market and see something I think I can get a good price for, I pick it up and then see what I can get for it at the pawnshops."

"So you're saying you got everything you pawned legitimately?"

"Jake, you sound like you're accusing me of stealing stuff and then pawning it."

"Well, you have been identified as pawning stuff recently and the robberies have all taken place recently. It all sounds too coincidental."

"Jake, who's saying I pawned things taken in the recent robberies?"

"Someone from Park Avenue Pawn was in here and identified Tommy Benson as the person pawning stuff there recently."

"I've never been to Park Avenue Pawn. I don't even know where it's located."

"You've never been in Park Avenue Pawn?"

"That's what I'm telling you."

"Well, someone has. And that person used the name Tommy Benson."

"I don't know anything about the robberies other than what I've heard at the bar. I will tell you I had nothing to do with them and I challenge anyone who says otherwise."

"Ok Tommy. I'll take your word for it for now."

"What do you mean for now?"

"Tommy, someone is committing these robberies. When we find out who it is, it's not going to be good for that person."

"Well, it's not me."

"Ok, Ok. Let's go back inside."

The two guys came back into the bar, and immediately separated; one to his seat, and the other to his job, but both definitely agitated.

"What did you find out?" Ron asked.

"Tommy says he didn't do it. He admits to being at some of the pawn shops but says everything he takes there he got fair and square."

"You believe him?"

"His story sounds credible."

"He looks upset."

"Give him a beer on me. That'll calm him down."

"Sure."

Ron poured a beer for Tommy and set it in front of him.

"Tommy, it's on Jake."

Tommy pushed the beer to the guy next to him.

# Chapter 33

The plan was all set. Lou and Sue would be going out on a date. Kelly and Karen planned on staying at Kelly's in case Sue or Lou called and needed their help.

Karen got to Kelly's about six o'clock with beer and pizza.

"Come on in Karen. It might be a long night."

"I brought a pizza and a twelve pack of Coors Light."

"Good. I got some chips and dip for us as well."

"We should be all set for the night."

"Yeah. There are a couple of good movies on TV tonight so it won't be so boring waiting."

"Good. Where do you want me to put the pizza?"

"Put it in the oven. I'll turn it on low so it stays warm."

"Got it. You want a piece?"

"Maybe later."

"How about a beer?"

"Sure."

Karen got herself a slice of pizza and brought two beers into the living room. Kelly had already selected a movie and started it. The credentials were just scrolling across the screen. The title appeared in big letters, "Sleepless in Seattle".

"I love this movie," Karen said.
"I know. Me too. The old ones are the best."

Lou picked up Sue right on time at seven o'clock. Sue had made it abundantly clear at the bar she would be spending the night at Lou's. When they left her place, she had a small bag with her. They got into Lou's vehicle and left. They went past the bar after the old factory building and turned right. They continued up to Route 44 and turned right. After a few lights, they turned right on Route 177. They took 177 back down to Unionville and made a right on Route 4. In another five minutes, they had reached their destination as they turned right at the stop sign and crossed the Farmington River. It had taken twenty minutes and in that time, they had made a complete circle ending up right by Sue's place. Lou didn't turn right to go to Sue's but instead continued past her street and made a right on the next street. He pulled in to a parking space by the bank just up from the local market. They got out and Lou locked the vehicle.

"Follow me Lou. There's a back way to get to my place where we won't be seen."
"I'm right behind you."

Sue led him down a side street. The street only had a few buildings on it. After the last building, she made a right and took a path down to the end of her street. Then, they crossed the street while still in the shadows of the woods and went into her home through a back door, making sure not to change any lights in case the house was being watched.

"Good idea leaving the back door unlocked Sue."

"I figured we'd only be gone a few minutes so it wasn't a problem."

"So what do you want me to do?"

"Let me get us a beer and we can go up stairs into the back spare bedroom. The shades in that room don't let any light outside and there's already a nightlight on. Just wait here."

Lou could hear the refrigerator open and then a closet. Sue was back with a six-pack and some chips. She led the way up the back staircase. When they got into the spare bedroom, Sue closed the door and turned on the radio.

The bedroom had a queen size bed, a nightstand, a dresser with a TV and radio on it and a recliner. There must have been six pillows on the bed. Lou looked around and then asked, "Where's the bathroom?"

"It's the second door on the right down the hall."

"Just in case I need to go."

Sue put the chips on a nightstand and opened two beers. She handed one to Lou.

"So do you think we can watch the Red Sox?"

"They don't go on for fifteen more minutes, but I suppose. Just keep the volume down."

"Are you a Sox fan, Sue?"

"I watch from time to time."

"Ok, then a ball game it is."

Lou went through the channels until he found the right station. In another few minutes, the game started.

They watched for a few innings and drank a couple of more beers. After the fifth inning, Lou said, "I've got to take a leak."

"Second door on the right."

"Got it."

He walked down the hall. Then, Sue saw a light go on in the distance.

"Lou, don't use the light. It'll let anyone watching know someone's here."

Lou quickly turned the light off. When he was done, he flushed the toilet.

"And don't flush the toilet."

"I already did," He said as he came back into the bedroom.

"Lou, if someone were trying to break in, they might hear the toilet flush."

"Oh."

"Or see you turning the light on and off."

"I guess I'm not very good at this stakeout stuff."

"You just need to think about what you're doing and what might give us away."

"Ok. I'll try harder."

Lou went to sit in the recliner and Sue said, "Why don't you come over here and sit with me on the bed?"

Lou didn't need to be told twice. He kicked off his shoes and hopped on the bed. They both watched the game for another hour. At the seventh inning break, Sue went back down stairs and got a few more beers for them. When she came back up, Lou had made himself more comfortable on the bed having taken his shirt and slacks off. Sue set the beers on the nightstand.

"Are you getting a little bored with the game?"

"Yeah. And I'm not sure anyone is going to try to break in tonight."

"You think the robber didn't get the message?"

"I don't know but I would have thought something would have happened by now."

Sue got on the bed.

"So what would you like to do?"

Lou leaned over to her and kissed her. She reciprocated. They continued to kiss and Sue put her hands under Lou's tee shirt. She stroked his chest and then allowed a hand to wander lower. Lou was aroused.

"Do you think we should?"

"Why not?"

"What if someone tries to break in?"

"We'll hear it if someone comes in. We'll have enough time to react."

"I don't know Lou."

He moved her hand back down to where she had just been. She went back to what she was doing.

Lou took Sue's maneuvers as a sign. He unbuttoned her blouse. It didn't take long and all of their clothes were on the floor next to the bed. The foreplay continued. Both of them became more excited. The two began to breathe heavily. Sue allowed Lou to take charge. A few minutes later, they were both moving in unison on the bed.

Sue was the first to climax. As she did, Lou joined her. They kept at it for a few minutes and then they both lay on the bed totally exhausted.

The baseball game was now over. Sue changed the channel to the news and put her head on Lou's shoulder. In a few minutes, she was asleep. Lou reached to the nightstand and picked up the remote. He switched the TV off. In a few minutes, Lou was asleep also.

At some time during the night, Lou was awakened by a noise. He sat up in bed. Sue felt him stir.

"What is it?"
"Shush. I think I hear something."
"What do you think you hear?"
"I thought I heard someone on your porch. There it is again."
This time Sue heard the squeaking sound as well.
"Someone's on my porch."

Lou quickly got up and got dressed. Sue did as well. They both went out of the bedroom to the top of the stairs. They stood there for a minute but didn't hear anything at first. Then, they heard footsteps outside the door on the porch. Lou was first to tiptoe down the stairs. He moved the shade slightly on the door so he could see out. He made out the figure of a person on the porch turning and starting to walk down the steps. Lou thought the person was dressed in jeans, sneakers and a hooded sweatshirt.

He whispered to Sue, "You open the door quickly and turn the light on when I run out and catch the robber."
Sue did as instructed.
The door opened and the light on the porch came on. Lou raced out and tackled the person who had just stepped off the porch.

"I've got you now," Lou exclaimed.
"What the hell are you doing?" the person shouted out.

Sue came out and stood on the porch. When she looked at Lou and the person on the ground, she said, "Lou, that's my paper delivery."

Lou got to his feet and helped the young man up.

"That's Brian Crane. He delivers my newspapers."

"I'm sorry Brian. I thought you were a burglar."

"I'm just delivering the papers man."

"You woke us up when you were on the porch Brian. I'm sorry. Are you all right?"

"Yeah. Just a little scratched and dirty."

"You want to come in and clean up?"

"That's ok Ms. Walker. I'll be ok."

"We're sorry Brian."

"No problem."


Brian walked away. He had parked down the street and had delivered papers to the other houses on the next street before going to Sue's house.


"What time is it Sue?"

She looked at a clock in her hallway as she closed and locked the door.

"It's five in the morning."

"I guess no one is coming to rob your place on this night."

"I guess not."

"Well, at least we had a nice date night."

"We had sex Lou, that's about it."

"Isn't that what people do on a date?"

"Not everyone."

"I had a good time Sue. Didn't you?"

"It was ok."

"Ok. I thought we had an outstanding time."

"We didn't catch the robber."

"But we did have a good time."

"I'll agree with you there. It was an interesting night."

"Somehow, that's not the phrase I would have used to describe our night."

"Ok Lou. We had a good time. Let's get back to bed and catch a few more hours of sleep before we've got to get up."

"If you say so."

Lou and Sue went back up stairs. Lou took all his clothing off again and got under the covers.

"What are you doing?"

"I thought we might go at it again when we wake up."

"We'll see."

Sue shed her clothing as well. Lou moved close to her and wrapped himself around her. Sue was turned away from him and allowed Lou the snuggle. It didn't take long and he was snoring.

# Chapter 34

The movie finished a little after nine. Karen smiled when the movie ended.

"I love that movie."

"Yeah, it's a good one."

"Want to watch another one?"

"Let's see what else is on."

"How about this one?" Kelly asked as she had stopped the channel listings on the movie title The Perfect Storm.

"Sure."

They sat and watched the movie for a few hours. When it was done, Karen said, "No calls from Sue. It doesn't look like anything is going to happen tonight."

Kelly had gotten up and was taking stuff into the kitchen.

"Guess so. You want to spend the night?"

"Nah. I've got plans for first thing in the morning so I want to go home and take a shower."

"You can take it here if you want."

"I need a change of clothes anyway."

"We're about the same size. You can take some of my stuff."

"Kelly, you trying to get me to stay over?"
"Yeah."
"Ok. But you only have one bedroom."
"That's ok. We can both sleep in my bed."
"Kelly, what will people think?"
"No one has to know."
"Guess you're right."
"Why don't we turn the TV off and hit the sack now."
"But my shower."
"You can take it in the morning."
"You're right. Ok, let's go to bed."

They turned the TV off and went to Kelly's bedroom.
"Want PJ's?" Kelly asked.
"What do you wear?"
"Something light."
"Give me something light also."

"Kelly, what do you make of us not hearing from Sue or Lou?"
"I don't know. Either nothing happened or they're waiting to tell us in the morning."
"I'd hope they'd call if someone tried to break in."
"That's what we agreed to but I guess they changed their minds or it didn't happen."
"You would think if whoever is doing those robberies, they would have gone to Sue's house after all the things said at the bar last night?"
"Yeah. You'd think."
"Maybe the robbers were not at the bar last night."
"Maybe. Let's see what they have to say tomorrow."

Kelly turned the sheet and blanket down. Then, she went to her dresser. Kelly took out a pair of shorts and a sheer almost see through top. Then, she took out another set and threw them to Karen. Kelly was already half undressed when Karen looked at the PJs Kelly was putting on.

"Kelly, you're bad."
"What do you mean?"

Karen held up the top she had caught. It was one of those fishnet type tops. She could see right through it. Kelly got into bed.

"Come on in Karen. You might like it."

Karen shed her clothing and put on the shorts and top. Kelly watched as Karen changed. Then, Karen got under the covers. Kelly leaned over and turned the light off. Then, she turned her attention to Karen.

"I've never done anything like this before," Karen said.
"Just relax and go with it."

Kelly touched Karen. Then, she helped Karen take her clothing off. Kelly did the same.

In the morning, Karen woke up with Kelly wrapped around her. They were both naked. Kelly's hand was on Karen's breast. She carefully moved it to the side.

"Morning Karen," Kelly said as she stirred.
"Good morning Kelly."
"Yes it is. Last night was terrific wasn't it?"
"I've never done that before Kelly."
"But, wasn't it good?"

"I guess so. I can't believe how many times…"

"It's ok, women know what women like."

"Yeah. But what was that thing?"

Kelly reached over and picked it up off her nightstand. She held it out for Karen to see.

"It looks real."

"Even feels real, just not attached to a man's body."

"Is that what we used?"

"It is, and you definitely liked it."

"I did. Have you ever done this with anyone else?"

"Sure. I've had Sue over a number of times. Now she's one who really gets off."

"She does?"

"Yeah."

"Do you think she's slept with Lou last night?"

"I'm sure she did. Sue isn't one to pass up an opportunity."

"So she goes both ways?"

"So do I. I like guys also. But sometimes I like to be with another woman. It's usually more intimate plus once a man is spent, he's usually done for the night. That's not the way it is with us."

"I found out."

"And wasn't it fun?"

"I can't remember ever getting so exhausted where my whole body went limp. And it did last night."

"Welcome to my world. It's all in what you know."

"But with another woman?"

"Hey. Too many people put up barriers. In most cases, those who object don't know what they're talking about."

"You're probably right."

"Didn't you have an opinion yesterday?"

"I did."

"Do you have the same opinion today?"

"No."

"See. You had formulated an opinion based on lack of knowledge. Now that you have been enlightened you've changed."

"I see what you mean."

"We'll have to do a threesome sometime with Sue. Then, you'll really look at things in a different light."

"I think I've got to get going Kelly. I do have plans for this morning."

"Ok. Towels are in the bathroom. Take what you want out of my closet or dresser. I'm going back to sleep."

Kelly pulled the covers up over her head and did exactly that.

Karen took a shower and put her clothing back on. She would stop at her place and get clean clothes.

She let herself out and drove home. When she got to her place just off New Britain Avenue, she noticed her front door was ajar. She cautiously went inside.

# Chapter 35

Karen looked around her place. Nothing seemed to be missing. Then, she looked at the wall where her TV used to be. It was gone. She went into her bedroom. A few of the dresser drawers were opened and the contents messed up. She quickly went into her walk-in closet and turned on the light. She looked up at the top shelf. Her small safe was gone.

"Oh no."
She picked up her cell phone.

Kelly answered on the second ring.
"Kelly, its Karen. My place was robbed last night."
"Really?"
"Yeah. My TVs gone and I had a little safe in my closet. It's gone also."
"The whole safe?"
"It isn't that big although I couldn't lift it up. I got it at Home Depot and had Tommy install it for me."
"Tommy huh?"

"Yeah. He helped me get it into my place and put it up on the shelf for me. There's no way I could have picked the thing up."

"What was in it?"

"I had jewelry, money, my passport and a few other papers in it."

"Did they get your gun?"

"No, I have it in a box under my bed and it's still there."

"You're lucky the robber didn't find it."

"Yeah. At least I still have my protection if I need it."

"Wow. And here we thought Sue would be robbed last night."

"I'm going to call the police and have them come over."

"Didn't you have plans for this morning?"

"I did but I guess I'm going to have to change them."

"Too bad Karen. Is there anything I can do?"

"No. I think I'll go over to the 'O' Bar after the police are done here. By then I'll need a drink."

"Then I'll probably see you there."

"Ok. Bye."

After hanging up, Karen called the police department. The desk sergeant told her he'd have an officer stop over in about a half hour. She waited for the officer to come. While waiting, she took the time to go through her dresser and the rest of her place making sure she know exactly what had been taken. About forty minutes later, her doorbell rang.

"I'm Officer Cassidy. I understand you were robbed last night."

"Karen Ascroft. Yes, I stayed over at friends last night and when I came home this morning I found my door open. It wasn't broken into or anything. Just left open. But not by me.

Looking around, I noticed my TV was missing along with a small safe I had in my closet."

"Ms. Ascroft, do you live alone?"

"Yes."

"Was anything else taken?"

"Not that I can tell."

Officer Cassidy made a few notes in his book.

"Can you describe the contents in the safe?"

"Sure. I had a few pair of earrings, a couple of necklaces, four rings, my passport and a few documents containing my savings and investment accounts."

"You might want to contact your bank and any institutions you had money at and have your account number and password changed."

"That's a good idea."

"Were any of the jewelry items worth a lot of money?"

"One ring had belonged to my mother. It was a pretty big diamond. It was probably worth thousands. One of the sets of earrings was a one-carat diamond. I think I paid about three thousand for them."

"Ok."

He made another note in his book.

"What kind of TV was it?"

"One of those smart TVs."

"About how big?"

"It was a fifty-five inch Sony TV."

"Ok. Did you have the smart TV features activated?"

"You mean did I use it?"

"For things like renting movies or seeing things over the Internet?"

"Yes. Why does that matter?"

"Because once you activate the TV features, your account information is stored in the TV. Someone taking the TV only needs to turn it on and hook it up to an Internet connection and the features you activated are still active."

"What can they do?"

"If you used anything like Netflix, the robber can continue to do so and you'll continue to be billed."

"I guess I'll have to call my internet provider and let them know. Than I'll close my account with Netflix."

"Don't close it. Just have your password changed."

"Why shouldn't I close it?"

"Because my department can use your IP address to try to backtrack anyone who tries to use your account. We'll work with your internet service provider and try to trace the things stolen from you that way."

"Oh. I didn't know you could do those things."

"It takes time. Plus, the culprit has to try to use your TV in order for us to put a trace on it."

"Is there anything else I should do?"

"That's it for now. I'll write up a report. Again, no forced entry, so no clues there. Your case will be put in with the other robbery cases we've been working on in the area."

"Have there been a lot?"

"Quite a few recently. We're already working on them."

"I know a few people who have had their places robbed recently."

"How do you know them?"

"Some friends of mine I know from the 'O' Bar have been robbed. They told me about them."

"We've been investigating a number of robberies involving patrons of the 'O' Bar. I'll add your name to the list."

"Do you think someone from the bar is doing these crimes?"

"Could be. But, I can't talk about it yet."

"Thanks Officer Cassidy for coming over."

"You're welcome Ms. Ascroft. I'll call you if anything comes up or if I need any additional information."

Officer Cassidy left and Karen needed a drink. She looked at the wall clock; it was two minutes past noon, so she closed and locked her door and drove to the bar.

"Hello Karen," Jake said as she took up one of the many empty stools at the bar. It was just noon.

"Jake. I'll have a beer and shot of Jack."

"Starting a little early?"

"I just came from my place. I was robbed last night."

"Your place? I thought you guys had worked out a sting for Sue's place to be robbed."

"We did. Only, the robber apparently had other plans."

"Were you at Sue's with her and Lou?"

"No. I went over to Kelly's and ended up spending the night there. When I got home this morning, my front door was open."

"What did they get?"

"My TV and my safe with my jewelry and some other stuff in it."

"Who knew you wouldn't be home last night?"

"I don't know. I only made my plans when I was talking with Sue, Lou and Kelly here last night."

"Who was sitting near you?"

"I don't remember."

"Do you think you might have talked about going to Kelly's and not being home?"

"Yes. We did talk about it but I didn't know I was going to stay overnight until late last night and that was only after Kelly suggested I stay over."

"If the person doing the robberies was in here last night, then he might have overheard you talking with Kelly, Sue and Lou. But he'd have no way of knowing you were going to stay overnight."

"That's right."

"So your place must have been hit earlier rather than later."

"You think so?"

"That's the only thing that makes sense."

As they were talking, Sue and Lou came in. Sue sat next to Karen and Lou next to Sue.

"Nothing happened at my place last night."

"I wouldn't say nothing," Lou rudely scoffed.

Sue waived Lou's comment off.

"My place was robbed last night."

"Your place?"

"Yeah. I ended up staying overnight at Kelly's. When I got home this morning, my door was open."

"What was taken?" Lou asked.

"My TV and a small safe I had in my closet."

"Did you have anything of value in the safe?"

"Yes. I had jewelry, my passport and a few other things in there."

"Karen, I can't believe we set this whole thing up for someone to rob my place last night and they got you instead."

"Me either."

"Do you think someone from here did it?"

"I was talking to Jake and he thinks someone in here might have overheard us talking and knew I wouldn't be home."

"But how would the robber know what you had at your place? We didn't talk about your place at all."

"I don't know but someone didn't care what I had."

237

"Did you call the police?" Lou asked.

"Yes. Officer Cassidy came over and took my statement. He said he'd have my information added to the other cases his department is pursuing of the patrons of the 'O' Bar."

"So he thinks they're all related?"

"He said he couldn't comment."

"That's what they all say until they make an arrest," Sue added.

"He said he'd be in touch."

"Well, don't hold your breath," Lou remarked. "That's the same line everyone else has been given who reported being robbed. Meanwhile, another house is robbed."

# Chapter 36

Karen finished her drink. Lou couldn't stop talking about the night he and Sue had. He talked about how they drove around for twenty minutes and then parked a street over so anyone looking wouldn't see them go to Sue's place. He talked about how slow the night went watching baseball waiting for someone to try to break in. Then, he ordered another round of drinks for Karen, Sue and himself.

"After the ball game finished, we decide to call it a night."

"About what time was that?" Karen asked.

"I'd guess it must have been midnight."

"I'd agree Lou. Remember the news had just gone off."

"Oh yeah."

"So you left Sue there to fend for herself if someone came after that?"

"No. I stayed the night. We both slept in the spare bedroom at the back of the house."

"I see. You and Sue spent the night together."

"Oh yeah. We spent the night together. And what a night it was."

"Lou, don't make it sound so bizarre. We had a good time."

"I'd say."

"Then we slept in, got up, had a brunch breakfast and wandered over here."

"Well, not right away if you know what I mean."

"Lou, you dog," Jake said as he had overheard much of the conversation.

Kelly Jones came in and sat down next to Lou.

"Did you hear about Karen getting hit last night?"

"She called me when she got to her place this morning. I know all about it."

"Oh yeah, she stayed with you last night."

"We watched a few movies and when we didn't hear from you or Sue, we called it a night."

"Our night went slow as well. Then we called it a night also. But, I'll bet I had a better night than you did."

"I wouldn't be so sure about it, Lou."

"Sue was very hospitable."

"I'll bet she was."

"And what exactly did you two do?"

"Now wouldn't you like to know?"

"What did you do? Get it on with each other?"

She didn't say anything further.

That shut Lou up. He didn't know where to go from there.

"What's the plan from here Sue?" Karen asked.

"I don't know. I thought for sure we set the right trap last night. It just didn't work out the way we thought it would."

"The officer who stopped by told me my case would be added to the rest of the robbery cases they're pursuing involving the patrons of the bar."

"Did he say what they're planning to do?" Jake asked.

"No. In fact, he specifically said he couldn't comment on what the police are doing."

"See, like I told you guys. The Police have put these robberies on the back burner. Losing a TV and some jewelry just isn't worth them spending their time looking into the crimes. Oh, they'll get around to looking at the robberies closer after a while but the other things like seat belt violations, domestics and speeding come first."

"Sue, you sound so negative," Kelly said.

"It's because it's true. If someone were killed during one of the robberies it would have been called a Home Invasion. Then, there would have been press coverage and headlines. The police would have to be engaged. But you take something like a TV, computer or jewelry theft and unless there is an arrest, it doesn't even get reported."

"Now that you mention it, I haven't seen hardly anything on the news or in the papers about these robberies," Karen stated.

"So what do we do?" Lou said matter-of-factly.

"We can continue to pursue answers ourselves," Jake said.

"You have ideas, Jake?" Lou asked.

"I do. Why don't one of us go to the Gold Digger and convince the guy who actually saw the person pawning some of the Taft's stuff to come in here and see if he can identify the person he saw?"

"Sounds like a good idea to me," Sue added.

"I'll do it," Jake said. "I already talked to the other clerk, Tracy. And I did take a look at their security tapes. Let me give it a try and see what happens.  I'm off tomorrow so I can go down there in the afternoon and see what I can find out."

"Let us know if we can help," Lou added.

"I will."

"Now that we have a plan, let's have another drink," Lou said.

"This one's on me," Jake said.

He got the drinks for each of them and had a beer as well.

# Chapter 37

The next day, Jake dressed in jeans, sneakers and a blue pullover Henley tee-shirt, and drove to the Gold Digger Pawn shop. He walked into the shop. A man who appeared to be in his mid-thirties was working behind the register counter.

"Excuse me, I'm looking for Bob."

"I'm Bob."

"My name is Jake Wilson. I met with Tracy a few days ago about some things being pawned by someone committing robberies against some of my restaurant's customers."

"Oh yeah. I recall Tracy telling me something about that."

"Do you have a few minutes to talk to me?"

"As you can see, business is pretty slow right now. So how can I help you?"

"Tracy had showed me a tape from your security system. We could see someone in the shop wearing a hooded sweatshirt from the bar I work at trying to pawn something."

"Yeah. She talked with me about it."

"She called me after talking to you. She said you didn't get any information on the person who was pawning the merchandise."

"Oh yeah. I remember. I called our owner because the guy wouldn't give me his ID. In fact, he wouldn't even tell me his name. Real shady guy."

"Do you think you'd recognize the guy if he came in again?"

"Sure. That wasn't the first time I've seen him in here."

"Do you think we could look at some of the security tapes of the other times you think you saw that person in here?"

"Absolutely not."

"Why not?"

"Because the tapes have all been scrubbed clean."

"Well, can we look at the same tape Tracy showed me from two weeks ago. Maybe it'll refresh your memory."

"Can't do it. That tape has been scrubbed also."

"Are you sure?"

"I'm sure. When I came to work the day before yesterday, the guy who owns this place was in here wiping out all of the old tapes. We've a revolving tape system covering two weeks but he cleaned every one of them that day."

"Why would he do that?"

"I talked with him after Tracy called when she showed you the security tape. He didn't like it. I think that's why he scrubbed all the tapes."

"So there's no record of anyone coming in here to pawn stuff?"

"Not before yesterday."

"Bob, I know this might be an unusual request. Do you think you could come to the 'O' Bar on Friday night to see if you recognize anyone there?"

"Probably not. My boss would have a fit."

"He doesn't have to know."

"I don't know."

"What if I gave you a hundred bucks?"

"Well, that kind of changes things. How long would I have to be there?"

"I'd think an hour or so would do it."

"A hundred for an hour. I could come by on my dinner break."

"Then you'll do it?"

"I didn't say I would. I have to think about it."

Jake pulled out a twenty. He put it on the counter.

"What's that for?"

"There's another hundred if you show up at the 'O' Bar on Friday night, say around seven."

"I'll think about it."

"We really need your help."

Jake turned and left. Since it was his day off, he decided to go to the 'O' Bar to have a beer. He drove there and parked out front.

"Hey Jake. Did you not read the schedule right? Its R-O-N today."

"Hey Ron. Yeah. I just came back from the Gold Digger Pawn shop and stopped in for a beer."

"What can I get you?"

"A Stella."

Ron poured the beer and set it in front of Jake.

"So, what did you find out?"

"Just like Dave told me, the Gold Digger Pawn shop is pretty shady."

"Why do you say that?"

"I talked with the person who was on duty when someone wearing a hooded sweatshirt with the bar's name and logo on it was there."

"And what did he tell you?"

"This guy Bob, the salesperson, told me he had seen the same person in there a number of times pawning stuff."

"So he knows who the person is?"

"Not by name. He said the person doing the pawning would not identify himself and usually had a hood over his head so the security cameras wouldn't be able to see his face. It really didn't matter anyway since all of the security tapes have been wiped clean."

"What do you mean wiped clean?"

"It looks like the shop owner doesn't want anyone looking at their security tapes. Bob said he saw the owner cleaning all of their tapes a two days ago."

"Too bad. If they still had some of the old tapes, you might have been able to identify the robber."

"That was my thought also."

"So where do you go from here?"

"I told Bob we'd give him a hundred bucks if he would come in here on Friday night and see if he can identify the guy who had pawned the stuff when he was working."

"Did he go for it?"

"He said he'd think about it.'

"Do you think he'll show?"

"I don't know. I gave him a twenty as good faith money. Hopefully, he'll feel obligated to come in and collect the other hundred."

"It sure would help move things along if we could get a positive ID for whoever's been doing these robberies."

"Yeah it would."

"What time did you tell him to come in on Friday?"

"I said seven o'clock. By then, the bar will be pretty full and whoever's been doing the robberies should be here. If we're right and the robber is from here. Maybe I'm wrong. I just don't know."

"Do you think you're taking a big chance hoping this Bob guy will identify someone?"

"If he shows and ID's someone, I think it will go a long way to solving the crimes."

"You're probably right. Let's hope he shows up."

# Chapter 38

While Ron was servicing the bar area, and Jake was nursing his day-off beer, Officer Cassidy arrived at the bar. He walked in and stood by the waitress station talking to Kim.

"I'm Officer Cassidy. I'd like to speak to someone about the recent robberies against some of the people who frequent this place."

Kim looked around.
"Do you want to speak with some of the people who were robbed?"
"Let me start with some of the staff who might know something."
"You might want to talk with Ron Alderman, today's bartender. He's standing over there, behind the bar." She pointed at Ron and Jake.
"Thanks."

Officer Cassidy went to the middle of the bar and sat down.

Ron came forward.

"What can I get for you Officer?"

"You're Alderman, aren't you?"

"I'm Ron Alderman. I met you the last time you were in here. How can I help you?"

"As you know, I'm looking into some local robberies, and this bar seems to run through all of them."

"And we've had two more in the last week."

"This is becoming a full time job for me so I'd like to know all that you know."

"You might want to talk to Jake Wilson, the other bartender." He pointed to Jake who was standing by another patron at the other end of the bar. "He's been looking into the robberies more than anyone else."

"What do you mean looking into them?"

"He has a theory about the robberies and he's doing some research. He's really thorough like that."

"Is he a former police office or something?"

"No, I don't think so."

"Then, he shouldn't be meddling into things where he doesn't have any real experience."

Officer Cassidy got up and went to the end of the bar where Jake was standing. He sat down.

"Mr. Wilson, while I appreciate your help, with the previous list and everything, I understand you've been doing your own sleuthing regarding the robberies. Not smart."

Jake looked in Ron's direction.

"Yes, Officer. It's just I know how busy you guys are. I'm not hurting anyone."

"Why didn't you just leave it to the police to investigate these robberies?"

"There are some unusual circumstances described by some of the robbery victims where I thought I might be of help."

"Such as?"

"It seems in a few instances, someone wearing a hooded sweatshirt was either captured in a picture at the place of a robbery or showed up at some of the local pawn shops."

"So, what's so unusual about that?"

"The sweatshirt worn by the person in question came from this bar."

"I don't know what that has to do with anything."

"We only sold one hundred hooded sweatshirts last summer and have a list of everyone who purchased one."

"Why would you have a list?"

"All the sweatshirts were purchased before we placed the order. They were a little expensive and had to be embroidered."

"And where did this lead you?"

"I've been able to account for all but eight."

"Did you talk with these eight?"

"Yes. Three were women. Two of them had purchased the sweatshirts for a man as gifts, and the gifts were sent out of state. The third woman is someone who comes in here regularly and was out of town when some of the robberies took place so she couldn't have been involved."

"And the other five?"

"Two sweatshirts were XL in size. The figure in the photo is pretty small. I'd say five-five and small in stature. The picture shows a well-fitted sweatshirt. Definitely not an XL on a small frame."

Officer Cassidy took out a pad and pen. He made some notes.

"That's good information Wilson. Maybe you should have been a cop."

"Call me Jake. Everyone does."

"Ok Wilson. What else have you come up with?"

"I'm still trying to track down the owner of the three un-accounted for sweatshirts. We've got one in our lost and found box. I'll get it. This belonged to someone, but I don't know who. And sometimes it's out of the box, and shows back up again. Weird."

Jake went to a closet and came back with a sweatshirt in hand. He held it up.

"So that's what we're looking for?"

"Yep." Jake turned it around so Officer Cassidy could see the other side."

"I see. It has the bar name and logo on it."

"Yes. And when I visited a few of the local pawn shops, they had a guy in there wearing one of these attempting to pawn some of the merchandise that might have been stolen in the robberies."

"What pawn shops did you visit?"

"Central Connecticut Pawn, Park Avenue Pawn and Gold Digger Pawn."

"I know all of them. What did each of them tell you?"

"Central Connecticut Pawn is owned by a friend of mine, Dave King. He's been pretty helpful pointing out how the business works."

"We know King. He runs a clean shop."

"He said he couldn't specifically remember anyone coming to his place trying to pawn something wearing a monogrammed sweatshirt like this one in the last month."

"And the other places?"

"I visited the Gold Digger Pawn shop twice. The first time, the salesperson there, Tracy, showed me their security tapes where we saw someone trying to pawn stuff and the person had on one of these sweatshirts."

"Did they get the name and other information of the person?"

"No. Tracy wasn't the person on duty when the suspect was there. Another salesperson, Bob, was on duty. I talked to him as well but he didn't have any contact information."

"What was Bob's last name?"

"I didn't get it."

"Well, we've had some issues with Gold Digger in the past. They tend to run a pretty loose shop."

"That's what I found out."

"And the other place?"

"Before we go to that place, let me finish up on Gold Digger. I was hoping to convince Bob to come here to see if he could identify the person I saw on their security tape."

"And did he?"

"Not yet. I just want him to look around and see if he recognizes anyone."

"So, when is Bob supposed to show up?"

"I hope pretty soon, but he didn't make a commitment."

Jake didn't tell him about the twenty bucks or the hundred if Bob were to show on Friday night.

Cassidy made another note in his book.

"I'll have to get that tape."

"Don't bother. When I talked to Bob about the security tape, he said the owner of the shop wiped all of the security tapes clean two days ago so there's nothing there."

"Still, I'll have a talk with them. Now the other one."

"My friend Dave King made a few phone calls to other pawn shop owners he knows. He got a hit at Park Avenue Pawn and came over here Friday night with the employee of Park Avenue who was working a couple of times when some of the merchandise lost in the robberies was being pawned."

"What was the name of the person from Park Avenue?"

"Roger Skylar."

"What did he tell you?"

"He said one person had been in to his shop a number of times over the past few weeks pawning stuff. He knew the stuff was hot because no one comes in a few times in a short period of time with similar items unless they're stolen."

"Did he get the name of the person?"

"He did although he said the name is probably a fake."

"Well, did he say the person showed ID?"

"Yes. And the ID matched the name the person gave."

"Was it a picture ID?"

"I didn't ask that question."

"If it wasn't a picture ID, it could have been a fake. And as I think about it, even picture IDs aren't a guarantee."

"What name did this Roger give you?"

"Tommy Benson."

"Do you know Tommy Benson?"

"Yes. He comes in here regularly."

"Maybe this Tommy Benson has used the information he gets here at the bar to commit these robberies?"

"I've talked to Tommy about the information I've gathered. He told me he's never been at the Park Avenue Pawn shop and Roger said Tommy wasn't the person he saw at his shop even though the person doing the pawning identified himself as Tommy Benson."

"Well then it might be someone else in here using Benson's name."

"Looks that way."

"I'll talk with this Roger Skylar and see what else I can get out of him."

"He's been very cooperative Officer."

"Anything else you've got Wilson?"

"Not that I can think of right now. You can reach me here most days if you want to talk more."

"Thanks Wilson."

Officer Cassidy made a few more notes in his book. He was about to get up when a woman sat down next to him.

"Officer Cassidy."
"Ms. Ascroft."
"Nice seeing you here. And, call me Karen."
"I'm here on official business."
"Too bad. I thought you might be taking some time off."
"Not today. I've been assigned to investigate all of the robberies that have taken place recently involving the patrons of the 'O' Bar."

Ron came over, "What can I get you Karen?"
"I'll have a martini. Want one Officer?"
"Can't drink on duty."
"Too bad. Maybe you and I can get together sometime outside of work?"
"Maybe."
"Are you married?"
"No."
"Seeing anyone?"
"Not at the present."
"It's sounding better all the time."
"I've got to be going Ms. Ascroft, I mean Karen. I have quite a bit more to do to find the person doing these robberies."
"You know where I live. Come by anytime. By the way, what's your first name?"
"Charles."
"Charles is a nice name. Do you mind if I call you Charles?"
"I don't mind if I'm not on official business. Otherwise, it's good to maintain professional recognition."

"Then Charles it is when you aren't on official business and Officer Cassidy when you are."

"Thanks Karen for understanding."

"Anytime, Officer Cassidy."

Officer Cassidy got up and left.

# Chapter 39

Ron and Jake were getting a little annoyed with their help staff. Bill Michaels had been filling in for Bobby. Bill was much slower than Bobby at doing the job and he kept getting the storage racks wrong for the bar glasses. Ron had to speak with Bill numerous times for putting the wine glasses in the cooler and the beer glasses on the back shelf of the bar. Bill was switching the glasses around when all of a sudden there was a loud crash. Bill had knocked over a whole tray of wine glasses shattering them all over the floor behind the bar.

"Just great," Ron said out loud.
"I'm sorry Ron. I didn't mean to."
"Just clean it up Bill. Wet vac is in the closet."
"Ok."

It took Bill fifteen minutes to pick up all of the broken glass. The whole time he was cleaning up, Ron stayed at the other end of the bar not wanting to make matters worse. When he was done, Ron walked around the bar to see if anyone wanted anything.

"Can I have another martini?" Karen asked.

"Sure."

Ron made it for her.

"Can't get good help, huh?" Karen said.

"He means well."

"Maybe, but Bobby is better."

"Yeah. Bobby looks like he's taking a long time to get things done but he's never in the way and never a problem."

"Bet you can't wait for him to come back to work."

"Got that right. So Karen, what's up with you and that Officer?"

"Nothing yet. He came by my place when I called the police station to report being robbed."

"And?"

"That's it. I think he's kind of cute. And he's single."

"Now, how do you know that?"

"I asked."

"You going to try to hook up with him?"

"I'd like to but I'm not sure he's interested."

"Why do you say that?"

"He was all business. I suggested but he didn't bite."

"He's just focused right now. Give it time. He might come around."

"I hope he does."


Ron went down the bar taking care of the other patrons who wanted something. He stopped at the end and talked with Jake.


"So, where are we at with the robberies, Jake?"

"Officer Cassidy is going to talk with Roger Skylar the guy from Park Avenue Pawn. He wants him to come back in and check out the staff."

"The staff? Does he think someone who works here is committing the robberies?"

"He just thinks, as we do, that someone who is in here regularly is doing them."

"When is he coming in?"

"He said he'd get back to me after he talks with Roger."

"Didn't Roger check everyone out in here already?"

"I guess he focused more on customers and Cassidy doesn't want to exclude anyone."

"That would be interesting if someone who works here was the dirt bag."

"Sure would. I'll let you know when they plan on coming back."

"Well, here comes the rest of your detective group," Ron said looking at the door as Sue and Lou came in. They took up stools next to Karen and Kelly.

"What's up Karen?" Sue said.

"Not much. Just having a martini.

Ron walked over to the group. "What'll it be?"

"I'll have a Bud," Lou said.

"I'll have the same," Sue added.

They all wanted to know where the case stood. Ron gave them all an update as Jake walked over from his end of the bar. Jake told them he'd let them all know once he heard from Officer Cassidy as to when he'd be back.

"We'll all be here. Just tell us when," Sue stated.

"Yeah, I can't believe he thinks it's someone who works here," Lou remarked.

"He didn't say for sure, Lou," Jake said. "He just said he wants to make sure all the i's are dotted and t's crossed."

"But what if it is someone who works here?" Karen asked.

"I pity that person," Lou said.

"Why?" Kelly asked.

"Because if it's true and you women get a hold of him, there's going to be trouble."

"Lou, we're not violent," Sue said.

"Oh, I know how women can be."

"You do, do you?" Kelly asked.

"Oh yeah. Show me a group of women who all feel violated and I'll show you a vigilante group," Lou declared.

"Us?" Sue said. "We're peace loving women."

"Sure you are," Lou said taking a drink of his beer.

Bill Michaels walked back behind the bar and picked up a tray of dirty dishes. He turned to take them to the kitchen and a plate flew off the top of the pile and broke on the floor. Everyone looked in his direction.

Jake said, "That guy has got to go."

"When's Bobby coming back?" Lou asked.

"In a day or so. He was in here yesterday picking up his paycheck and said he's coming back this week."

"Good thing," said Ron. "I'm not sure we have enough glasses and dishes to last us another week if Bill is still here."

They all laughed. Bill had heard them and gave them a dirty look.

"He'll be back in the kitchen doing dishes in a few days Ron. You'll survive," Kelly commented.

"I hope."

"Just hope his new habit of breaking stuff doesn't carry over to the kitchen," Karen said.

"He's just nervous working out here," Jake added. "He'll be alright once he gets back to his normal job."

"What if he's the one doing the robberies?" Karen asked.

"Who? Bill?" Jake asked.

"Yeah Bill," Karen replied.

"How would he even get the information on everyone who has been robbed?"

"I don't know. But he works here."

"So do I," Ron who had been listening added.

"Hell, it could be anyone."

"We'll just have to wait and see what Officer Cassidy comes up with."

"Hopefully, it will not take too long."

"He's on the case full time now," Jake said. "I'm guessing things will start to come together real soon."

"Hope you're right," Lou said.

As the night wore on, the regulars all started to filter out. About ten o'clock, Kelly said to Sue, "I just don't want to go home alone. I'm pretty scared that these robberies might escalate into something worse."

"Kelly, don't be so dramatic."

"I'm not being dramatic. I just don't like it that there have been more and more crimes happening."

"Then, why don't you get someone to go home with you?"

"Like who?"

"Tommy Benson's single. I'm sure he'll go with you. And there is always Lou."

Lou heard his name.

"Who? What?" Lou asked.

"We were just talking Lou. Kelly doesn't want to go home alone and I suggested she get you or Tommy to go with her."

"Hey Kelly, I think it's a good idea. I'll go with you if you want."

"Thanks Lou but you're here with Sue."

"True. I don't think she'll mind."

Lou looked at Sue, "Will you?"

"You can go home with anyone you want. Just pick up your vehicle in the morning."

"See, she doesn't mind."

"Thanks for the offer Lou but I'll see if Tommy wants to go with me."

Lou felt rejected.

"You can still go home with me, Lou," Sue stated.

Lou smiled. "I'll have another beer Jake."

Kelly got up and walked to where Tommy was seated.

"Hi Tommy."

"Kelly."

"Got any plans for tonight?"

"Not really."

"Want to come over to my place with me?"

"What do you have in mind?"

"All this robbery stuff has me nervous and I'd like company."

"Didn't you get robbed already?"

"Yeah."

"Well, I don't think a robber would hit the same place so soon."

"Just the same, you want to come over?"

"Sure. Let me finish my beer."

Kelly walked back to her seat.

"So?" Sue asked.

"Tommy's going with me."

"Have fun," Sue remarked.

Kelly paid her tab and got up. Tommy was walking her way. They walked out together.

# Chapter 40

Kelly drove herself and Tommy to her place. They went inside.

"So what do you want to do Kel? Want to watch TV?"

"I haven't replaced the big one that was stolen yet. Insurance companies move like snails."

"Want to listen to the stereo?"

"No, I have a small TV up in my bedroom. Let's go up there."

"Sure."

"Want a beer?"

"Ok."

"I'll get them. You go up and see what's on."

Tommy went to the bedroom. He turned on a light next to the bed. Then, he picked up the remote and turned the TV on. He browsed through the channel listings until he found what he was looking for. He selected music from the 70's.

Kelly came into the bedroom with two beers in hand.

"Couldn't find anything worthwhile on the TV?"

"I thought the music would be fine."

"Sounds good to me. I'm going to change."

She walked into the adjoining bathroom. Tommy sat on the edge of the bed. He could see her from time to time through the partially opened door, as she got undressed. At one point, she turned facing the door and was completely naked. Tommy started to get excited. When she came out, she had on a sheer tee shirt revealing her body. She looked terrific.

Kelly walked over to the bed and stretched out. Her tee shirt rose up well past her knees. Tommy stood. He took his shirt off. As he started to undo his belt, she said, "Let me do that."

Tommy stood in front of Kelly as she undid his belt. Then, she undid his pants and slid them off. Tommy was quite excited and it showed.

"What do we have here?" She said as she pushed his jeans to the floor.

She put a hand on each side of his waist and pulled him close to her. Tommy put his hands on her shoulders and slid the tee off her. She kissed him. Then, she made sure he was ready. Tommy was having a hard time holding back.

She extended her hand to his and coaxed him down onto the bed. Tommy couldn't keep his hands off her. He explored her body, then, he kissed her passionately and they began to move as one. His motion started slowly and accelerated. They were both breathing heavily when Tommy could hold out no longer. Kelly followed. Tommy continued for as long as he could. Kelly clutched Tommy's back and held him tight. Then, she let out a big sigh. He pressed harder.

"Easy Tommy. It hurts a little."
"Sorry Kelly."
"Just take it slow."

He did. A few minutes later, she sighed again.
"That was better."
"I'm glad."
"What do you want to do now?"
"Let's just lay here and listen to the music."
"Ok."

The two embraced. Tommy kissed Kelly a few times and then they both fell asleep.

\* \* \* \* \* \* \*

Lou had gone home with Sue. He had left his vehicle at her place. While they were driving, she said, "You could have gone home with Kelly if you wanted."
"I'd rather be here with you."
"You'd have gotten laid whether you went home with me or her."
"Doesn't it bother you that I might have slept with Kelly tonight?"
"Not at all. We're not an item and I don't have any strings on you."
"That's pretty open thinking, Sue."
"Lou, I try to keep an open mind about those kinds of things."
"Really?"
"Yeah. People who shut their mind to different things are missing out on a lot of what life has to offer."
"How far have you let yourself think?"

"I've done more than just think Lou. For example, a lot of people are against same sex or multiple partners. Not me. Some of the best sex I have had has been with multiple partners."

"No kidding? Exactly what are we talking about here?"

"I've been with more than one guy at the same time."

"Wow. And how did it work out?"

"I got off with each one."

"Each one?"

"Yeah. And it was great."

"You're telling me you had two guys do it at the same time?"

"No. Three."

"Three?"

"Yep. And it was fantastic. When one was done, there was another and then another."

"Isn't that called a gang bang?"

"That's a crude term Lou."

"Well, isn't it?"

"I'd rather think of it as making love with multiple partners at the same time."

"I don't think I could do it with other guys present."

"Oh, you could. You just need the right woman."

"And you're that woman?"

"I'm just saying I have had multiple men at the same time and it was really good."

"And what about the same sex stuff?"

"I don't know about men with men but I've been with other women and it can be just as good."

"How can that be? Aren't you missing something?"

"Lou, there's tools."

"Like a vibrator?"

"That's one and there are others."

"So us guys can be replaced by plastic or rubber."

"Sure can. And it doesn't go soft."

"Sue, I don't know if all this talk is getting me horny or afraid."

"Afraid of what? Me?"

"Not you but I don't think I could do it with other guys with or without a woman."

"That's closed minded thinking Lou."

"Ok. I'm closed minded. I plan on staying that way."

They arrived at Sue's and walked to the porch.

"Do you want me to come in?" Lou asked.

"Sure. We can pick up where we were last night."

"Is it just going to be me and you?"

"Lou, you're getting carried away."

"That's just it, I don't want to get carried anywhere."

Sue put her hand on Lou's cheek and gently slapped him.

"Lou, Lou, what am I going to do with you?"

"I've got some ideas but they only include you and me."

"Let's get inside."

# Chapter 41

Karen was cleaning her house when someone knocked on her door. She opened it. Officer Cassidy stood there. He was in uniform and looked handsome. He was six-foot two, had jet-black hair and hazel eyes. She could tell he kept physically fit by the broad shoulders, a thin waist and trim look in his uniform. Both forearms had tattoos, and the way his arms looked was scarily inviting.

"Ms. Ascroft."

"Charles or should I say Officer Cassidy."

"Call me Charles."

"Are you on duty or off?"

"Actually, I'm on duty, but it's just the two of us here right now."

"What can I do for you?"

"I have a few questions for you if you have a few minutes."

"Sure. Come in."

Karen was dressed in navy blue shorts that were cuffed at her thighs, with a white tee shirt. She had on a pair of navy blue Keds sneakers and had her hair pulled back in a ponytail.

"Sorry for my appearance. I was just doing some house cleaning."

"No problem."

"Let's sit in my living room."

He followed her to the living room and sat on the couch. She sat next to him.

"I'm going to visit some of the local pawn shops this afternoon and wanted to make sure of my facts before I go there."

"Sure. What do you want from me?"

"First, do you have any of the paperwork for the TV you had or for the safe that was taken?"

"Like receipts or manuals?"

"Yes."

"I do. After they were stolen, I went through my files and found the receipts for both of those things."

"Can I take a look at them?"

"Sure. The receipts are in my desk in my bedroom. I'll get them."

She left the room and went to her bedroom. He could hear her opening the desk drawer and then heard her say, "Here they are."

"Charles, I've found them."

"Good."

"I've got some other paper work in here as well that you might be interested in."

He stood and walked to the bedroom. When he got there, she had taken most of her clothing off and was on the bed.

"Why don't you come here and sit next to me?"

One look at her body convinced him. He took off his gun belt, shirt, pants and vest. Then, he joined her on the bed. They helped each other finish undressing and then she was all over him.

"So muscular."
"You're pretty fit yourself."

She ran her hands over his chest and then down his body. He explored hers as well. Then, they embraced. They kissed and she took control.

They made love together for a few minutes all the while continuing to kiss. He eventually couldn't hold off any longer. He let out a big sigh. She did also. They remained in that position for a little while longer.

"That was nice. Now, why did you come here?"
"Originally to ask a few questions."
"And now?"
"And now I've got to get back to work."
"Can we do this again?"
"Sure. But, next time, I'll make sure I can spend more time."
"Next time, I want you to spend the night."
He kissed her and got up.

"I've got a few things to do this afternoon and have to be going."
"Can you come back?"
"Maybe. Why don't we meet somewhere?"
"How about at the 'O' Bar tonight around seven."
"That will work for me. I probably need to talk with Jake Wilson anyway."

"So, I'll see you around seven."

He dressed and left. Cassidy drove to Hartford. He got off at Prospect Street and in a few minutes was on Park Avenue looking for Park Avenue Pawn. It didn't take long and he stopped his unmarked vehicle in the parking lot of the pawnshop.

"I'm looking for Roger Skylar."

"I'm Roger."

"I'm Officer Cassidy. I've been assigned to look into a number of robberies that have taken place in and around the town of Farmington recently."

"Are these the robberies committed against the patrons of the 'O' Bar?"

"Yes."

"Someone I know had asked me to go there last Friday night to see if I could identify anyone who might have been pawning stuff in here recently."

"I know. Jake Wilson told me about it."

"Then you know I was unable to identify the robber."

"Yes. But, did you take a look at all of the staff working at the 'O' Bar?"

"Not in particular. Why does that matter?"

"What if the person doing these crimes is someone who works there as opposed to being a patron?"

"I never gave it a thought."

"I'd like to ask you to go over there with me tonight, and take another look, especially at the staff."

"I guess I could do that."

"What time would you like me there?"

"How about six-thirty?"

"Sure. I'll be there at six-thirty."

"See you then."

Officer Cassidy left and went back to his office. He had some paperwork to do before going to the 'O' Bar. While at his office, he called the 'O' Bar and asked for Jake Wilson.

"Jake here."

"Jake, it's Officer Cassidy. I've arranged for Mr. Skylar to come with me to the 'O' Bar tonight around six-thirty. I want him to get a good look at the staff and see if he recognizes any of them."

"Sure. Tonight being Friday is one of our busy nights so we'll be at full staff."

"Great. I'll be there a little after six."

# Chapter 42

Another Friday night arrived. As usual, most of the regulars were at the bar before six. The guys from Harttt Landscaping were at the middle of the bar. Pete Harttt was seated along with his significant other Heather, Lou Adams and Sam Marino were standing behind them talking with Frank Johnson. Rick and Sally Taft were seated to Pete's left and Mary and Hal Carson next to them. Pops sat on the other side of Heather. Paul Aaron sat next to Pops along with Big Ed Martin. Professor Ryan, John and Pat Walden next to Ed. Kelly Jones, Karen Ascroft, Trish Howland and Jenny Connors filled out the remaining seats at the end of the bar except for the last one.

"Full house tonight?" Ron said to Jake.
"It's Friday night. What else would you expect?"
"I guess."

Jake went over to the end of the bar.
"Hi ladies. Jenny, can you tip the last stool forward so no one sits there."

"Sure. You expecting someone?" Jenny asked.

"Yeah. I've got someone coming here in a little while and I'd like to save that seat."

The women all looked at Jake.

"Who is the mystery person Jake?" Kelly asked.

"Nothing like you're thinking. You'll see later."

"Jake's got a woman coming in?" Karen declared.

Jake put an empty beer bottle in front of the seat Jenny had leaned forward so it would look like someone was sitting there.

Sue Walker came into the bar by herself. She saw the girls at the end of the bar and went over. She went to the open seat next to Jenny.

"Who's sitting here?" She asked.

"Jake has someone coming in and wants to keep the seat open."

She pulled the seat back and sat down. Jake immediately came over to her.

"Sue, I've got someone coming here soon and I want to keep that seat open."

"Jake, you let me know when your friend arrives and I'll give up the seat."

Jake thought about it for a minute and figured that would work, so long as Sue was willing to get up when asked.

"So, anyone know who is so special that Jake is reserving a seat?"

"He wouldn't tell us," Jenny said.

"I'll have a beer Jake," Sue said. "And give the girls another one on me."

"Sure Sue. You still spending your winnings from the casino?"

"Jake, you know that was all a setup," Sue said.

"Yeah, I know. I just wanted to see your reaction."

"Boy that scheme didn't work out," Karen said.

"Sorry about that Karen. I thought for sure we'd catch the robber at my place that night. Who would have thought you were the target for that night."

"I'm still not over it."

"Do you ever get over being robbed?" Jenny asked.

"I guess not."

Frank Johnson was talking to Lou, Sam and Pete about the weather for the upcoming weekend.

"It's supposed to be a nice day on Sunday. You guys want to have another golf outing?" Frank asked.

"I'm in," said Lou.

"Me too," said Sam.

"How about you Pete?" Frank asked.

Pete looked at Heather. He had the look of a little boy wanting to ask a question but was afraid to.

"Don't look like that Pete. If you want to play golf with the guys on Sunday, go ahead. I can find something to do."

Now Pete felt even worse.

"I don't know guys."

"Go ahead Hon. I was planning on spending the day at the beach anyway. With a good book."

"I'm good company Heather, if you want some" winked Lou.

Pete looked at Lou with a look of contempt.

"You already said you were in for golf," Sam said.

"I guess I'm golfing then," Lou said sheepishly.

"Ok. I'm in," Pete declared.

"Let's meet at Tunxis at ten. I'll make the tee time reservation," Frank declared.

"Who's going to be partners?" Lou asked.

"Let's see," Frank said. "Last time we all played together you were paired up with Tommy Benson. Sam and I were partners. Seems to me you and Pete should probably be a team to try and beat us."

"How's your game Pete?" Lou asked.

"We are talking golf now right Lou?"

They all laughed. Heather turned around looking at Lou, "I don't know about his golf game but he's right on his game in other areas."

Lou didn't respond.

"I've been playing a couple of times a week and I'm shooting in the mid 70's."

"Ok. It's Pete and me. Frank and Sam. Those are the teams."

"What are we playing for?" Pete asked.

"Bragging rights and a C-note," Lou stated.

"Sounds good to me," Pete said.

"Remember to bring you're "A" game on Sunday Pete," Lou stated.

"He'll be ready," Heather said.

The Carsons and Tafts were having a discussion while Ron stood in front of them.

"Do you want to order anything to eat?" Ron asked Hal Carson.

"Order some nachos," Mary Carson told Hal.

"Yeah, we'll have some nachos. Have them put chicken on them."

"Got it. Anything for you, Rick?"

275

"We'll share the nachos, if you guys don't mind. The portion is huge," Rick replied.

Ron went to the register and entered the order. The Carsons and Tafts went back to their discussion.

"Why hasn't anything been done about the robberies?" Sally Taft asked.

"I'm just glad we weren't robbed," said Mary.

"I lost some jewelry that meant a lot to me," declared Sally.

"Not to mention my computer with all my pictures on it and some other stuff I didn't have backed up."

"That's too bad," Hal said.

"We've gotten a new computer now and I made sure it came with an external backup drive. We're not going to lose everything if it happens again," Rick said.

"What if a robber steals your new computer and the backup drive?" Mary asked.

"They're in different locations in our house," Rick said. "But I guess if we lost both, we'd be out of luck again."

"We use an internet backup service," Hal stated.

"We should look into something like that Sally. Mary's right. If we were robbed again and lost the backup drive, we'd be in the same boat were in a few weeks ago."

"It took me two weeks spending most of my days re-entering business data to get back to almost where we were before we lost our computer," Sally said. "And I was able to recover some of our photos from our cell phones. But we lost a lot of data. I wouldn't want to have to try to recreate it all again."

"Can you send us the contact information for the internet company you're using?" Rick asked Hal.

"Sure. I'll send it to you in the morning."

"Thanks Hal."

Ron put a big platter of nachos in front of the group along with forks, napkins and serving plates. They all filled their plates and continued talking.

Paul Aaron, Ed Martin and Pops were having a discussion about the Red Sox.

"You think the Sox can keep it together and make the playoffs?" Paul asked.

"Only if the pitching stays healthy," Ed replied.

"And the Yankees stumble," Pops said.

"Well, they could get the Wild Card," Paul added.

"Lately, it's looking like that will be their only way in," Pops said.

"We've had a few good years recently so it's not out of the question for the Sox to win it all again," Ed said.

"I hope so," Paul said.

"We'll see, we'll see," Pops added.

Professor Ryan and the Waldens were engaged in a conversation about the community college.

"I see there's another building going up on campus," John Walden stated.

"Yeah. Enrollment was up another fifteen percent last semester and is expected to continue to rise in the future."

"It's sure nice to see the local community college doing so well," Pat Walden stated.

"It is. We've got a pretty aggressive program under way to up the enrollment to ten thousand over the next five years."

"Wow, that's pretty aggressive," John said.

"It is. But, with all the press about giving people the skills they need for today's workplace, we've been encouraged by the enrollment. And the government has made it easy to procure funds for expansion."

"Isn't the school limited by the property it has for expansion?"

"Somewhat. We bought a residence across the street from the school a few years ago and put some of the administrative offices in there. There's a few acres of land over there that might get used for expansion."

"Isn't that a little dangerous for crossing Route 6?" Mary asked.

"It would be but the school is looking at constructing a tunnel under the street or putting a raised walkway over it," Professor Ryan said.

"Something like that would solve the access issue," John said.

As all of the conversations were going on, Bobby came in and walked up to the end of the bar by the waitress station. Lou and the guys clapped. Everyone at the bar stopped what they were doing and gave out a cheer.

"Hey Bobby. Ready to come back to work?" Jake asked happily.

"I'm just picking up my paycheck Jake."

"How's the hand," Lou shouted out.

Bobby held up his hand for everyone to see. A regular band-aid had replaced the gauze bandage and he looked ok.

"Jake, give Bobby a drink on me," Lou declared.

"Thanks anyway Lou but I'm still on medication and can't have any alcohol."

Jake went to the register and pulled out a stack of envelopes. He selected Bobby's and handed it to him.

"You hanging around Bobby?" Ron asked.

"No. I've got a date tonight."

"You have a good time Bobby and we'll see you tomorrow," Jake added.

Bobby took the envelope, turned and headed to the door. After he went outside, he turned to the right and walked past a vehicle pulling into the parking lot. He stopped at the end of the building and took out a cigarette, lit it and took a drag.

The vehicle going past him went half way down the row and pulled into an empty space. Officer Cassidy and Roger Skylar got out.

# Chapter 44

Officer Cassidy and Roger Skylar walked into the 'O' Bar. Jake saw them coming in and walked over to greet them.

"Thanks for coming back Roger, and Officer Cassidy. I've arranged for you to have a seat in the corner at the end of the bar so you'll be able to see just about everyone coming and going."

"Will he be able to see all the staff from that position?" Officer Cassidy asked.

"I talked with my manager and he's going to have the entire staff come out to the bar over a half hour period bringing food out for the waitresses. That way, you'll see everyone who is working without tipping anyone off as to what you're doing."

"Sounds good."

Cassidy had shed his official uniform in preparation for the undercover surveillance, and Jake led them to the corner of the bar where Sue and Jenny were sitting.

"Sue, this is the person I was saving the seat for."

Sue looked at Roger Skylar and Officer Cassidy, "Jake, I'm surprised at you. I didn't think you swung that way."

"It's not what you think."

Karen knew Officer Cassidy was coming to the bar that night. She turned to Officer Cassidy, "Hi Charles, or is it Officer Cassidy?"

He leaned over to her and whispered, "I'm on duty."

She corrected herself, "Nice to see you again, Officer Cassidy."

Again, he leaned over to her and whispered, "I'm doing undercover work tonight Karen. Call me Charles."

"Ok, I'm sorry. You told me you would see me here tonight but didn't say what role you'd be playing."

"It's not playing Karen. I'm gathering information."

"You go ahead and gather Charles. Come see me when you're done."

Officer Cassidy turned his attention to Roger Skylar. Roger was engaged in a discussion with Sue. She was insisting he take the seat at the bar and he would have no part of it. He wasn't going to ask a woman to get up so he could have her seat.

"The seat is yours. I'm only sitting here so no one would take it. Jake and I worked it out earlier."

"Listen Ms."

"It's Sue."

"Listen Sue. I'm not about to ask a woman to get up so I can have a seat. I can stand here and talk to you and still do what I'm supposed to be doing."

"And what is that?"

Roger looked at Jake and Officer Cassidy.

"Sue is one of the people who were robbed," Jake said.

"Oh. I'm Roger Skylar. I own Park Avenue Pawn in Hartford. One of the people who has come into my shop a number of times recently pawning stuff had on a sweatshirt with the bar name and logo on it. We think the person might be someone who frequents the bar so I'm here to see if I can identify the person."

"Weren't you in here last week?" Jenny said.

"I was but didn't see anyone I recognized.

"Officer Cassidy thought it would be a good idea to take another look and see if I missed someone."

"Oh. What can I do?" Sue asked.

"You stay and talk with me, Sue," Roger said. "That will give me the cover I need to look at everyone."

"How about you Officer Cassidy?" Sue asked.

"I'll be sitting over there at that table," Officer Cassidy pointed to an empty table by the door.

"I'll go sit with you," Jenny said.

Karen gave her a dirty look. Only Jenny saw it. Karen had told Sue about her visit from Officer Cassidy. As they walked away, Sue said to her, "Karen, Officer Cassidy and Jenny are going to sit at a table by the door while we help Roger."

"And how are we supposed to be helping Roger?" Karen said. It was apparent she was unhappy about Jenny going to sit with Officer Cassidy.

"We're supposed to give him the names of anyone he recognizes in here."

"Ok. I guess I can do that."

She watched as Jenny and Officer Cassidy sat.

Officer Cassidy and Jenny walked over to the table. She brought her drink with her. The table they sat at was in Kim's area, so she came over.

"What can I get you?"

"I'll have a seltzer and lime," Officer Cassidy said.

"I'm all set," Jenny said.

"Call me Charles, Jenny," Officer Cassidy said.

"I don't want to scare anyone off before Skylar has a chance to carefully look at them."

"Ok, Charles. So is undercover work as interesting for you as it is for me?"

He just looked at her.

"How do you know Karen?"

"Why do you think I know her?"

"By the look she gave me when I offered to come sit with you."

"She's one of the people who were robbed. I had to interview her at her place and check things out."

"And did you?"

"Did I what?"

"Check things out."

"Jenny. I'm on official business. I don't think it's appropriate to talk about non-work related stuff."

"Well, when you're non-official, maybe we could get together and do some undercover work together."

Officer Cassidy thought he knew what she meant. He looked at Jenny. She was around thirty. He put her at five-eight, 140 pounds, brown hair and brown eyes with an attractive figure. He was beginning to hope these robberies weren't solved too quickly.

"I'd like that," he replied.

Over the next hour, there was a steady flow of personnel to the bar. Each time, it was a different person bringing the food to the bar from the kitchen. Roger could easily see the face of each person as they came and went. He took the time in between staff viewing to look around the bar at all the patrons in case he had overlooked one of them on his last visit, or a new one came in that wasn't here the last time.

At seven o'clock, the manager came to the bar.

"That's it Jake. I've had everyone come to the bar to be seen."

"Thanks George. I'll talk with Officer Cassidy."

Jake came out from behind the bar and walked over to the table by the door.

"My manager says he has had everyone walk out to the bar over the last half-hour. Hopefully, Roger recognized someone."

"Thanks Jake. And tell your manager we appreciate his cooperation."

"No problem. My boss wants this thing resolved soon as well."

"I can understand that."

Officer Cassidy got up and walked over to Roger.

"Anyone you recognized?"

"Yeah."

"Which one?"

"Remember when we drove in to the parking lot?"

"Yeah."

"There was a guy outside smoking a cigarette. I'm pretty sure he was the one who pawned the stuff at my shop."

"Why didn't you say anything?"

"I figured he was just outside having a smoke and I'd get a better look at him in here."

"And did you?"

"No. I didn't see the guy again."

Jake had gone behind the bar. He walked to the end where Roger Skylar was standing.

"So, recognize anyone?"

Officer Cassidy said, "Yeah. He thinks he recognized the guy outside when we came in. The guy was having a smoke and Roger thought the guy would come back in."

"I wanted to get a better look at him but I'm pretty sure he was the same guy."

"Did he come back inside?"

"I didn't see the guy again after that."

"Too bad. He was right here."

"If it was someone you saw outside, it must have been one of our patrons. My manager had all of the staff in here walk out to the bar after you arrived so it can't be one of them."

"It must be one of the patrons. Someone who left just as you were getting here?"

"Looks that way."

"Where do we go from here?"

"It looks like it's someone who comes here regularly. We'll need to keep up our efforts. I'm sure we'll catch the person," Officer Cassidy stated.

"Do you want to do anything else tonight?" Roger asked.

"No. I guess we're all done for tonight," Officer Cassidy said. "Unless he's still standing outside, and I don't think we'll get that lucky."

"Then, if you don't mind, I'm going to stay here with Sue for a while."

Officer Cassidy looked at Sue. She smiled, "Official Business."

Officer Cassidy shook his head and laughed.

"Have a good night."

He turned and went outside. Jenny followed him out.

"So are you off duty now, Officer Cassidy?"

"Looks that way."

"Got any plans?"

"What did you have in mind?"

"Let's take a ride to my place. I'll come up with something."

"I like the sound of that."

They left together. Getting into his vehicle she said, "You can bring me back to pick up my car later."

"Ok."

She got into the unmarked car. It had some official equipment in it like a police radio, computer and other official police stuff.

"What can you do with the computer?"

"I can check license plates, registrations and other official things like that."

"I wonder if you have anything on me in there."

"Let's see."

He entered her name into the computer. It came back and displayed her name and a speeding infraction from two years ago.

"So, you have a record."

She was impressed with what he had showed her and figured she'd be even more impressed with what he hadn't shown her.

They arrived at her place and went in.

"Now it's time for more undercover work," Jenny said. "Follow me."

She led him through her place and down the hall. They walked into her bedroom.

"Can you stay the night?"

"Probably not. I've got some things I still have to do at the station tonight."

"But I thought," he stopped her in the middle of her sentence as he put his arms around her and kissed her. She didn't protest as he lifted her from the floor and onto the bed.

A few minutes later, the lights in the house went off.

# Chapter 45

Jake and Ron were cleaning up the bar at the end of their day. Ron was stacking cleaned glasses into a rack.

"Isn't that Bill's job?"

"He's outside having a smoke."

"Do you know if Roger ever got to take a good look at Bill tonight?"

"I'm not sure. I thought George said he had everyone bring something out of the kitchen so Roger could get a good look at everyone."

"I wonder if that included Bill."

"He probably had Bill bring something out. George is pretty thorough."

"Yeah, you're right."

"Sure will be good when Bobby gets back here tomorrow," Ron said.

"So you don't have to keep stacking the glasses?"

"I'd rather do it than have Bill drop another tray. He scared the crap out of me the other day when he dropped the wine glasses."

"I know what you mean. He might be a good dishwasher but he's terrible as our assistant at the bar."

"Bobby's back tomorrow. Everything will settle back down."

"What do you think is the next step in trying to find the robber?"

"Officer Cassidy said Roger saw someone here he thinks he recognized but the guy left before he could positively identify him."

"No kidding. So the robber has been here."

"Looks that way."

"Jake, does anyone else know the police think they have identified the criminal?"

"I'm sure Sue and Jenny overheard Officer Cassidy talking and maybe others heard him as well."

"Isn't that the problem the bar has had all along? People overhearing things."

"Yeah. Kind of an occupational hazard."

"So what did he say is the next step?"

"Officer Cassidy just said he'd have to stay with it. I think he's going to try to get Roger to come here again."

"Did he say that?"

"No, but that's the impression I got."

"Well, it looks like he thinks the trail is pretty hot so I'm thinking he's got something up his sleeve he's not telling us about."

"I hope you're right. Do you have anything you're planning on doing?"

"I'm pretty much out of ideas right now."

Jake was about to turn the lights off. He picked up his cell phone by the register and went to put it into his pocket.

He noticed he had missed a call. He checked to see who had called. He could see he had missed a call from Dave King. Then, he checked his voice mail. Dave had left a message.

"Jake, it's Dave King. When you get this message, give me a call. I had one of my guys over at Gold Digger earlier today dropping something off and he saw a guy in there wearing one of those sweatshirts with the name and logo from your bar. He said the guy looked to be pawning a computer."

Jake called back. His call went to Dave's voice mail. Jake looked at his watch. It was one o'clock in the morning. He'd try Dave again tomorrow.

Jake closed up. He and Ron went their respective ways. When Jake got home, he turned on the TV and watched the rerun of local news from a few hours earlier. He had a beer and tried to relax. The phone message from Dave had him thinking.

After a half hour, he decided to go to bed. While he tossed and turned quite a bit during the night, he finally woke to the bright sun shining in his bedroom window around seven thirty. Jake made a cup of coffee and toast. He took a shower and got dressed. At eight-thirty, he called Dave.

Dave answered on the second ring.
"Dave, its Jake."
"Hey Jake. I was hoping to hear from you last night."
"We were pretty busy at the bar and I didn't notice your call until I was closing up."
"Yeah, I saw where you returned my call at one a.m."
"Sorry about that."
"Oh, I didn't mean I got it at one a.m., I mean I got it this morning from you sending it to me at one a.m."
"Good, then I didn't wake you up."

290

"No you didn't. Listen, I had one of my guys dropping something off at the Gold Digger shop yesterday and he said he saw a guy in there who was wearing one of the sweatshirts you showed me. I had told all of my staff about your investigation in case one of them saw someone who might fit the description you gave me."

"Did he get a good look at the guy?"

"Yeah. He said he's sure he can ID the person if he sees him again."

"Great. You think you can get your guy to come over here tonight and see if he recognizes anyone?"

"Sure. His name is Dominic Garibaldi."

"Sounds like mafia."

"Na. He's a good guy. You'll like him."

"Have him come over around seven."

"I'll call him and see if he can be there. Then, I'll call you back."

"Thanks Dave."

Jake hung up. He put his phone on the table and poured another cup of coffee. A few minutes later, it rang again.

"It's Dave. We're all set. Dom and I will be there around seven."

"Thanks Dave. I owe you one."

Jake called Ron.

"Ron, I just talked with Dave King. He's got someone who saw a guy pawning something at Gold Digger yesterday and the guy was wearing one of our sweatshirts."

"I thought Dave owned Central Connecticut Pawn?"

"He does. He said he was having one of his guys dropping something off at Gold Digger when his guy noticed someone wearing a sweatshirt with the bar name and logo on it."

"What is he going to do?"

"He's coming over to the bar tonight at seven."

"You sure Dave's guy is going to be able to identify the same person who had been doing all the robberies?"

"Dave's guy, Dom, said he saw a man wearing our sweatshirt pawning a laptop at Gold Digger. I'm going down to Gold Digger to see if I can find the laptop. If I can, and if it's one of the ones stolen from one of our patrons and if Dom can positively identify the guy, we'll have solved the case."

"That's a lot of ifs Jake."

"Maybe that's what it's going to take to solve the robberies."

"Ok, my fingers are crossed for you, and everyone else."

Jake hung up. He had things to do. At 11:45 a.m. Jake went down to the Gold Digger. Tracy had just opened the front door.

"I didn't think I'd get to see you in here again Jake," she said as Jake walked in.

"Hi Tracy. Listen, a friend of mine saw a guy in here yesterday pawning a laptop. I'd like to buy that laptop if you still have it?"

"Let's see."

She walked to the back room to a rack of stuff.

"These are the things that came in yesterday. They haven't been checked into our inventory yet. What kind of laptop was it?"

"That I don't know."

She went through the rack. There were TVs, a desktop, cell phones, a couple of boxes of stuff and under one of the boxes there was a laptop. She checked the whole rack and didn't find another laptop.

"This must be the one."

"Can we check your security tape?"

"Sure."

Tracy rewound the security tape and hit play. After a few minutes, Jake said, "There, see that guy?"

Tracy looked.

"Yeah."

"He's wearing one of the sweatshirts from the bar."

Again, the angle of the camera wasn't positioned where they could see the person's face but they could see the laptop the person had in his hands.

"Look there," Jake said. "It has a sticker on the cover."

Tracy looked. Then, she turned the laptop over that she had taken out of the rack and it had the same sticker on it.

"It has to be the one."

"Can I buy it?" he asked.

"Sure. But I'll tell you what. If it's in the rack, it hasn't been entered into our inventory yet. Why don't you take it and see if it belonged to one of your patrons. If it did, you'll want it for evidence anyway."

"Won't your boss get mad at you?"

"Nah. If he asks, I'll say the police came in and recognized the laptop and took it. It happens more than you'd think and my boss doesn't like making waves."

Jake was about to leave.

"Why don't you take this as well," Tracy said handing the security tape to Jake.

"Thanks Tracy. I owe you one."

Jake picked up the laptop and tape and left. He had what he came for.

293

# Chapter 46

Jake showed up for work at four. He walked behind the bar carrying a laptop.

"What's with the laptop?" Ron asked.

"I went down to the Gold Digger today. The person working there, Tracy was a big help in finding it."

"What's so unique about this one?"

"It's the one Dave's guy saw being pawned at Gold Digger yesterday by someone wearing one of our sweatshirts."

"No kidding? Are you sure it's the same computer?"

"No doubt. Tracy let me look at the security tape and that's the same one the guy was pawning."

"Do you think it belongs to one of out patrons?"

"I don't know but I plan on finding out later tonight."

"What's your plan?"

"If we can get everyone in here, I plan on asking them if the computer belongs to one of them. If it does, we're almost there. Then, around seven, Dave and his guy, Dom, will be here so Dom can identify the guy who pawned the laptop."

"Sounds so mysterious. Just like on TV."

"Let's just hope it all works out."

"Ok. Want me to do anything?"

"No. Just don't say anything to anyone."

"Got it."

Over the next two hours, Ron and Jake went about their business. To their delight, Bobby had come back to work around five o'clock. He got right into his routine giving Ron relief from having to stock the shelves with glasses.

As Bobby was straightening things out behind the bar, he picked up the laptop that Jake had placed by the register.

"What do you want me to do with this?"

"Oh, just put it in the closet. It's Jake's."

Bobby took the laptop from the bar and put it away.

The bar filled up pretty quickly but some of the regulars didn't show up for some reason. The Waldens weren't there, nor was Professor Ryan. He probably had a class to teach at night. Paul Aaron was out of town on business and the guys who worked for Hartt Landscaping were still on the job.

"What if the laptop belongs to one of the patrons who isn't here?" Ron asked Jake.

"We'll have to take our chances."

Jake looked at his watch. It was seven o'clock. He waited a few more minutes hoping to see Dave King and his employee Dom come through the door.

A few minutes later, the door opened and two guys entered. They walked over to where Jake was standing at the end of the bar.

"Hey Jake."

"Dave."

"This is Dominic Garibaldi. He's the guy I was telling you about."

Jake and Dom shook hands.

"Dave said you got a good look at the guy who was at the Gold Digger Pawn shop yesterday pawning a laptop."

"Sure did. Dave had given us a description of a person he said has been involved in some recent robberies. He said they guy might try to pawn some of the goods at our place. It was just by chance I saw someone matching the description when I was dropping something of at Gold Digger."

"Thank goodness you did," Jake said. "Take a look around and see if you recognize anyone in here?"

Dom looked around. There were quite a few people in the bar. He walked from one end of the bar to the other.

"Don't see the guy."

"Are you sure?"

"I'm pretty good with faces."

"Take a seat here Dom. We still have a few of our regulars who aren't here. Hopefully they'll come in shortly and you'll recognize one of them."

Jake turned to the register to get the laptop. It wasn't there.

"Ron, do you know where the laptop is?"

"Yeah. I had Bobby put it away."

"Can you get it?"

"Sure."

Bobby had been in the kitchen dropping off dirty dishes and glasses when Ron went to find him. He was still in the kitchen talking with Bill.

"Bobby, where did you put the laptop that was in the bar earlier?"

"It's in the closet by the front door. Want me to get it?"

"That's ok. I'll get it."

Bobby went back to talking with Bill.

Ron went to the closet, found the laptop and brought it to Jake.

Jake stood on a chair, "Everyone can I have your attention?"

The bar went silent.

Jake reached down and picked up a laptop and held it high.

"Does anyone recognize this laptop?"

He turned it over so everyone could see the front and back.

"Hey, that's my laptop," Sue Walker said. "Where did you get it?"

"I picked it up at the Gold Digger Pawn shop earlier today."

"How did you know it was there?"

"My friend Dave King, who owns Central Connecticut Pawn, called me and said one of his guys, Dom over there," Jake was now pointing at Dave and Dom seated at a table, "called and said Dom saw someone pawning a laptop while he was dropping something off at Gold Digger."

"How did he know it was something stolen from one of us?"

"He didn't. But the person pawning the laptop was wearing one of our logo sweatshirts. Dave had told all his employees to be on the lookout for anyone wearing one of them and trying to pawn stuff. I had the opportunity of watching some of the security tapes at the Gold Digger shop and saw someone wearing one of our logo sweatshirts pawning this laptop. I put it all together and guess what. We got a hot lead."

"Can I have my laptop back?"

"I'm sure you can but not until after we catch the robber."

"How do you intend on doing that?"

"Dom saw the person who pawned this laptop. He can identify him."

Everyone looked around at everyone else.

"Well, who is it?" Lou asked.

"Dom?" Jake said.

Dominic stood up to address everyone.

"I haven't seen the person yet."

Just then, the door opened and Officer Cassidy walked in. He walked over to Jake. The place was very quiet.

"I called Officer Cassidy and told him we had a break in the case of the robberies and he agreed to come over here."

Jake took a few minutes to update Officer Cassidy about what had transpired up to this point. He handed Cassidy the tape Tracy from Gold Digger had given him.

"Can you ask your manager to have all of the employees come out here?"

"Sure."

Jake went down the hall. A few minutes later, the staff from the restaurant side of the place started to walk into the bar.

Dom looked carefully at each person as they walked into the room.

Bill was one of the last to walk in.

"That's him," Dom said pointing at the entrance from the hallway.

Jake walked over and grabbed Bill's arm. He pulled him in front of Officer Cassidy.

Dom said, "Not him. The other guy."

Jake turned and looked. Bobby was the only person left in the hallway.

"Bobby Rose?"

"He's the guy I saw pawning that laptop at the Gold Digger."

Officer Cassidy took a hold of Bobby's arm and stepped back into the hallway with him.

"What do you have to say for yourself?" Cassidy asked.

"So I pawned a laptop, its no big deal."

"It is if you can't explain how the laptop came to be in your possession."

"Someone sold it to me."

"And who is that?"

"I'm not saying anything."

"You're under arrest."

# Chapter 47

Officer Cassidy took Bobby into custody and took him back to the police station. When he got there, he called Roger Skylar and asked him to come down to the station.

Roger was happy to comply and showed up about an hour later. Bobby was put into a five-person line-up.

He took his time looking at each person.

"Can I see their hands?"

"Why do you want to see their hands?"

"The last time the person was in my shop, he had bandages on his left hand."

Cassidy spoke into the microphone. "Put your hands out in front of you."

Each of the five did.

Bobby's left hand had a bandage on it.

"That's the guy who's been pawning stuff at Park Avenue Pawn."

"You can't ID someone based on a bandage."

"I know. I just wanted to see if one of them had a bandage still on his left hand."

"Well, can you say without a doubt that is the person you saw at your place by looking at his face?"

"He is. In fact, I've got him on our security tapes and I'm sure your experts will say he's the guy."

Roger handed a tape to Officer Cassidy.

"Thanks, Roger, for coming down."

Roger shook Officer Cassidy's hand and left.

Officer Cassidy said he was finished with the line-up. Bobby Rose was taken away and put into a cell.

Officer Cassidy took the tape Roger had provided and the one Jake had given to him from the Gold Digger shop to a lab at the station. He asked the lab technician to play the tapes for him. There wasn't much on the first tape in the beginning other than Roger straightening things up at the Park Avenue Pawn shop.

"Can we fast forward this thing?"

The technician played the tape on fast forward speed stopping at each point where a customer came up to the counter.

"We're looking for a guy who's wearing a hooded sweatshirt with 'O' Bar written on the back and a picture of a martini glass displayed on it. Keep running the tape and stop it if you see anything like that. I'll be right back. I have to use the bathroom."

Cassidy left the lab. The technician continued to review the tape. When Cassidy came back in, the technician was filing something in a cabinet.

"I thought you were going to continue to look at the tapes for me?"

"I did. I printed a picture of the guy wearing the hooded sweatshirt at the first place." He handed the picture to Cassidy.

"Then, I put the second tape in and stopped it once I saw a person on the tape wearing the same sweatshirt."

"Oh."

"Take a look. It's stopped with a person wearing the clothing you described standing at the counter at the second place."

Officer Cassidy and the technician walked over to the computer screen displaying a bunch of slanted lines because the tape had been paused. Cassidy could see a man in the picture at the counter at Gold Digger Pawn. He could just make out the letter 'O' in the blurred screen.

"Watch," the technician said.

She pressed play and the video played clearly. Cassidy could see the hooded sweatshirt clearly.

"Can you stop it right there?"

"Sure."

"Can I get a print of that shot?"

"Just plain paper or a glossy?"

"Which is clearer?"

"A glossy will hold up better over time. And they're usually clearer."

"Why not give me one of each?"

"No problem."

The technician pressed a few keys. The printer started to hum. When a page came out, she handed it to Cassidy. Then, she put a page of special paper into the feeder and printed the picture again. When it was finished, she handed the glossy print to Officer Cassidy.

"Thanks."

"Want me to file the tapes?"

"No. But, can you put them on a memory stick for me?"

"Sure. It'll only take a minute."

"That way, I can take the pictures with me and keep them in my file until the case goes to court."

"I'll be right back."

The technician went and got a memory stick and copied the pictures from the tapes. Then, she gave it to Officer Cassidy.

"Just plug this into any USB port and you'll be able to see the pictures."

"Thanks. The DA will just hold the stick up for effect. It works all the time. Even if the stick were blank, just the suggestion of hard evidence like a picture gets a suspect talking."

Officer Cassidy took the picture prints and the memory stick with him. He went back to the interview room. He pressed the intercom on the wall and asked that Bobby Rose be brought there. A few minutes later, Bobby came in.

"Have a seat Mr. Rose."

"I don't know why you arrested me Officer."

Officer Cassidy opened a file and pulled out the black and white printout showing Bobby at the counter at the Park Avenue Pawn shop."

"Isn't this you, Mr. Rose?"

Bobby looked at the picture.

"Yes, that's me."

Then, Officer Cassidy took out the other picture. This one showed Bobby standing at the counter at the Gold Digger Pawn shop.

"And, isn't that you?"

"So?"

"That picture was taken when you pawned this laptop." Officer Cassidy reached down and picked up a laptop off the floor. He put it on the table.

Bobby looked at the laptop and again at the picture. It was pretty clear that the laptop in the picture with the decal on it was the same one Officer Cassidy had put on the table in front of Bobby.

"Yeah, that's me. I got that laptop from someone I know and needed some extra cash."

"That may be, Mr. Rose. But it's the circumstances under which you came to have possession of the laptop that's questionable."

"What do you mean?"

"You see, that laptop belongs to Ms. Susan Walker. It was stolen from her house a few weeks ago. And in the security video from the Gold Digger Pawn shop, that's you pawning it."

"I don't deny that I'm the person in the picture pawning the laptop, but I'm not admitting to gaining possession of the laptop under questionable circumstances."

"Look Mr. Rose. I have first hand witnesses who have come forward and will testify you have been pawning stolen merchandise for some time now. We've got pictures of you with some of the merchandise and you've been caught red-handed in that picture right there."

"I think I want to talk with a lawyer."

"Oh, you'll get to talk to a lawyer. But, first, I'd like to ask you a few more questions."

"Was anyone else involved in these robberies?"

"Why should I tell you anything?"

"Because, if you do, I'll put in a good word for you with the DA."

Bobby thought about it for a minute.
"I'd like immunity in writing before I'll say anything."
"I'll see what I can do."

Officer Cassidy left the room for a few minutes. When he came back in, he had a piece of paper with a few sentences written on it. The police chief had signed it. Bobby picked it up and read it. When he was done, he asked for a pen. Then, Bobby signed the paper.

"That document gives you immunity from prosecution provided you give us all the facts surrounding this matter and that you're innocent of the robberies."

"Ok. Here's what I know," Bobby said as he fidgeted with his fingers.

"I'm the person pawning those things. I don't make much money working at the 'O' bar and needed some extra cash. They never let me serve the customers, so I don't get the tips. So, I go to tag sales and flea markets looking for stuff I can resell on craigslist or at the pawnshops. One day, when I was working at the bar, one of the customers was in there having a beer. When he went to pay, he dropped some jewelry on the floor and I just happened to be walking by when it happened. I picked it up and handed it back to him. When I asked him if the jewelry was his, he said he had come into possession of it recently and was looking to sell the stuff. I asked how much he wanted and he told me. I knew his asking price was pretty low so I offered to buy it. I paid him cash and told him if he had any other stuff, I'd be interested in buying it. Over the next few weeks, he sold me a number of different things, which I either put up on craigslist for sale or took to one of the pawnshops in the area. It was a pretty good arrangement. Most of the stuff I pawned."

"Did you know the things you were buying were stolen?"

"I'm not stupid, Officer. But, I didn't ask any questions. I needed the money."

"So, you took the stolen goods and pawned them for the money?"

"Like I told you, I bought the stuff. After a while, it became apparent the stuff was coming from some of the people who come in to the 'O' Bar."

"Even then, you continued to go through with your end of the arrangement?"

"Look. I didn't steal anything. I paid cash for everything I got and just pawned the stuff I purchased."

"Ok. How many times did you purchase things to pawn?"

He thought for a few minutes. He started to count.

"Twelve."

Officer Cassidy knew of most of the dates of the robberies. His list had a few less than twelve names on it.

"Can you list all of the times you bought things from the robber?"

Cassidy put a pad and pen in front of Bobby. Bobby made a list of the dates. Cassidy held it up and read the dates. He took out a calendar and looked the dates up.

"Looks like you got the items after weekends?"

"My day off is usually Monday. That's when I usually met with my supplier to see what he had for me. And, I usually went to the pawn shops the same day if I got good stuff."

"Ok, so who was your so called supplier?"

"Frank Johnson."

"I don't think I know him."

"He's at the bar all the time."

"Does he have one of those hooded sweatshirts?"

"Probably. He played on the baseball team sponsored by the Bar so I'm pretty sure he has one."

"Ok Rose. You're free to go for now. I'll be talking with Mr. Johnson. If your story holds up, you'll be free and clear. Until then, don't go moving or anything."

"So I can go now?"

"Sure."


Bobby got up and left. He went to the 'O' Bar to pick up his paycheck. When he walked in, Jake said, "You've got some nerve coming in here."

"I've been released. I didn't do it."

"That's not what the eye witnesses said."

"Sure, I pawned stuff. But, I didn't steal anything."

"If you didn't, who did?"


Just then, Officer Cassidy walked into the bar. He walked up to Jake.

"Do you know a Mr. Frank Johnson?"

"Sure, he's right over there," Jake said pointing at Frank.

Officer Cassidy went over to him.

"You want to come with me, Mr. Johnson?"

"I guess Bobby told what you needed to know."

"He did. Now, you're under arrest, Mr. Johnson."

Bobby watched as Officer Cassidy talked with Frank. When Officer Cassidy started to walk towards the door with Frank Johnson in tow, Bobby said, "See, it wasn't me. Frank did those robberies. I didn't know he was doing them. He sold me some stuff that he stole and I either pawned some of the things or sold them on craigslist. I didn't know."

"Here's your paycheck Bobby."

Jake handed it to him and Bobby turned and left.

Officer Cassidy escorted Frank Johnson out of the bar. He took him to the station just down the street on New Britain Avenue, and they went into an interview room.

"Mr. Johnson, Mr. Rose has told me all about the relationship you and he had with respect to the items you stole. We tracked some of the items back through the pawnshops Mr. Rose took the merchandise to and he was positively identified as the person pawning the merchandise."

"He's so stupid. I knew I should have picked someone smarter."

"So you're admitting to doing the robberies?"

"Those people all deserved it. They boast about what they have and think they're better than everyone else."

"So you robbed them?"

"It was easy. Some of them even let it be known where they keep a secret key to get in. How stupid is that? You don't have to be a genius to pull these robberies off. You just have to be observant and a good listener. And I probably would have gotten away with it if I didn't sell the stuff to Bobby."

"Why did you?"

"He said he had a place to sell the stuff no questions asked plus, he had the cash."

"Here's a list of the dates Mr. Rose said he bought stuff from you. Can you put names next to each date?"

Frank took a look at the list. He picked up a pen and wrote down names next to each date. When he was done, he handed the list to Officer Cassidy.

"Why did you leave some of the stuff laying around the Bar after some of the robberies?"

"I didn't. Bobby must have dropped some of the stuff he purchased from me. He was just sloppy. I couldn't believe it when Jake turned the lost and found box over and some of the stuff dropped out right there on the bar."

"Ok, I can understand some of what you're saying, but what about some of the other robberies?"

"Like which ones?"

"Mr. Wilson?"

"Yeah. He didn't have much. He had an older style TV that weighed way too much for me to carry plus no one buys those kind anyway."

"Did you take anything from him?"

"Only some tools out of his garage. And I think I only got a few bucks for the stuff I took from there."

Cassidy looked over the rest of the list. All of the names of the victims he had talked to were on it. He'd follow-up on the other names and contact them.

"I have no further questions Mr. Johnson. The guard will take you back to a cell."

Officer Cassidy went back to his desk and called the 'O' Bar. Jake answered.

"O Bar, Jake Wilson speaking. How can I help you?"

"Mr. Wilson, its Officer Cassidy. I just finished interviewing Mr. Johnson and he confessed to the crimes. I was able to get him to list out all the victims he robbed. He listed twelve in all."

"Twelve? Who were they?"

Officer Cassidy read the list. He let Jake's name be the last one. When Jake heard his name, he said, "Me? I don't think I'm missing anything."

"Check your tools in your garage."

"I will."

"I'll be contacting all the people on the list including the ones I haven't interviewed yet. If you know any of them, you might want to let them know."

"Officer Cassidy, did Frank say why he did all of these robberies?"

"He said he wanted to get back at everyone who made fun of him or treated him unfairly over the years. He claimed that everyone he robbed had wronged him in some way at some point in time and robbing them was his way of getting even."

"Really?"

"That's what he said."

"And, did he say anything about Bobby Rose?"

"Johnson said he sold a lot of the loot to Mr. Rose. Apparently, Mr. Rose bought things from Mr. Johnson and then resold them to pawnshops or through craigslist. It looks like Mr. Rose played no role in the robberies at all."

"So Bobby is cleared?"

"It looks like that's the way it will work out. My report will detail everything. You can contact the station in a few days and get a copy if you want one."

"Thanks for calling Officer Cassidy."

"I'll be in touch."

Jake hung up the phone. Ron walked over to him, "What was that all about?"

"Frank robbed my place as well."

"Isn't he in custody?"

"Yeah. That was Officer Cassidy. He said Frank listed everyone he robbed and I was one of the names on the list."

"Jake, don't you think you'd know if you were robbed?"

"That's what I told Cassidy. He told me to check my tools in my garage. I can't believe I was a victim in Frank's spree. He told Officer Cassidy the robberies were his way of getting even with everyone who wronged him in the past. I have no idea how I wronged him in any way."

"You know, some people can be real sensitive."

"Yeah, but to rob your friends."

"Maybe that was part of the problem. He didn't consider them friends."

As they were talking, Bill came out of the kitchen carrying half a rack of glasses. Somehow, he clipped the corner of the bar and dropped the whole rack on the floor. There was broken glass everywhere.

Ron looked at Jake, "Think we can get Bobby back?"
Jake just shook his head.